I0670057

Deceit

A Life of Lies

Mark R Hopkins

1

For Grandmother

Thank you for teaching me courage and strength—I would not have been able to have written this without your teachings throughout my life.

I love you and miss you every day.

"Three things that can never be hidden: the sun, the moon, and the truth"

Buddha

Author photo by Ty Herndon

Edited and formatted by
www.onlinebookservices.co.uk

For more information about the author, please check out his website:
www.writermarkrhopkins.com
or visit his Amazon Author page:
www.amazon.com/markrhopkins

Table of Contents

Foreword

One really doesn't know how, when, or where a homicide will happen. But what one does know is that inevitably a murder will occur. It might be at the darkest hour. It might be in the blazing sunlight of midday. It might be in a church, a school or even in your own home. I never really thought about this until I became a forensic detective. My life was fairly basic but ended when I arrived in Red Cove. Not physically, of course, but a piece of me was taken. I think, or so I've told my shrink that a piece of my soul was buried with Tessie. It's hard to explain, but she was me. She was you. She was everyone. Over the years, I've learned that with every case you investigate, you also see a piece of yourself, not only in the actual case, but also in the victim.

Chapter One

The body was found in room 201, a corner room of the Red Cove Travel Inn, a motel frequented by prostitutes, drug dealers, and the occasional suicide.

Fleetham Police Department had never encountered a more gruesome scene. In fact, it was a scene that hasn't ever happened—and yet it occurred in the middle of a warm summer night.

The body of Tessie Johanan, 'a known piece of white trash', or so the sheriff said, was found lying on the bed, hands bound to either side of the headboard with her feet strapped to the foot of the bed. A gag made from her panties was stuffed in her mouth, her abdomen ripped open, with the contents of her bowels hanging out, and the shape of a heart cut into her chest, she resembled a macabre version of the Vitruvian Man

When Sheriff Robert Binder arrived at the scene, after receiving a call from the Red Cove's manager, Josef Priti, it was clear this wasn't the typical suicide or accidental overdose usually associated with such establishments. While displayed in a typical restraint pose, Tessie's body had been almost totally gutted. There was obvious bruising, and what appeared to be ligature marks around the neck, although no strangulation device had been found nearby.

As Robert stood in the room waiting for the coroner to arrive, his thoughts raced, confused as to why the town had to suffer. The town... and Tessie.

3

A few minutes later, the coroner's car pulled up as he lived just down the street from the motel. The call had come from the sheriff's dispatcher requesting that a body be pronounced dead and a crime investigation started. Walking up to the door of the motel room, he opened it and stepped inside where a night of horror unfolded before him.

"Whoever done this to Tessie sure did a number on her! I don't understand how anyone could have had the guts or conscience to destroy her body like this." Robert told the coroner, shaking his head. The coroner, Jim Sanchez, was a young émigré from El Paso. Having graduated with a degree in forensic pathology, he chose Fleetham as a haven for his work. His thinking was—small town, little work—easy salary. While he had been mostly right, he was about to find out that he was sadly mistaken to think his life had little purpose.

Jim, while full of intelligence and knowledge, had a bizarre fascination for the morbid, an obsession that fueled his desire in school. His father had been a mortician, so growing up in the shadow of death was perfectly normal to him.

Jim and Robert peered over the bed. The room told a story of an unfortunate night. It told the story of a night of fornication. It told the story of lust. It told the story of deceit.

"Poor Tessie, she should have known better and left this lifestyle," Sheriff Robert Binder told the coroner as the body was removed. It was obvious to both men that she had been the victim of a night of lust gone wrong. Her clothing was nowhere to be found, and when she was lifted on to the gurney, it was evident that she'd been brutally raped. A clot of blood dislodged from her vagina and fell on the mattress.

4

As Robert looked down at the abused body, rubbing his greasy, bald head, he mumbled, "You know, a few years ago I nailed her. I couldn't help it. I arrested the little slut for possession of something—I can't remember what. She begged me not to throw her ass in jail—so she made a deal with me. I'd nail her, then let her go."

Jim, amazed but not all that shocked, thought about what he'd just heard.

The pillar of the law department? What the hell? How can he use his power to control people?

In order to preserve any evidence, Jim encased the corpse in the body bag, along with the fitted sheet. Shockingly, they were alone during the body removal as there was no deputy in the sleepy town of Fleetham. Tessie was gone, apart from the clues that were left behind.

***

The sheriff governed the land. *The land is mine. I make the law here.* It was Robert's motto and had always been since he became sheriff in 1988. His father had been the sheriff back in the 60s—only ending when his son won the election. He won the only way a small-town election is won. With a vengeance. A vengeance to control. A vengeance to succeed.

Having just overseen a body removal at the motel, Sheriff Robert Binder was now alone in room 201, as Jim had left to handle the processing of the corpse and its examination. With the body and Jim gone, he could now begin his investigation of the crime scene. The door was blocked off, and yellow crime scene tape

5

had been strung around the entire perimeter, leaving Jim free to 'have at it'.

"Base, over?"

Dispatch, "Base. Go ahead, sir.".

"What's the ETA of the damn forensics team? This is taking long enough as it is!"

"ETA thirty minutes, sir. I've spoken to the detective. He's confirmed your location and should be there soon. Over."

"Ten-four."

As Robert ended his brief radio conversation, he sat on the bed, knowing he shouldn't, but just couldn't help it. Seeing the motel room he'd been in many times before, he couldn't help but wonder why she was killed. "Goddamn. The Lord sure works in mysterious ways…" Robert whispered.

In the distance, he could hear the traffic on the lonely highway that stretched as far as the eye could see. If you drove 300 miles east, you'd end up in Dallas. If you drove 300 miles west, you'd end up in Lubbock.

Fleetham was the definition of small-town America. It was home to state football championships, small-town politics, a constant battle between the Methodists and Baptists, and the occasional festival.

Resting in the innards of the town, a history of death could be found. A history very close to Sheriff Binder as it had engulfed his family for generations. His family, while considered 'well-to-do Baptists', held something else closer—they were masterminds in the art of lies.

Fleetham, the sleepy little town in north central Texas now harbored one of America's most gruesome murders. Likewise, it was the home to every white-

6

headed, senior citizen who had appeared on an AARP commercial.

With only 900 citizens and some change, it was the kind of place any boring couple could only dream of. With the exception of being 300 miles from the nearest mall, or half an hour from the nearest super-center store, it was a pretty quiet abode. Nestled in the cul-de-sac of mesquite trees and salt cedar, Fleetham surpassed any Thomas Kincaid village painting. With its century-old brick streets, to its art deco movie theatre, the atmosphere was nothing less than calm.

Frederick Fleetham Binder and Olivia Rose Binder were Robert's grandparents and namesake. The Binder family had resided in Fleetham since its conception in1882. Having originally migrated from colonial Virginia, the Binders had left behind a stockpile of money and fortune. Seeking peace and tranquility in post-civil war America, the Binder's landed in Fleetham and built what was now a historically protected structure, the largest home in the city. Sitting on the corner of Main and Marietta, its *Gone with the Wind* style front porch would stop a passing tourist and entice them to explore this century-old monument of beauty.

The original home had been transformed into a funeral home. But nonetheless, the beauty still remained. Having lived in Virginia for quite some time, along with their family and a small portion of their fortune came the slaves. As the 'coloreds', as Robert called them, had been long freed, the hired help who remained with the family, stayed out of loyalty. Like the loyal valets of Edwardian England, the southern slaves stayed with their owners long after being given their freedom.

7

With a house full of domestic staff, the family could now focus on building up the area. As the Binders were the first settlers in the land, naturally, they had named the area. With the belief that old man Frederick must be the sole contributor to everything related to his family, he chose the name Fleetham—his middle name. As a man with a large ego, an insatiable drive for success, and a non-existent conscience, he forged forward and built the town into what it was today.

Having inherited his grandfather's sense of determination, perseverance and strength, Robert had the foundation to become a successful lawman. However, he too lacked a conscience.

Chapter Two

As he sat on the bed, thinking about the death of one of his tricks, he wondered why. *Who would do this? In Fleetham, of all places, who would kill someone who doesn't really matter?*

"Base? Where the hell are the forensics people. I've got shit to do and want to see Tessie's body before she's on her way to *Slaughterville*."

"Sir, dispatch said they're five minutes out, over."

"Base, pull up the security footage from the last week. I want to see what the hell happened in this room. Over."

"Ten-four."

Five minutes later, a black SUV, brand new from the looks of it, slowly pulled into the gravel drive of the motel. With the recent drought that was ongoing throughout most of central Texas, the slightest bit of friction on a dirt road instantly blew up clouds of white, west Texas sandy dust. Shadowing itself in the sand, the halogen headlights shone on the cracked windows of room 201.

A wave of wheat-colored hair poured out of the door the second it was slung open. It was the first thing Robert saw. Stepping out of the SUV, with a rather pissed off look, was the director of the forensics team, Alison Chaney—but to the law enforcement world, she was known as 'The Bitch'.

9

Having built a solid reputation for no-nonsense investigations, and life in general, Alison could be very difficult to handle. She carried herself with the confidence of a soldier, her head held high, shoulders back, and chest thrust forward. To Robert, she looked as if she were poised for battle.

"It's about damn time you showed up! The body has already gone. As soon as this investigation begins, the sooner I can go home and go to bed. What we've got here, Detective Chaney, is a hog killin' of a no-good piece of white trash." Robert snarled.

"Thank you for that fine forensic analysis. However, if you'll let me review your notes, I'm sure that we can begin momentarily," Alison snapped back.

As Robert was becoming more irritated by the minute, he raised his voice and retorted, "You always speak like you have a doctor's in smartness. Talk normally so people can understand you. And while you're at it, send in some more of your people. There's a pile of shit, literally, over here in the corner. There's six inches of guts by the pillow, and I don't know where her clothes are at. I can't do this alone! And my notes are in my head!"

At Alison's insistence the two of them donned protective clothing to preserve the crime scene, and Robert began questioning his rationale for even staying. He could have been at home with a beer and a smoke, watching the Braves' game. "But no, I'm here, wading through guts and blood of someone who is better off dead," he muttered to himself, voicing the thought that was running through his head.

As the words exited his mouth, he was reminded of his night with Tessie and a faint smile formed on his lips. A smile of pleasure, not of happiness. A smile of

10

self-gratification, not of emotional enjoyment. A smile of an abusive night of random sex… at her expense.

"Alison, let me quickly brief you, so I can get going. She was strangled with something that we haven't yet found. We did all the searches around the body but haven't looked through the entire room yet. She was disemboweled and a piece of skin on her chest was removed. Oh, she was also raped."

"Wait," Alison interrupted. "Go back to what you first told me—she had a piece of skin removed from her chest? Was there a specific shape or was the entire chest wall removed? I've never seen anything like that!"

"Yeah, well, it wasn't her entire chest and tit area, thank God, but a small, heart shaped cut-out, exactly above her heart. I think it's exactly where… I'm not a doctor or nothing." The thought entered Robert's mind about what Tessie must have been feeling during her attack. Granted, he knew he had hurt her a few years ago, emotionally, and physically, but he never dreamed of killing her. His rape had been something out of instinct, as he usually overpowered the women he slept with… but he always made sure they weren't severely injured. As Robert would say, "they were only worn out."

"Do you think she knew her assailant? It sounds like a crime of passion to me… rather than a random murder," Alison chimed in.

As she finished her sentence, she looked around the room, seeing the worn-out bedspread, faded curtains, and nicotine stained wallpaper, and quipped, "Jesus Christ, why would anyone want to be here, let alone sleep here?"

Robert chuckled at this, and mumbled, "I don't think 'ole Tessie had much sleep tonight, darlin'. I mean,

11

you didn't see her. It's a sight you can't forget. When you see a belly ripped open and all the innards half hanging out—I mean, it ain't the same as watching a Bette Davis movie and wishing the lead actress would marry the lead actor—this is real life here."

Only half listening to him, Alison slowly walked around the room, surveying the area. Wearing her plastic shoe covers to avoid contaminating the scene further, she carefully stepped around the bed. The bed, nothing more than a mattress and box springs sitting on a frame, dominated the east wall. With its faded, olive-green bedspread wadded up in a pile against the headboard, Alison could see exactly how much Tessie was—for lack of a better term—tortured. The amount of blood was not really that surprising considering what had happened... all the while, the questions kept being repeated in her head, *this isn't a crime of passion... premeditated maybe? ... but what exactly? Is it a pleasure kill?*

Seeing the pool of clotted blood on the threadbare fitted sheet, Alison glanced over at Robert, who was thumbing through his latest text messages on his mobile.

Realizing that she was the only human who remotely cared about the deceased girl, she turned her attention back to the middle of the bed—obviously where Tessie had been laying. Running her gloved hand across a clean corner of the sheet, she felt intense sadness, yet an odd feeling of relief. "In a way, I think she is happy she's dead, don't you, Rob?"

Robert, who wasn't remotely paying attention to her, whipped around to face Alison, and asked, "did you really just ask me if I think she's happy she's dead?"

12

Trying to speak through his snorting laughter, Robert bellowed to Alison, "I guess she's thrilled she's sitting up in glory land now!"

Rolling her eyes at hs comment, Alison turned her attention back to the bed, where she spotted something peeking out from under a pillow from the corner of her eye.

A condom. Quickly changing gloves, Alison reached for the unrolled piece of what appeared to be lubricated rubber and looked at it. Rolling it around in her nitrile covered hands, she realized that something wasn't quite right.

The texture. A used condom had a jelly like consistency when manipulated in your hand.

This condom was, yes, jelly like, however, it was full of something.

"Put your gloves back on and look at this."

As he pocketed the nearly dead mobile phone and eyed the creamy-white piece of rubber in Alison's hand, his thoughts raced.

"Robert, look at this—what's it full of? It's certainly not the aftereffects of last night's soiree! Something is bunched up at the bottom of it… look!"

As Robert slid a glove on his already sweaty hand, he held the condom, rolling it around in his palm. The sensation was unlike anything he'd ever encountered. The more his hand manipulated it, the more the color changed… completely. Now, a faint pink color shone through…

"Rob, stop!" Alison yelled.

A lightbulb clicked in Alison's head the moment she saw the pink coloring. The heart cut-out.

"Whoever done this, shoved it in this rubber!" Robert mumbled.

13

As the two stared blankly at one another, the thoughts of what happened started to creep in. As they bagged the rubber condom, a tear began to trickle down Alison's cheek.

"Ya know, I'm always so stoic... I never show emotion. You simply can't when you do what I do—hell, you can't as an adult. But I can't handle this for some reason. I hurt, for Tessie," Alison admitted.

Tuning her out, Robert glared out the window, thinking about the night's events. As he was lost in his thoughts, his radio crackled to life.

Dispatch, "Unit, over."

"Base, go ahead."

"Sir, we have video footage from the last week at the motel, but today's is missing. Over."

"What do you mean it's missing? Dig deeper. Over and out."

Chapter Three

"Alison, I'm going home. I've had enough of this sadness. Of this death. Tessie's dead. Her autopsy will be going on—there's nothing for us to do." Robert declared, looking exhausted, an immense amount of stress apparent.

"When the rest of forensics arrive, please let me know what you find. I'll call you tomorrow to discuss the details. I really can't handle anything else today."

Without waiting for her to reply, Robert strolled out of room 201, shedding his blood-soaked shoe covers at the threshold of the door. After stepping outside, the rush of fresh air hit him. The air, though thick with Texas humidity, was such a welcome relief, considering his last few hours. Looking up at the clear sky, he said a prayer, "God, take care of me. Take care of Tessie. Help me figure out what happened. Help me find whoever did this." As he whispered his prayer to whatever entity was listening, the hair on his neck stood-up, and his eyes watered. At that exact moment, he lowered himself into a genuflect position and began to sob. "Forgive me. Please forgive me, Lord. I give myself to you and beg for your mercy over the years of failing you."

Crying heavily now, he remained, head bowed, arms folded on his knees. He knew he had been unfaithful to his wife, family, and career, but he never truly knew the impact of his transgressions until now—until this very moment.

Slowly getting back to his feet, he wiped his eyes, blew his nose on his sleeve, and trekked to his patrol car. Typical for Texas summers, lightning bugs were flitting around the car. In a way, it was a sign of relief for him. "Tess, I know you're here and I know you're watching over us. I'm sorry, baby doll."

As he uttered those words, his voice cracking, he climbed in his car, turned the engine over and slowly drove down the highway. With no intention to head for home, as he'd suggested to Alison, he took a left on Highway 70, and headed for the hospital.

In the quaint town of Fleetham, the hospital, which also housed the walk-in clinic and the morgue, was a few blocks west of Red Cove Travel Inn.

With the middle of the night in full force, he drove to Fleetham Memorial Hospital. Seeing the empty parking lot brought back many memories of this place. Having visited both his parents, his wife, his son, and countless friends in the establishment, he was well versed with the layout. His memories of the hospital were both happy and sad. He had sat at his father's bedside as he drew his last breath. He had sat in the waiting room as his mother screamed during the last moments of her life. He had sat in the nursery lobby, awaiting the birth of his son.

"Life is born here. Life comes to die here." The infamous words he used to tell his son when he asked questions about the buildings in town.

Standing on the entrance steps to the hospital, the overwhelming stench of disinfectant lingered in the air... the stench, as Robert would usually say, was of 'that brown shit' they scrub the floors and walls with. As the motion sensor of the electronic sliding doors sensed his presence, the rush of cold, sterile air hit him in the

16

face. Stepping inside the hospital, he sensed something wasn't quite right, but couldn't place it.

A black woman, about Robert's age… or so he thought, sat at reception.

"Hmmm, hi, can I help you?" Terri, the night receptionist, asked.

Flashing his tarnished badge, but knowing he needn't bother, as everyone in town knew him, he informed her that he needed to visit the morgue.

"I have a case that I'm leading and need to speak to the coroner. I saw him earlier when the body was removed but need to discuss case details with him tonight." Robert explained.

Attempting to sound less 'country', and more official, Robert went on to say, "If you'll give me the access code, or let me down to the mortuary, I'd be happy, ma'am."

The receptionist, who was actually sixty-eight, looked up from the word game she was playing on her mobile phone, cleared her throat and asked, "I know who ya are. You're the lawman who arrested all those potheads down the street from me. Lord, the things that happen in a town of this size… who would believe us, seriously!" Terri laughed at her own comment.

Robert, becoming more frustrated by the minute, straightened his posture, and said, "Yes, so about that access code? Can you let me downstairs to see Jim?"

With that, Terri popped out of her chair, placed the telephone system on night mode and escorted Robert to the elevator. Entering the access code, the elevator descended into the pit of the hospital.

Standing in the elevator, trying to focus on the events that had unfolded, he couldn't help but think

17

about how many poor souls had taken the same trip that he was taking right now.

Landing at basement level, the doors opened, and Robert was led to a series of locked doors. Entering code after code, Terri took the pair to the last set of folding doors, with eerily flickering, fluorescent lighting overhead—perfect for the entrance of the morgue—illuminated the sign, 'Morgue'.

"This is no longer a cliché, this is really happening," Robert intoned, voicing his thoughts.

"I'll leave you here. I can't go any farther with you, plus, I don't want to. I think it's jinxed." Terri said, with a tremble in her voice.

"Sheriff Binder, you know what they say, don't you? They say that if you open a door, the sprits come. That's why I ain't going with you—plus, a receptionist can't." She said, as she headed back to the elevator, almost sprinting.

Pushing the stainless-steel doors apart, Robert entered the morgue. The ice-cold sensation sending shivers down his spine, as his hands touched the steel doors. Entering the morgue, the ambience and atmosphere changed. Entirely. No longer was he calm and content, in an airline seat looking out at the fluffy, whipped cream-like clouds, he was now, basically in the pits of the abyss.

"Jim, where the hell are ya? We've got to talk," Robert called out, his voice slightly echoing in the room. The morgue, as Robert observed, was typical. Blinding white walls of ceramic tile. Stainless steel ceiling tiles. White mosaic tile flooring, probably, as Robert suspected, original to the building—1963. The lighting in the room showed its true age. Ceramic covered metal dome shades shrouded flickering, fluorescent bulbs,

18

which dominated the room. Aside from the typical surgical gurneys, sliding. stainless steel instrument tray tables and foot-controlled sinks, there was an array of drain tables used during autopsies.

A sensation of chills ran through his entire body. A feeling he hadn't had in many, many years.

Remembering the first time he felt the sensation, it was when he was staring at a suicide victim. Oddly enough, at the same motel. That suicide victim, whose name he couldn't remember as he had intentionally put it out of his mind, had died of a self-inflicted gunshot wound to the head.

As Robert thought more about the memory, the images became clearer. The victim had used a shotgun. Being a hunter, as well as a law officer, he knew how the pellets of a shotgun worked—they didn't send one single slug, rather they sent a cloud of death to any victim in their direct path.

With that memory fresh in his mind, he walked over to the morgue refrigeration units housing those waiting on a procedure.

Robert chuckled as his twisted mind suddenly had a thought, *they're waiting on their butcher appointments*.

His rubber soled shoes squeaked on the tile floor as he slowly walked up and down the row of stainless-steel refrigerators doors. With all the nameplates blank, he wondered where Tessie could be.

"Jim, man, are you here? I'm waiting for you, man," Robert yelled, his voice reverberating as if he were in a well.

At the end of the row of 'body holders', as Jim used to call them, was Tessie.

"Tess... sweet, baby girl," he whispered.

19

Not hearing a sound after calling out for Jim Sanchez, he grasped the ice-cold handle of the refrigerator door. If this moment could have gotten any worse, he wouldn't have believed it. The sensation of just holding the handle alone would be one that would force anyone out of this job, and room for that matter.

Taking a deep breath, attempting to calm himself, he pulled once. The click. It was a sound you'd never forget. Robert thought, *it's the click of an empty Glock. It's the click of a pen signing a death certificate. It's the click of a beer pull tab.* With that, he chuckled again.

With his hand firmly gripping the handle, he pulled once more. As the door opened, a rush of ice-steam flooded out mingling with the smell of stale cigarette smoke and the metallic iron odor of blood.

The motel followed me back to the morgue, he thought, as the odor overwhelmed him.

Gripping the gurney, he pulled the corpse out. While the body bag was in place, Jim hadn't zipped it fully, leaving Tessie's distorted, frozen face exposed.

The eyes. Robert couldn't stop staring at her eyes. Her beautiful, chocolate brown eyes were replaced with frozen, hazy orbs of gelatinous sadness. Not having dealt extensively with death and forensics, he had forgotten the postmortem changes associated with death, and preservation of bodies, in general.

"Dammit, girl, what happened to you?" Robert asked the lifeless corpse. Pulling the refrigeration gurney out farther, Robert was able to fully observe the body bag. The maroon bag held what at one time had been one of Robert's prizes. Now, having asked for forgiveness for that event, it held one of his secrets.

20

As Robert grabbed a pair of too small rubber gloves from the sink a few feet away, he slowly unzipped the body bag. Hoping Jim wouldn't catch him in the act, he thought he should hurry up and take a closer peek at the body.

Pulling the zipper down to the bottom, he quickly opened it fully, exposing the gruesome scene. Having been in the freezer for about two hours, her body had begun to freeze completely.

The postmortem hue that her skin had taken on was that of a porcelain doll. As she had died in the supine position, her blood had drained from her face and top portions of her body, leaving them bone china white.

As Robert examined the body, engrossed in what he was looking at, a squeak of a shoe sounded a few feet away when Jim appeared from his office.

"Rob, man, what are you doing? I can't leave you alone anywhere. Get back from there. You know you're not at all authorized to be back here, let alone be knee deep in a corpse!" Jim said abruptly, highly infuriated.

"Terri let me come back here. I told her I was working on a case. Obviously, I am. I'm the sheriff in charge, buddy."

Robert, knowing he had royally screwed up, ripped off his gloves and threw them in the body bag.

Slamming shut the refrigerator door, without any regard for the body, he said, "Then do your job. I came down here to see what progress had been made. I didn't know you were napping in the back! I want to see her body during the autopsy. I want to see exactly what happened to her."

As Jim was processing Robert's hostility and irritation, he heard a buzzing sound. Realizing it was

21

Robert's phone, he barked, "Dude, your phone keeps going off. Will you do something about it?"

With Robert fully aware of what Jim had said, he reached down and pulled his phone out of his pant pocket. Nine missed calls. All from his son.

Chapter Four

Robert's son, Seth Binder, was a hero in his father's eyes. Seth was one of the few in Fleetham, who as any Fleetunian would say, had made it in life.

Seth, a very successful physician, graduated as valedictorian of Fleetham High School. Having been a rather unpopular teenager, he focused his studies and time on his education. Applying to Texas A&M, his mind was welcomed with open arms. Graduating with a degree in biology, he was accepted into medical school. Focusing on emergency medicine, he gained the respect of the senior physicians in the hospital.

Using his knowledge and experience, he moved away from the large city to settle in the nearby town of Fleetham—about forty-five minutes away, tucked in the alcove of the west Texas cotton fields. With his new career at the Auburn Medical Clinic as chief physician… well, the only physician, he earned the admiration of every citizen he treated. While the citizens of Auburn loved Dr. Binder—Dr. B, as the younger patients called him, the older, wiser patients were still wary of him.

With Auburn Medical Clinic as Seth's day job, he frequently handled night calls at Fleetham Memorial. Fleetham Memorial, which Seth described as a 'humble pile of rotting memories, sub-par nurses, and a hell of a paycheck'. As the night call physician for the last few years, the bulk of his medical experience at the hospital had been minor injuries, with the occasional cardiac arrest. Overall, it was an easy night for Seth… usually. He tended to his patients, flirted with the nurses, and ate the institutional food—only because he was hungry.

***

As Robert checked his phone, he realized Seth must be working tonight. After sliding open the locked screen, as well as having multiple missed calls, he saw that he had three text messages from his son.

As he squinted through his farsighted eyes, his arms barely long enough to make the text come into focus, he read the messages, whispering to himself, *"01:29 Hey, dad can u call me ASAP!!!*

01:38 I heard about Tessie! Call me!

01:51 DAD! I'M IN THE ER TAKING A CALL. COME SEE ME NOW!"

As any concerned parent, seeing the message and calls made Robert anxious and worried. Jim continued to stand next to Robert, concerned that he had destroyed some sort of evidence or contaminated something on the corpse.

I'll worry about that later, Jim thought to himself, as he dismissed Robert's actions from his mind.

Waiting for Robert to finish looking at his phone, Jim closed the refrigerator door, turned to him and asked, "Now, as you probably damaged the body or added some form of evidence that doesn't need to be here, what do you want, again?" The anger building gradually… his dark neck slowly getting darker by the minute.

"Jesus, Jim, calm down. You're going to have a stroke. Listen, I need to go see Seth. I think something is wrong. He sent several messages, which aren't written the way he normally talks to me. I'll be right back, but I want to see her on the table when I return, so I can go over this with a fine-tooth comb. When are you going to begin the autopsy?" Robert finally managed to say in one long breath. All the years of practicing smoking cessation had helped him in the simplest of tasks.

"Tsk, tsk," Jim replied. "I'll begin the procedure tomorrow. It's late and I'm tired. We don't have all her clothes and items from the motel yet, anyway. I'll begin first thing in the morning."

As Robert processed the information, which he really didn't want to hear... as he was a 'give it to me now' man... he nodded, snorting up his runny nose and adjusting his uniform pants to show his dominance in the situation. With Jim standing in front of him, watching his every move, he commented in a joking yet cruel way, "the irony, Robert, is that you're not the guy running the show here, yet somehow, you seem to think that. Or at least you still have your 'I'm the stud' stance going right now."

With that, Robert whipped around, heading towards the double doors that led into the hallway. Realizing that he needed an access code to navigate through the staff elevator. which he had taken earlier that evening, he opted for the stairwell. As his years of police experience had caught up with him, he quickly noticed that he wasn't in the best shape of his life. Trekking up the stairs, one by one, randomly stopping to catch his breath, Robert finally reached the main floor.

'Ground Level', the sign read. Walking out the fire exit door, he veered left. The mid-century-esque sign overhead read, 'Emergency Department, Nursery & Labor/Delivery'. Knowing his destination was directly ahead, he continued down the hallway.

25

The hospital hadn't seen a birth since 1991, however, the peaceful nursery and its memories remained. Peering through the window, directing his focus away from the implanted wire in the glass, he closed his eyes, if only for a moment. Seeing the nurse in her pink nursing uniform and yellow paper mask, holding his son up to the window, so the proud father could admire him. That moment, which Robert often recalled whenever he visited his son at work, was 'the happiest time of my life'.

Snapping back to reality, he continued along the hallway, pausing at the emergency department entrance. The bay doors, usually reserved for emergency medical technicians and ambulance staff, remained open—the hospital's security, while present, was extremely lax.

"Dad, man, I've been waiting for you. I've called and called. I heard about Tessie at the motel and knew you'd have responded to the call. Mom said she read something on Facebook about it." Seth huffed out as he rushed over to his dad, barely managing to get the words out without being incoherent. Seth's mom—Judy, Robert's ex-wife—a teacher and typical, small town girl, did what she was supposed to during her earlier years. She studied hard, married a Christian 'good-ole' boy', and had a child—but the years of being the *Stepford Wife* had taken its toll. The divorce happened after Judy caught him in bed with one of her former students.

The affair, however, would have landed Robert in jail, but she'd just turned eighteen.

The divorce was the talk of the town for weeks, even months. Everyone was talking about poor Judy, who remained silent through the ordeal, teaching and just living. That's all Judy did... live. Just barely, but she lived.

26

"Yeah, well, someone ripped her up... but how did you hear about this again? No one has released a public statement. Your mom said... what, again?" Robert asked.

"Mom said she read it on Facebook. About Tessie's death.' Seth explained, seeing both the worry and the concerned look in his dad's expression. Rubbing his eyes, Robert knew that he had understood and heard every word his son had said but couldn't understand how it was possible. He hadn't released a public statement yet, and everyone who knew about the death—at least those he was aware of, were present in either the motel room or the morgue.

The Timex, the last remaining gift that he'd kept from his ex-wife, read 03:09. The exhaustion had returned with a vengeance, but as usual with Robert, he'd blocked it out. "Son, I'm okay, I'm just tired. Tomorrow, Jim will perform the autopsy and see what the hell happened. In the meantime, Alison and I will have a look at the rest of the items in the motel room.

"Seth, I can't discuss this anymore now. I don't have the authority until I make a public statement at least. Let's worry about it tomorrow. I've got to get home and hit the sack... I hadn't realized, but I've been up all damned night."

With his dad standing in front of him, Seth saw his physical exhaustion. Hoping he could help his dad additionally, he suggested, "I'll help Jim if you need me to, Dad. Remember, I'm a doctor. I've seen and experienced everything. In fact, I can start tonight if you want me to."

Too tired to discuss it any further, he said, "No, it will be started tomorrow. Forensics and the crime department won't allow another soul in the room, let

27

alone, interfere with the investigation. But thanks, anyway. I'm off. I just wanted to come down since you blew up my phone all night."

"Okay… well, I've got a few patients to see and I have to finish signing off orders. I'll stop by tomorrow and see you. Are you back at the station again?"

Yawning and rubbing his eyes constantly, he nodded and mumbled, "Yeah. Night. Call me tomorrow or something."

He'd never been so tired in his life. His day had been an adventurous one, for sure. The emotions alone were enough to cause someone to crumble. Leaving his son in the ER, he cut through the ambulance bay doors, a shortcut that led him straight to the parking lot in front of the hospital. As he neared his car his brain instantly came to life.

If anyone would have been anywhere near Robert, they would have had serious concern for his mentation. "How did Judy hear about it? How come it's even public knowledge yet? Did Seth really hear it from her?" He said in his thick, southern drawl, in something louder than a whisper.

Opening the car door, he paused and glanced over his shoulder.

Peering out the window was an elderly woman. *One of the few patients Fleetham's hospital houses,* he thought. Though the hospital had two upper levels, he could clearly see her face. Maybe it was because he was so physically and mentally exhausted, but for some reason, his senses were hyper-sensitive. Robert kept gazing at the woman. Realizing immediately that this was just another patient in for pneumonia or a gallbladder attack, he collapsed into his car.

28

Before taking off down the road, he sent a text message to Alison, *Headed home. I will be back tomorrow sometime. Going to autopsy tomorrow. Will keep u informed. Get some rest.*

Chapter Five

Arriving at his house, Robert crawled out of his car, shuffling down the sidewalk to his door. His house, which had been a last-minute decision before the divorce was finalized, was nothing special. In a decent neighborhood, it stood alone on the corner. Shrouded by pecan trees and crepe myrtle bushes, the vast yard held memories, however thin, of its former beauty. The house had been built during the 1960s. Its 'ready-built' façade, popular during that time, still shone through its 21st century additions. The home, previously owned by someone Robert couldn't remember or even remotely care about, was all that he had in life... apart from his son and career—all other possessions were lost during the divorce. The divorce, which quickly turned bitterly nasty had taken all of Robert's belongings, including items that he'd worked so hard to acquire. Judy, while a sweet schoolteacher, turned into 'Satan's sister', as Robert would say.

With a few hours of sleep under his belt, he awoke to the sound of his phone buzzing. He hadn't realized how late he had actually slept, but the number of missed calls was an indicator. The current caller being Alison.

Answering in a thick, nasally voice, "Yeah, Sheriff Binder here."

30

"I have called you. I have sent you messages. I have had the base office radio you. What the hell is wrong? It's 11:39 a.m., for Christ sake!" Alison yelled.

"I got home at four-ish. I'm sorry, Ali. I stopped by the ER to chat with Seth, then crashed as soon as I got home." Robert yawned through every other word to Alison.

With his phone on speaker, he dressed while listening to her brief him on the latest news.

"First of all, the motel room. I'll be here most of the day with the entire forensics team. All the guests have been questioned, but there's one who I want you to deal with. I think there's something not quite right. Anyway, we found several things of interest in the room that your Fleetham bunch need to handle."

Tripping over a pair of boots that were laying in the middle of the floor, Robert struggled to process the morning's events. Having had zero coffee since yesterday morning, he wasn't truly mentally equipped to handle the flood of information. "If you'll hold your tits, I'll be there in a minute. Damn."

With that remark, Ali hung up the phone without a closing salutation. "That bastard has no clue how important this is." Making a gagging noise in disgust, she rolled her eyes at the thought of him even showing up. Alison's entire forensic team was on site and had questioned each motel guest, as well as the staff—all three of them. For the most part, they had cleared any suspects who existed in the immediate vicinity of the murder. As her team combed through each item in the room, as well as taking samples of carpeting and bed linens, Alison couldn't help but wonder what made this particular murder stand out so much to her. There was

31

something weighing heavily on her heart and mind at that moment. Something she couldn't quite grasp.

Nonetheless, her mind was made up. As with every case she managed, she would solve this one.

She'd bring peace to the victim's family. She'd send the criminal to prison to pay for *its* actions. She always used the pronoun *it*. Alison believed that by not signifying the killer with the he/she word, she could, in a sense, disassociate all emotions she had for them, whether good or bad.

So, in her private journal of case notes, *IT* was always dramatically printed.

Walking around the room, completely covered in her personal protective equipment, she wrote notes about what she saw. Unlike others in the field, her notes consisted of the use of all senses. That's to say that Alison would often write what something smelled like. What something looked like. What something felt like. What something sounded like. Obviously, all senses, with the exception of taste, were used. Until today.

With her criminal profiler, Aaron Duncan, standing next to her, she looked at him, chewing her lip. He was young and boyish compared to the men in Fleetham. Aaron didn't live in town, however, but had been brought in specifically to assist with the murder investigation. A native of Houston, he lived in the Dallas Metroplex. Working with the Dallas PD, he was the top profiler in the state. And with his enormous success, word was buzzing around the law enforcement realm that he was to be transferred to the FBI, to manage their high-profile cases—a job that one could only dare to dream of. A job that would be perfect for him.

As Alison looked at his youthful face, she was reminded of her college encounters during the nights of

32

binge drinking and sorority parties. *He would have been my target back then*, she thought.

Shaking her head slightly, trying to rid herself of the immature thoughts in her head, she asked him, "After initially surveying the scene, do you have any idea as to what we are looking at here?"

"Well, I knew you'd ask sooner rather than later, which would have been my choice, but… I've only been here about an hour, so I can't say for sure. I do know this. The person or persons—I'm saying that, because we truly don't know if more than one person was involved—is intelligent but lacking the commonsense factor. I think, after reading your notes that they would either be a social outcast, a loner or someone who is sociable but wears a mask daily." Aaron explained, all the while, looking through the nightstand drawer.

"Actually, Aaron, the thought crossed my mind that the killer was someone who was weird. Ya know? That's why I want Robert to interview that guy."

"There's nothing wrong with the guy, Alison. He's retarded… I think. Anyway, from what the motel manager was telling me, he is just a weird dude."

"Wait a minute, I wrote something down. This is why I think Robert, and you for that matter, need to see him." Scanning her notes, Alison mumbled aloud.

With her notebook in her right hand, and her left index finger scanning and moving from side to side, she found what she'd been searching for. A note written earlier that morning, about an event that occurred during her initial interviews of the motel staff and customers.

Has a Fleetham Baptist Church shirt on. Collects comic books and reads Playboy. Has had four arrests. Check accuracy! Drinker. No teeth. Check drug arrest record? Has a heart tattoo on his left F/A (forearm).

33

"Here it is. The heart on his arm. I knew I wrote something down like that. He has a rifle. A heart tattoo. Who knows if he has had a drug arrest. I'll have Robert verify that later." Alison said excitedly.

"Alison, lots of people have tattoos. It doesn't mean he killed her. He's more than likely going to come back totally clean. Don't waste your time on him, but if you want me to, I'll sit down and chat with him myself. Right now, I want to finish looking through this nightstand." Aaron demanded.

With the forensic team in full force, the tiny motel room appeared to be getting smaller by the minute. That ten by ten room had never seen so many people— at least not that many sober people.

As one team member began to lift an article of bedding, another would be closing a drawer. As Aaron was reviewing the contents of the nightstand, which surprisingly housed several items, he knew he'd found something worthwhile.

Apart from the *Gideon Bible*, placed there in the hope of people learning about the teachings of Jesus Christ, he found a hypodermic.

Taking his gloved hand and a pair of long tweezers, he picked up the syringe and needle. A tiny amount of liquid was visible in the barrel of the syringe, prompting him to have the liquid tested as quickly as possible. "If this murder was drug induced, or related to that in any way, then you have your answer as to who committed it."

With Aaron's assistant nearby, he took the syringe and needle, and placed it in a metal-lined box— sealing it, in the hope of preventing an accidental needle stick. With Alison hovering over his shoulder, he could sense the sheer determination in her posture and her

34

voice, as she stated, "See, I told you 'Little Sammy' was the one. I don't want to say I'm right, but I was right." With a slight chuckle in her voice, she kneeled beside Aaron, looking into the drawer where the needle had been. Taking a gloved hand, she removed the drawer.

Asking a question, which he already knew the answer to, Aaron said, "Why are you taking the entire drawer?"

With a wry smile, Alison looked up and said, "to catch our killer. I have a feeling about this, Aaron. Have you ever known something was just right? I know. I feel it. I know he did this."

Opening an evidence bag, she slid the drawer into it, sealing it with a zip tie issued by the department. With its contents sealed, she turned her attention back to the nightstand. Sitting atop the surface, apart from an expensive metal lamp, was a pair of sunglasses, a pack of menthol cigarettes and a bottle of off-label pills.

After touching the drawer of the nightstand earlier, she was mentally prompted to remove and change her gloves to not transfer evidence from surface to surface. Picking up the bottle of pills with her newly gloved hand, she gave it a shake.

"My God," Alison whispered to herself.

The pills, a bottle of Hydrocodone/Acetaminophen tablets, had been filled within the last few months, but oddly, was still full. No tablets were missing.

"Fifty-eight, fifty-nine, sixty. They're all here. The prescription quantity at the bottom says sixty. I don't understand. If someone were going to drug her, why not actually give her a pill?" Alison pondered, instantly becoming confused.

35

With the question still hanging in the air, a cloud of dust began to grow larger and larger from an approaching car, coming off the road. Robert had arrived, bringing with him a thermos of coffee. "Sorry, y'all, I had a rough night. I need a pick me up. What's going on here? Fill me in on what's happened since I went home last night." Robert insisted.

Surveying the room, with his left hand shoved in his pocket, his right holding his coffee, he scanned from top to bottom. Already seeing obvious changes in the room since last night, he realized how much information he potentially missed by not arriving earlier. With the bloody sheets now removed, leaving only a stained mattress protector, he could still see her. He could still see the pain that was left behind. The memory of the pain. The pain that followed the memory of the pain. He would never forget last night. He'd never forget Tessie. Robert tried to put it out of his head, *but there are things*, he reminded himself, *that… just don't ever leave you, no matter what happens.*

Chapter Six

Maintaining his composure and knowing that he felt emotional because of the recent lack of sleep… at least that was the lie he needed to tell himself… he reviewed the day's events, as told by Alison.

She detailed the bottle of pills, syringe, and needle, including the interview with 'Little Sammy'. With her concern about the individual conveyed to Robert, Aaron interjected, and reminded both of them that he was innocent until proven guilty. "Alison had it in her head that he was the one who drugged her with the needle, cut the piece of skin from her chest, and ripped her intestines out."

"Wait just a damned minute here, who did you say? There's not a dangerous bone in his body. I've known him for years and he's never hurt anyone. He's just retarded. Hang around Fleetham long enough and you'll see him walking the streets. I once ran him out of the grocery store for trying to buy a cigar with a coffee cup full of pennies." Robert laughed as he explained this.

"Take it from me, y'all, if there's anything worth saving, it's that boy's life. Don't put him through this. He's just a bit slow, but he's certainly not a murderer." Robert exclaimed.

"Yes, Robert, you've said that twice now, but remember, we must question everyone. I've already spoken to all the guests and staff members here, but he's the one I'm concerned about. We have a profiler for a reason. Let's utilize him." Alison begged.

With the investigation in full force, Robert briefed Alison on the events that had taken place last night at the hotel. "Ya know, Seth knew about the murder. He said my ex-wife told him."

Not surprised by this bit of information at all, and knowing how small-town gossip turned into a viral, social media medley, Alison listened to it, then immediately put it out of her mind. Turning her attention back to the bed, she searched for additional evidence that hadn't been collected yet. With the body removed, she was able to see the mess left behind. The forensics team surrounding the bed pulled the mattress cover back, bagging it in a red biohazard bag. Exposing the mattress, Alison and the rest of the forensics team were able to see the true terror that Tessie had to lie in. The mattress, originally purchased, as Robert said, "over a decade ago, from the looks of it," had a plethora of stains—sporadically placed, as if someone… or something, had had multiple spills. Spills… this was the term Alison kept repeating in her head, to avoid the true reality of what was actually on the mattress.

Covering the windows with a black plastic bag to block out the Texas morning sun, a bottle of Luminol was sprayed over the entire surface of the mattress. Having only about thirty seconds to see any trace evidence of blood, the investigation team huddled around the bed, waiting for the chemical to react with the iron elements found in blood.

After exactly thirty seconds of waiting—per Alison's watch—which felt like an hour to her, the mattress didn't change color. Verifying that the chemical had been correctly packaged, a second application was added. Again, after the waiting period was over, no change in color was seen. "I felt certain that something would be on there and I'm literally shocked to see nothing at all. It would have shone even if the surface had been cleaned," Alison stated, sounding obviously disappointed.

"Aaron, what else are you seeing here? I know you people use the actual crime scene to build your profile of each killer, right?" Robert asked.

Aaron, who wasn't truly paying attention to anyone, focusing all of his attention instead on the motel room, he turned and simply replied, "Yeah". As he slowly walked in front of the bed, Robert thought he looked like one of those British policemen you see on the TV. As Aaron stopped in front of the corner dining table, he turned and told Alison, "I need to talk to your suspect. Now."

Alison, who immediately grinned from ear to ear at the statement, as she had the gut feeling that she was right, called the Fleetham Police Department. "Hello, this is Detective Chaney, I need to speak to someone about one of our suspects." Not giving the other woman on the phone a chance to reply, she went on to request, "I need the arrest record for Samuel Harper, oh, and for Tessie Johanan, and anything else you find. I'll be down at the station in a few."

"Ma'am, can you hang on a minute; I'm searching the database in our computer system, and there's nothing on Samuel Harper. He doesn't have another name... other than 'Little Sammy'." Dispatch explained.

The operator, who Alison learned was also dispatch, given the raspy voice echoing over Robert's radio, apparently didn't understand the importance of this. "Y'all, I'm going to run down to the police station and see what I can find out. Robert, will you please see what the progress is on the autopsy?" Alison politely demanded. With that, she grabbed her keys from the depths of her pocket, and strolled out the door, heading to what she thought would be the arrest of her career.

Chapter Seven

Driving down Main Street in Fleetham, Alison let her mind wander. With the quaintness of small-town life, she wondered what it had been like for Tessie that night. The night she was killed. "Jesus Christ," Alison muttered.

Turning left, passing the bank, she envied the boring lives of the tellers and loan officers. As Alison continued to think about office life and their mundane routine, at that very moment, she wished she had less stress and excitement in her life. "They just don't know how it is," she thought aloud.

Accidently running through a stop sign, Alison chuckled to herself, thinking, *I just broke a law*.

Pulling into the police station parking lot, she sat in her car for a moment. Wondering what the potential criminal, 'Little Sammy' was doing, she also kept thinking about the autopsy result. Curious to know what the report would show everyone, she pushed the thought out of her head, and shoved the door open.

Standing in front of the door to the police station, texting, was Seth. He saw her, and not really realizing who she was, smiled and nodded. As Alison squeezed past him, hoping Seth would get the hint and move out of the way, she cleared her throat and said, "Pardon me, but I need to get through."

As Seth moved back slightly, Alison slipped through the door. Instinctively turning her head around, sensing that she was being watched, she saw Seth

41

standing in the exact spot he was in before, grinning. Alison thought his smirk was creepy. Scoffing quietly to herself, she half mumbled half whispered, "Pig."

Recognizing the coarse voice she had spoken to earlier, she strolled up to the receptionist desk.

Sitting behind the desk, hunched over a pile of files, was the dispatcher and receptionist, Sylvia.

Sylvia had been employed by the Fleetham Police Department since graduating from high school. Alison thought, this was the only life she'd ever known. Her dedication to the city of Fleetham was, something you just don't see anymore. Sylvia, a chain smoker for almost half her life, had the scars to prove it. As Alison kept looking Sylvia over, she realized her face resembled her GPS maps.

"How may I help?" Sylvia asked, clearing her throat. With her left hand gripping a Styrofoam coffee cup full of last night's scorched coffee, she slowly, but very loudly sipped.

"I'm Detective Chaney. I spoke to you earlier."

Looking over her grocery store readers, she opened her mouth to explain the information she had found to Alison, "I told you earlier, I didn't find anything. I thought I saw his name on an arrest record, but it was another Sammy."

Feeling a twinge of sadness at this bit of news, Alison was temporarily distracted by Seth. She could see him standing on the sidewalk directly in front of the police station. He wasn't doing anything in particular that she could see, except gazing through the window. As if he were staring into a looking glass, waiting for a response from an entity deep within, the expression on his face sending chills down Alison's spine. She turned

42

her attention back to Sylvia, "who is that standing in front of the window?"

"Oh... that's Dr. B. He's the doctor at the Auburn Clinic. He ran in here right before you drove up to ask a question about his dad."

Curious, Alison, while still gazing out the window asked, "His dad?"

"Yeah, his dad. He's the sheriff in town. I thought you'd know that."

Realizing that Seth was a miniature version of Robert, only with less fat and more hair, Alison nodded, acknowledging Sylvia's statement. Determined to find some shred of information on her main suspect, she started to scroll through her phone, finally finding the name she was looking for.

"Robert, do you have the video footage of the motel security cameras at your office? If so, I'm here now. I need to see them... There's absolutely nothing on this 'Small Sammy' guy."

"'Little Sammy', actually, and no I don't. I think they're available to be sent via email. The camera system is one of those new kinds, with Wi-Fi and all that. I'll run over to the motel office and talk to the manager. The problem is that the footage from last night wasn't found."

"Yeah, but well, forget it. Send it in an encrypted file. I'll use this as evidence to the court if there's something I need," Alison told him. Feeling an ounce of hope with the prospect of seeing the video footage, Alison finished the conversation with, "I ran into your son just now. He's here at the police station, or at least he was. Did he call you?"

43

"Seth was there? And no, I'd assumed he was at work. I'll call him in a minute after we hang up. What did he want with you?"

As per her very direct and blunt personality—she was a Scorpio after all—she asked Sylvia, with Robert still on the phone, "What did Seth, uh, Dr. Binder want when he was here earlier?"

Sylvia, not necessarily shocked by her question, but taken off guard replied, "Oh, he just ran in here asking about his dad and wanted to know something about the autopsy of that gal from the motel. I'd be lying if I said I was really paying attention."

Robert, having overheard what his receptionist said, asked Alison, "Okay, look, I've got things to do, so hit me up later if you're finished?"

With that, Alison hung up without telling him goodbye.

Awaiting the email notification, she quickly sent a text to Aaron, her criminal profiler.

Can you meet me at the police station? I need to go over some information, and I need your brain.

A few moments after the telephone call ended, the receptionist told her the email had arrived. Asking to sit behind the desk to review the information, Alison entered the encrypted password. With the video footage from the last few days in front of her, she took a deep breath, and readied herself for what she thought would be the evidence she needed.

As the video began earlier in the week, she followed the lives of those she thought of as less fortunate. Seeing the young mothers, who, along with their children, called Red Cove their home, Alison couldn't help but feel sorry for them. After the string of

44

women strolling past the vending machines and entering their rooms, she saw what she thought was a drug deal. Truly not caring about it, she continued scrubbing through the footage.

"He was right," she mumbled under her breath. "There's no footage from the night of the murder. The entire day is missing." Overhearing Alison talking to herself, Sylvia asked, "What does that mean?"

"It means that someone has altered this tape. The thing is who had access to it? Is this something 'Little Sammy' could have done?"

Choking and coughing on her coffee from an immediate inhalation of air, her laugh mixed with her wet smokers cough, nearly rattling the windows. "Hell, no. He didn't fix this tape. He only went through the third grade. He knows how to mow grass and move lumber from place to place. Though he's pretty decent at the grill when there's a hog to smoke." Sylvia chortled.

As she continued scrolling through the tape, it immediately skipped to the day after the murder—today.

With today's early morning footage beginning at 02:14, a split-second frame showed Robert standing in front of room 201. Slowly scrubbing the video, hoping to see something of interest, exactly three minutes after seeing Robert on the camera, something immediately stood out to her. To the very far left of the camera, barely in viewing range, she saw a man. Although the video quality was very poor, she thought the man appeared to be youngish. "Sylvia, who is this? See him? He looks like he's very short and stocky." Alison asked as she continued to squint at the computer screen.

"Hang on, let me get my spectacles on. My eyes ain't as good as they used to be," Sylvia scoffed, as she slid her glasses on, "Oh, well, looky here. There's ole

45

'Little Sammy'. What the hell is he doing in the middle of the night?"

Her concerned face slowly turned into that of a kid in a candy store. Feeling very sure of herself now, she tapped her manicured acrylic nail on the desk. Watching the man, whom Sylvia had identified as 'Little Sammy', she slowly moved the scrubbing button to the right, hoping to see more. As she waited, she began to wonder why he wasn't moving. After watching the clip again, she saw the same thing all over again. "He's just standing there. He looks like a statue, doesn't he?" Alison asked.

Feeling a tad frustrated by this, she continued to scroll through the video, into the afternoon, and then the present time—minus a few minutes. Nothing of interest caught her eye, but she would absolutely use this in the evidence listing. Waiting for Aaron to arrive, she decided to scroll through her work email, not seeing anything that required immediate attention. As she continued to kill time on her mobile, she looked up towards the large front window of the police station.

Seth was gone. Dismissing the thought, she continued to wait for Aaron. After she was ready to send a text to remind him, and in her own way, "bitch a bit", something she was an expert at, she saw his black FBI issued vehicle pull up in front of the building. Aaron, being a resident of a large city wasn't accustomed to parking in a small-town parking lot. It really wasn't a proper parking lot as it was only the shoulder of the main road. In Fleetham, you parked in front of any given building, hoping that you wouldn't ram your front fender on the curb.

That's exactly what happened. She could hear his plastic fender scraping against the concrete curb. The sound, as she had experienced all too often, was the sound of money. The sound of a soon to be broken front fender.

As Aaron strutted down the sidewalk, approaching the front door, Alison stood up to allow Sylvia to return to her duties. Walking to the front door, she opened it, feeling the humidity of the Texas morning; "Hey, we need to talk," She said in her most direct tone.

"Sure, what's up. Your boy get caught yet?"

Chuckling at his comment, she replied, "No, but I did see him on the video footage from the motel. Anyway, I want you to tell me something about the killer, please."

As the two walked down the hallway to an empty office, it became apparent that Alison had something specific on her mind to ask him. With his expertise in criminal profiling, he was renowned throughout the field for his ability to 'enter the killer's mind' and understand the nuances of what drives them to kill. Arriving at what appeared to both of them to be an office that hadn't been used in many years, they sat down at a card table.

"Life is so different here, Ali. I mean, I'm sitting at a card table, working on a murder case. This certainly isn't a metropolitan city of any form," Aaron joked.

"Okay, so here's my thing," Alison said. Pushing her frizzed hair from the morning humidity behind her ears, she cleared her throat and continued, "As I said before, I saw 'Little Sammy' on the video. He wasn't really doing anything. Just standing there. But it was weird. It was as if he was just watching or something. I haven't really worked it out yet."

With Aaron's response, almost pre-generated from his years of profiling murderers, he elucidated matters for Alison, "I think from the little evidence that

47

I have been exposed to over the last few days, the killer probably has psychopathic tendencies, and antisocial behavior."

Hearing the word 'antisocial', she recalled what she had learned about 'Little Sammy'. *Was he antisocial, she thought?* "Judging by the weird video, could you say that 'Little Sammy' was antisocial?"

"That's hard to say from seeing a five-second video. By the way, I haven't seen the video yet, so your statement isn't remotely accurate." Aaron protested.

As Alison nodded at his remark, making a mental note to show him the video later that afternoon, she pulled out her notebook. Preparing to ask Aaron a few questions to get a true insider's look at the tendencies he was describing, her mobile buzzed.

Glancing at her phone, she saw it was a text from Robert. *The autopsy will be performed at 14:00 today. When you finish at the station, I need to see you. It's important.*

Setting her phone aside for the time being, promising herself she would reply to him shortly, she began her interview with Aaron.

"Okay, so you think he's a psychopath, or at least has those tendencies?" Alison asked.

With her anxiety building, waiting for an answer, she abruptly added, "Also, would a psychopath have to be really smart to do this?"

Aaron, who was used to repetitive questions like this, ran his hands through his hair, leaned back in his chair and began, "A psychopath, tendencies or not, same-same. For the most part, they are usually very smart. I guess there's the dumbass who can still be one. But I digress. They're stellar liars and can make Jesus believe their stories." Laughing at his last comment,

48

Aaron continued, "If you've met one before, you would never forget them… once you figured out what their— for lack of a better term—affliction was. They're suave. Everyone wants to be around them. They're a true stud. Or princess. Whichever shoe fits."

Writing at a furious pace, Alison looked up and asked, "This doesn't sound like our guy, does it? He's far from suave from what I'm told."

Receiving another text, she raised her phone and saw another message from Robert. *Call your lab ASAP.*

Reading the message aloud to Aaron, she pushed her chair back, adding a bone-chilling, metal scraping against tile sound. "I need to go outside to get better reception. There's an issue the lab. Be right back. Can you run to the front desk and ask to see the last year's arrest records? From everyone in the county?" Alison requested.

Stepping outside, immediately savoring the fresh air, she dialed the number to her lab. The main operator answered, a youngish woman, maybe twenty? But Alison wasn't great at judging age. Definitely a foreigner. Maybe Indian? "Hello, this is Detective Chaney, I need to be connected to the forensics lab." Alison insisted.

After the call transferred through a series of clicks followed by silence, the man on the other end finally answered. Speaking in a very distinctive, pronounced English accent, he said, "Forensics lab, this is Dr. Anderson, how may I help you?"

"Hey, this is Alison, I had a message to call you."

"Ah, yes, I thought it was you. I must speak to you about something. Are you sitting down?"

Not really in the mood for a Londoner's sense of humor, she abruptly demanded, "What is it?"

49

Sensing her irritation at his remark, he cleared his throat and began, "It concerns the syringe and drawer you sent over here. Firstly, the hypodermic contained a very small amount of blood, which has been preserved and will be compared to autopsy DNA. Secondly, in the barrel of the syringe was a very small portion of what was determined to be Versed. The victim was more than likely given the Versed before the murder… or after. I'm only speculating, you understand."

"What else?" Alison asked.

"I also found a fingerprint. Several in fact. None on the drawer, but three were located on the hypodermic syringe. They have been recorded into official evidence and are currently being scanned for matches." Dr. Anderson concluded.

With this bit of information that she really wasn't surprised to hear, Alison told him to search everything he was given again, and look for additional strands of anything, drops of anything, anything at all.

"Okay, I've got to run, but call me on this number if you have new information. Goodbye," Alison ended the call and pocketed her phone.

Poking her head back into the station, she yelled for Sylvia to step outside. "Can you run fingerprints for me please?"

Not giving Sylvia a chance to reply, Alison also added, "And I need you to call 'Little Sammy' in too, please. Let Robert know."

Glancing at her watch, the autopsy time was slowly creeping up on her. *I need to hurry the hell up here and head over to the hospital,* Alison thought.

Back inside, Aaron was already waiting for her at the reception desk when he said, " Go to the hospital.

50

I've got this. I want to do my thing here, and I'll meet you at the hospital in about an hour or so. Okay?"

With a sudden sense of relief, yet still carrying an immense burden as she realized the amount of work that still remained, she smiled, turned around, and headed back to her car. As she left the station, she knew her next stop would be the most important. The autopsy was like adding the correct number to a Sudoku puzzle to achieve the right answer.

Chapter Eight.

Walking away from the police station, heading for the hospital, Seth couldn't stop thinking about seeing Alison. Having seen her before at the motel and around town, he couldn't get her out of his mind. His head was all over the place and included his main, reoccurring thought, *She's just my type. She walks like she doesn't take shit from nobody.* Smiling at this, Seth licked his lips, adjusting his shirt as he stepped down from the sidewalk and climbed into his car. "Hey, there, sister," he purred to his Porsche 911. His car, the trophy of his life thus far was something that everyone stared at. Living in a town of less than a thousand, he was the guy who didn't fit the mold. "I'm not a cowboy and I'm not a city boy. I'm just me," Seth used to tell his dates.

Sliding into his buttery-soft, leather seats, he cranked the engine and adjusted the air conditioning. Pulling his visor mirror from its resting position, he checked his hair and his appearance in general. "Hot damn..." Seth whispered. Getting a brief, but sufficient scent of his cologne, he smiled, thinking, *Oh, Alison, come to daddy.*

Releasing the parking brake, and moving his gear shift to reverse, he slowly backed out of the parking lot, hoping to catch one last glimpse of Alison. Realizing that this wasn't going to happen, he decided to head down to the hospital. Having already been told that he wasn't

52

allowed to attend the autopsy, he bit his lip and whispered, "here we go."

After five minutes of driving, he whipped his sportscar into the hospital parking lot and stepped out of the car.

Snapping his ID badge on the front of his collar and slinging his white lab coat over his shoulder, he strolled through the front sliding doors. Flashing his pearly white smile, covered with porcelain veneers, he nodded at Olga, the morning receptionist, and said, "Hello, there, beautiful. How's it going?"

With chills running down her spine, and a tingle in the pit of her stomach, she cleared her throat and replied, "Hello Dr. B, are you on call today?" Her face flushing with every passing second.

"No. I just dropped by to see Dr. Sanchez for a second. Is he in his office?" Seth asked, intentionally adding a sultry flair. Smiling again at Olga, but this time squinting slightly and with a crooked grin, he added, "You have a great day!"

With that, he left Olga flushed, tingly and flustered, but in a very positive way.

Walking to the elevator, he swiped the barcode side of his ID card through the reader slot, entered his access code and pushed the "B" button, destined for the basement morgue.

Chapter Nine

Having driven across town, which in reality was only about four blocks down the road, she arrived at the Fleetham Memorial Hospital. Unaware of her surroundings, especially the parking lot, she pulled her vehicle into an "expectant mother" parking space. Smiling, she thought, *Someday.* Getting out of her car, she strolled through the front doors of the building.

Waiting to greet her was the day-shift receptionist, Olga, a woman who had aged beautifully. She had the appearance of a graceful, old Hollywood star, mixed with the feistiness of a mad bull. Looking up from her crossword puzzle she said, "Hi, honey, what can I help you with today?"

Flashing her badge, knowing that this generation highly respected authority, she explained that she needed to be directed to the mortuary. Abruptly taken back by the question, expecting to be asked where the gift shop was, Olga cleared her throat, plucked a Kleenex from its box, and walked around the crescent-shaped podium. Taking Alison by the arm, which, oddly made her feel at ease, she led her to the elevator.

"Hun, you'll want to take the elevator down to the basement, turn left, and go through the double doors. Actually, there are a few sets of doors, but once you get there, you'll know."

Thinking about what she had just said, Alison laughed, "I think everyone would know if they end up in the morgue!"

Smiling in a very refined and poised way, Olga entered the access code so the elevator could begin its descent.

Alison, deep in thought with the comfort of Olga at her side, kept repeating a bible verse in her head that always comforted her as a child, *Isaiah 41:10: Fear thou not; for I am with thee.*

Dismissing the clout of religion after her teenage years, she nonetheless maintained the strength of calling herself a Christian. She, or so she told people, wasn't very religious, however, she was spiritual. Standing in the stainless-steel elevator, with the sound of *Moonlight Sonata* playing in the background, gave Alison a sense of contentment. Lowered by the elevator to the pits of the hospital, they finally arrived in the basement, where the vault of death was housed.

As they stepped out of the elevator, Olga directed Alison to the set of double doors leading to the morgue. Bidding her goodbye and explaining that only clinical and legal staff were allowed to cross that barrier, Olga returned to the elevator, ascending back to civilization. Seeing the double doors, which Alison presumed led to the most depressing room she'd ever visit, she slowly pushed them open to find Jim sitting at his desk. Alison announced her presence by half knocking, half tapping her nails on the double doors. Jim looked across from his computer screen, his glasses hanging off the bridge of his nose, obviously deep in thought and said, "Oh, hey, I was wondering when you'd stop by. I have some things for you to look at over here."

Perplexed, Alison quickly scanned the room for an extra chair, only finding a metal stool on casters. Jim motioned, arm outstretched, offering the stool to her. Assuming it was used during the autopsy process, she opted to stand in front of his desk, her mysophobia making her fear coming in contact with germs and blood. "I'm sorry, but I'll stand. Thank you, all the same. It's just the thought of…" Alison broke off, a disgusted look on her face. Grinning and half laughing, slightly irritated by her comment, Jim said, "Oh, loosen up, it's fine. But if you'd rather stand, be my guest. Now, I have some preliminary results to show you, as well as some evidence recovered from the body."

Giving it her undivided attention, she started to get herself into detective mode, leaving the phobia of medical procedures behind her. "What could you have possibly found in the body?" Alison asked, curious, yet nervous at the same time.

Barely allowing Alison to finish her sentence, Jim immediately interrupted, "Fibers. Two actually. Well, one fiber and one hair, to be exact. The fiber was a nylon strand, brown in color. The hair, well, I'm not sure what species yet, but it's an animal hair."

Alison's eyes sprang wide open with the second tidbit of information. Thinking she had misheard, she clarified, "You said animal hair? Are you absolutely sure, Jim?"

Knowing she'd clarify and re-clarify this information, as per the norm for a forensic detective, Jim replied, "Yes, I'm quite sure. The medulla of the hair is very small in humans, whereas, in an animal it's quite thick. Also, the cuticle of the human hair is imbricated, but the animal hair is spinous. You can also see the

56

differences in pigmentation. It's quite dense, compared to a human."

Understanding a fraction of what he said, Alison, scribbling furiously in her notebook, looked at Jim, "Okay, I know what the cuticle of the hair is. It's the shell basically, right? And imbricated. That's what?"

"Imbricated is scaly, in a way. And, yes, you're correct about the cuticle. The hair, once you see it under magnification, is denser than a dog's hair… say a poodle, for example. You'd expect a poodle hair to be softer than that of say a hog," Jim explained.

"I've sent the hair off to a hair analysis lab. I should have some kind of answer back by tomorrow. The fiber has also been sent off for analysis. It's quite curly. Could be from a sweater, carpet, or something similar."

Continuing to scribble her notes as he spoke, Alison stopped. Tapping her pen on her chin, she looked up, squinting, apparently ready to say something. Staring into a black hole, deep in thought, she formulated her question, without sounding arrogant, "I don't understand the animal hair, though. The fiber, yeah, but wouldn't you expect a human hair, rather than an animal? It's quite obvious that an animal didn't kill her."

Understanding the point she was trying to make, Jim told her, "Yeah, I know. Dr. Binder and I both agree. He noticed the animal hair when we began cutting away the bedsheet she was laying on in the body bag."

Immediately after hearing Dr. Binder's name, she snapped her head up, pushed her hair behind her ears and said, in an infuriated voice, "What did you just say?"

Her voice echoed through the sterile, stainless steel room. Jim's face, while already naturally tan, as he was fortunate enough to be born with olive skin, originating from Mexico, had turned an odd shade of

57

rose. Stuttering as he spoke, Jim reluctantly replied, "Uh, yeah, he came by a few hours ago, and uh, we started to talk and um, he offered to help me with the autopsy."

"Are you crazy? You can't involve another doctor in this case. He isn't associated with the Bureau. He hasn't even been cleared by federal security, for Christ sake! I swear, sometimes it feels like I have to completely involve myself in everyday situations..."

At that moment, the examination room doors to the morgue opened, stopping her mid-flow. Wearing a powder blue, paper surgical gown, covered in blood, was Seth. Still wearing his facial shield, but out of sheer common sense, she figured out who he was. "Hello, I'm Detective Alison Chaney, with the forensics team. I don't believe we've met?" Lowering his mask, and raising his facial shield, having already removed his gloves in the exam room, he said, "Hey, how are ya? I'm Dr. Seth Binder. I hope you don't mind, but I figured Jim here could use an extra set of hands... being as it's such a big deal and all."

Highly annoyed, yet melting inside from his silky-smooth voice, Alison said, "You've not been cleared at all by the security team. Do you often assist with autopsies?"

Smiling at her question, Seth quickly replied, "Not really, but I am a doctor and know what I'm looking at. Basically, it's surgery. And I don't have an arrest record or a license referral, so I'm good to go with your little security issue, ma'am."

Immediately catching his sarcastic tone, she nodded, hoping it would suffice, trying to avoid a long discussion with such a pompous man. "Jim, anyway, I need to show you something. Are you nearly finished out

58

here with this policewoman so you can come back to what we were doing?" Seth asked.

Standing up from his desk, he grabbed the mask he'd removed earlier and turned to Alison, "Listen, I've got to go back to work. You're welcome to hang out here and review the notes I've already made. I need to finish this exam and stitch her back up."

Excited to read his findings up to this point, Alison nodded, and simply replied, "Okay, great. Have at it." The irritation from Seth's presence still hanging in the air, she walked around to sit in Jim's chair, readying herself for what she hoped would be a long, insightful reading session. It was apparent that both men could sense and hear her annoyance, so nothing was said as they pushed the double doors open and disappeared into the exam room. With the two doctors gone, she adjusted the chair to the appropriate height, propped her elbows on the table, and opened the manila file folder. Inside, she found the typical postmortem photographs, both from the motel and the exam table, handwritten notes, and a typed county report.

Alison quickly scanned the county form, which was typical for any autopsy. Realizing it was only partially completed, since the autopsy wasn't finished yet, she transcribed some of the information into her notebook. The most pertinent bit of information was the birthdate: *August 5, 1991*. "She'd be thirty-four next month," Alison murmured. There was no other demographic information, other than her name and last known address, pulled from the Department of Public Safety information. Scribbling down her address, she flipped pages, and focused her attention on the photographs.

59

The pictures confronted Alison with the most gruesome images she remembered from the previous day, leading her to a somber moment. Normally, Alison lived in a bubble, blocking her emotions from the job, but today she was overcome by sadness. "Poor thing," she whispered to herself. Touching Tessie's face on the photo with her index finger, she began to study the images. The first photo that affected her so much was of Tessie lying in bed, posed as one of Leonardo da Vinci's masterpieces, had he been a killer. On the first page were Jim's handwritten notes.

Rope to feet secured to footboard. Rope to hands tied to headboard. Skin removed on chest. Heart shape. Golf ball shoved down throat. Linear incision/cut to ABD. Large and small intestine exposed.

White panties in mouth. Bruising to neck. Choked?

Realizing that this was the initial assessment of the body, she turned her attention to, as Jim called it, the incision on the abdomen. When she looked closer at the disembowelment, she cringed. Her arms were full of goosepimples and she felt a sudden wave of nausea. Normally, she had the strength of a lion when dealing with crime scene photos, and crime scenes in general, but today was different. Slowly taking a very deep breath, she held it for a few seconds—a trick she learned at the academy during training when tension was high. Feeling somewhat more relaxed, she transcribed his findings to her notebook. Turning the photograph over, she moved to the next.

In the second photo, judging by the background images, Tessie was now in the morgue. The autopsy was about to begin, as she had had the fitted sheet from the motel removed. The image was a macro shot of her stomach. The incision—which Alison felt comfortable calling it—was according to Jim's notes, 17.04 cm in length. Googling quickly, she typed, *inches to cm conversion.* With the search engine pulling up a table, she entered the centimeter amount, converting it to 6.71 inches.

Catching herself continuing to gaze at the photo, she couldn't understand why the incision was so clean. *Could 'Little Sammy' have done this? Is he even able to cut a straight line?* Alison thought to herself. Seeing the haunting images made her instantly realize just how precious life was. The gore of the body was there. The gore was real. Alison shuddered.

Unable to continue with her task, she kept her attention focused on this one particular photo. The incision to her stomach was very clean. It didn't look like others she'd seen over the years, or even in training. Remembering some of her previous cases where bodies had been severely damaged and mangled, she recalled very uneven, almost 'sawing' cuts and gouges. Not realizing she was talking to herself, she said, "someone with a steady hand." Knowing she needed to continue with her work, she set aside the photo, to remind herself to look at the image again. Feeling that she needed a break for a brief moment, she walked over to the double doors that led into the hallway and stepped outside. Though she was still in the depths of the hospital, stepping out of the morgue was overwhelmingly relieving. Feeling the chill from the constantly cold hospital air-conditioner, she inhaled deeply. Closing her eyes for a moment, she took herself to her happy place. Her happy place was one that she kept to herself. No one, not even her ex-lovers, or even her parents knew where it was. Her happy place was her grandmother's house.

Alison's grandmother was her rock and had died when she was in her mid-twenties. But to this day, Alison continued to relish every moment she had had with her. Her home, full of baked cookies and lemon fresh spray disinfectant, was her sanctuary. It was her home away from home. She felt safe there. And in this moment, going back to grandmother's house was her safe haven. It was her relief from the world. "Ahh." The sound escaped her mouth, louder than anticipated, but she didn't care. For that brief second, she was content.

Feeling a sense of calmness, she turned around and headed back to the morgue. Though the double entry doors were only about ten feet away, in the bright, white tunnel of death, it seemed like walking ten miles. *Imagine doing this every day, all day,* she thought to herself. Walking into the morgue, she resumed her position at Jim's desk and continued to go through the additional photographs.

Seeing the image of the piece of skin removed from her chest, she wondered why the killer had chosen to do this. Remembering a classic trademark of serial killers, the taking of an item as a trophy, she asked herself, "Was this their trophy?" Unable to persuade herself that the trophy was indeed the cut-out piece of skin, she nevertheless wrote it down in her book. A question mark was added to the statement, with the addendum, *Trophy? Skin was left in room and placed in condom.*

The cut-out shape to her chest was, as Jim's notes suggested, directly above the heart. The shape was freehand—that much she could see clearly. Not as much precision and time was used to cut into her chest, since there was a small area of skin that had accidently been

62

cut into along the perimeter of the wound. Jim had also written *postmortem wound* on the back of the photo.

Alison hadn't immediately seen that. There was minimal blood on the body, yet the skin in the condom at the motel was slightly bloody. "Of course, there would be blood, just not a lot of it," she muttered to herself. The condom had not been taken to the morgue yet, and she knew of several other items that were missing. As she was finishing reviewing the heart photo, a rap at the door indicated someone was entering the morgue. Walking in, notebook in hand, was Robert. Looking disheveled and tired, he addressed Alison, "Look, I don't have a lot of time, but I wanted to say that 'Little Sammy' has an old arrest in a neighboring town. I found the info from another county, but had it faxed over to my office. I'm waiting to receive it."

"That's awesome, maybe they will find something else, as well," Alison chimed in. Motioning Robert to the desk, she said, "I know you saw the body before it was removed, but here are some photos if you wanted to check them out."

"Nope. I can't bear to see her in that condition again. There are some things you just can't forget. That'll be one of them," he said quietly, sounding depressed.

"I want to show you something, though. Please?" she insisted, handing him the disembowelment image. Robert took a quick, deep breath, and glanced at the photo. All the memories came flooding back to him. Last night, walking into the motel—seeing her naked body tied down.

He told Alison, "Not that this is funny in any way, but it reminds me of hunting. We'd hang deer from a chain in the garage and gut them. Their guts would spill

63

out all over the damned place. Not that I'm comparing her to a dead animal, but still…"

The image immediately popped into Alison's head. Shrugging it off, not wanting to hyper focus on that gory mental image, she said, "Right, but look at the incision. It's so clean. I keep asking myself, could our guy have done this?"

Robert, now running the question through his head, looked at Alison. As their eyes locked, Robert squinted slightly and tilted his head to the side. Keeping his eyes on hers, he asked, "What do you think?"

"I haven't even spoken to the guy, but from what I've been told, he isn't the most intelligent man in the world. Maybe his cornbread just isn't done in the middle?" Alison spat.

Chuckling at her comment, he added, "He drinks a lot. He's had some addiction issues in the past. Sober him up enough and he might be able to gut someone. I think anyone is capable. Anyone."

With that statement, he handed her the photograph and said, "I've got to run, I need to finish up at the motel. The profiler is coming to the morgue in a minute, or so he says. He's a bit scatterbrained."

Bidding him goodbye, Alison replied, "See you. I'll call you with anything new."

Giving her the one-handed military salute, in a joking way, he opened the double doors and disappeared into the ten-mile white hallway of the hospital.

64

Chapter Ten

With Robert gone, Alison was left alone in the front area of the morgue. As she was wishing that the two men would finish their assessment, Jim strolled back into the room.

Still wearing his blue surgical gown, he walked over to the foot-controlled sink and washed his hands. "Ya know, this girl was high as a kite. I had Seth run a toxicology screen on her. Tox screen was positive for anxiolytics and opioids," Jim informed her.

Wanting to know what drugs were found, Alison asked, "Oh. really? Well, we did find a bottle of pills and that syringe with something in it."

Jim continued, "Yeah, I'm waiting for the syringe info to come back from the lab, but she had a very large amount of morphine as well as Versed. If she were sedated prior to the actual murder, it would have been a blessing."

Nodding in agreement, she said, "Mmmhmmm".

Curious for more information about what findings were made during the autopsy, she walked closer to where he stood and pointedly asked, "What else did you find? I need to know about the abdominal cut and the heart shaped area on her chest. Also, you had written in your notes about a golf ball?"

Remembering his notes, which she hoped she'd transcribed correctly, as his penmanship was horrible, she couldn't help but wonder why someone would actually want Jim's job. Momentarily zoning out, which was common for her during high stress situations, she quickly brought herself back to the here and now.

Jim added to his previous comment, "The cut-out was definitely postmortem. There was minimal bleeding to the wound itself. The skin flap that was removed would have bled slightly, but not enough to show a significant amount of blood. It was in the condom, right? With the lubrication of the condom, and the small amount of blood on the skin flap, what you saw is probably accurate and not altered."

Nodding, and scribbling faster than she'd ever written before, she held up a finger, gesturing for him to pause, and asked, "But the golf ball. What was that all about? And while you were working on her, did you see how straight the stomach cut was?"

Nodding and adjusting his mask, Jim replied, "I did. It was very clean. I was just telling Seth that I've performed autopsies where the body looked as if it had been a victim of a hacksaw. And that golf ball. I think it could be a trademark of the killer. That's why we need Aaron here. I called him earlier. Anyway, the golf ball wasn't what suffocated her. I really believe she had died long before any of this was done."

Alison sat down at the desk, absentmindedly going through the photos again. Trying to form the question in her head and make it sound as professional as possible, she flung the stack of photos on the desk and asked, "How did she die?"

Knowing the answer wouldn't be known for quite some time, and seeing her pain and frustration, Jim nodded. His kind eyes told her the answer she didn't want to hear, "*I don't know yet.*"

66

Chapter Eleven

As Seth lifted the heart from the chest cavity, he massaged it. Feeling its weight in the palm of his hand, he placed it in the metal tray on the scale, directly beside him. The digital display showed 276 grams. Knowing it was an appropriate weight, he set the organ on the table behind him. The table was barely visible beneath the cobalt blue sheet that covered it. Under the surgical drape, the vital organs of Tessie rested. The heart in the left corner, followed by both lungs, and dominating the table were the intestines. Spanning a length of about eighteen feet, though the actual measurement would be included in the report, Seth admired the workmanship of his creator. *He made nearly twenty feet of gut that piles up into a ball the size of a birthday cake*, he thought to himself.

Removing the liver, he could see she was a heavy drinker. Multiple areas of scarring were noted and recorded into his digital tape recorder. Hanging above the table, it served as an automated transcriptionist. Detailing every event of the autopsy, later to be typed into a report. As he was finishing his sentence into the dictation device above, Jim entered the room again. As he finished pulling his gloves on, he asked, "Find anything interesting while I was away?"

With his hand's wrist deep in Tessie's chest cavity, Seth said, "The liver was a mess. She obviously was an alcoholic. See the scar tissue over there?"

Turning slightly, acknowledging that the liver was directly behind him, he nodded in the general direction of the table. With Jim fully prepared to resume his job, he took a pair of scissor clamps and pulled the neck tissue back. Securing the clamps with a clip to the table, he examined the bones of the throat. With the golf ball having been removed at the beginning of the autopsy, he was able to clearly see the throat and all its organs that awaited his assessment. Excising the trachea, he could see the hyoid bone. Though not as dominant as Tessie's male counterpart would be, it was nonetheless present. "Seth, look, the hyoid is cracked. It's a vertical and horizontal crack. T-shaped. See?" Jim enthused, as he pointed to the area.

Seth turned his attention to her neck, focusing on what Jim had described, and added, "The ligature around her neck probably crushed it. The bruising is in a very thin line. Rope would have left a larger mark, don't you agree?"

Continuing to assess the neck region, Jim nodded and replied with a simple, "Mmhmm".

Taking a scalpel and removing additional tissue from her neck, Jim was able to see the bruising more clearly. The bruise, from his experience was definitely a ligature mark. Something had been used to strangle her. "This absolutely isn't postmortem. There's too much bruising." Jim added. Taking his attention off her neck for a moment, he quickly glanced at her eyes. Under close observation, her beautiful brown eyes showed Jim what he needed to see—the tell-tale signs of strangulation. Subconjunctival hemorrhage. The sclera—whites of the eyes—were filled with sporadic, circular areas of blood, which would be added to the report. Under each eye, several petechiae patches were seen as well. "I'll have to dumb this down for Alison," he told Seth.

As Seth continued to assess her lower abdomen, moving down to expose her reproductive organs, he commented, "Didn't you say she was raped? I checked her vaginal canal and didn't see any other fluid except coagulated blood. I swabbed the entire area, just in case."

Tilting his head in a moment of deep thought, Jim asked, "Really? She had several areas of trauma to her vaginal tissue, I remember. I quickly did a once over when she arrived."

As Seth removed her ovaries and uterus, it was clear that she'd had a tubal ligation. Her fallopian tubes had been stapled shut, though he didn't understand why. As Seth was a typical man, he never understood the concept of preventing life in the first place. He had a very strict pro-life stance, and even wearing a condom condemned his viewpoint. Being raised in a very religious home, he was taught the more conservative side of life. While showing Jim the tubal site, he asked him, "Did she have a lot of children? She's been sealed off at some point in her life."

Not knowing the answer, Jim shrugged his shoulders, more concerned about her eyes. It appeared to him that one of the eyes was bruised. He believed, as she died from strangulation that the bruise was related to the intense pressure caused by the ligature. In his report, he would conclude that the cause of death was by strangulation.

As Seth continued to evaluate the lower groin area, he moved into the vaginal region. With her pelvis floor exposed, he continued to excise tissue. Having the entire area open, he could then see the extensive damage to the vaginal walls. If rape was what was deemed to

69

have happened, he'd have to seriously re-consider the event. From the extensive clotting of blood, plus the extreme amount of damage, this was something that couldn't have happened during a normal rape. Approximately forty superficial lacerations were present on both sides of the vaginal walls. Her cervix was lacerated, and her clitoris had been removed. This wasn't noticed during the initial examination.

"Jim. Jesus Christ. They cut her clit off and sliced her to shit."

With this, Jim moved his attention to Seth's area of the body to see the gruesome work of her murder firsthand. "Were the body parts recovered at the motel?" Jim asked.

Shrugging, Seth gave Jim his answer.

"I've seen all I need to see. I'm going to go and type my report and check on the lab results. Are you good with closing her up?" Jim asked.

"Yes, sir, I've got this. Go fill Alison in. I spent five minutes with her and realized she needs to be kept informed at all times," Seth said, laughing lightly.

As Jim removed his gloves, plastered to his hands by his own sweat, he flung them off into the lab's kick bucket, usually reserved for dirty gauze squares. Removing his facial shield and mask, he flicked them both in the trash, along with his bloody surgical gown. Strolling over to the foot-controlled sink, he grabbed a chlorhexidine scrub packet, and began his ritualist performance of cleansing the death from him. Though he was covered from head to toe, in Jim's mind, scrubbing after the fact, removed the emotions and some of the memories.

70

"Seth, stay in this business long enough and you'll see what we do to cope. Just don't use me as an example." Jim quipped, laughing as he spoke to Seth.

Drying his now completely sterile hands, he shouldered the double doors open and walked back into the main morgue office where Alison was on her phone, texting.

"Okay, Okay, I can't stand it. Surely, you've got more information for me. My office keeps calling, wanting updates, and I'm ready to get this over with and arrest my boy," Alison demanded.

Grabbing his file and notepad, he made several comments on a few forms, and added additional comments to already written statements. Glancing at Alison, Jim announced, "The cause of death is strangulation. Her vaginal area was absolutely destroyed, and her hyoid bone was crushed... but that's expected. The thing is was she drugged? Did she die from an overdose? Or was she strangled? Bruising to her eyes say strangulation. Tox screen says drug overdose. That's the million-dollar question, but I really think it's strangulation. She has more visible signs of that than of being killed by a drug overdose."

Furiously scribbling as he spoke, she was surprised to feel a tear forming in the corner of her eye. "Wasn't she raped?"

Nodding, Jim gave her his answer. "I'm not going into the details of that. It's very sad. Very sad indeed. It will, however, be in my report for you and your office to read."

For some reason, Alison felt disappointed. Quickly going over and over that thought in her head, she asked herself, *is it because Tessie was so brutally*

71

attacked? Did I not hear the sentence I wanted to hear? Did she suffer?

Did she suffer? That was the question she wanted Jim to answer. To ease her heart, mind, and physical worry, she told herself, *No, Ali, she was given a sedative and didn't feel a thing.*

Chapter Twelve

Arriving back at the motel, to the infamous room 201, Robert randomly thought about his ex-wife. Before all their problems began, he would have been comforted to know that she was waiting for him at home. Ready to greet him with a smile that would melt all the day's stresses away. Until today, he hadn't realized just how much he missed her. She had been his rock—but in the same way as a rock sinks in water, so did their happiness.

With the rest of the crime scene officers winding up their investigation for the day, he kept his focus on the bed. The image of Tessie's body was seared in his memory. Closing his eyes, his mind drifted back to the previous night. Tired, both mentally and physically, he thought, *If people knew how hard this part of the job was, no one would do it.*

There were two members of the crime team left in the room. Each busying themselves with their assigned task. One was dusting the headboard, searching for fingerprints, the other writing something in his notebook as he looked at the motel room door. Not able to focus on what he needed to do, which would be easier with no one there, he stepped outside. Hoping to see the motel manager, he spotted Aaron pulling up in his vehicle. Usually spotless, but being in this small, dusty Texas town had wreaked havoc on his car. Smirking slightly, he thought, *If I ran out of paper, I could take notes on the hood of his car.*

73

As Aaron stepped out of the car, Robert decided to meet him in the parking lot. "I thought I'd see you at the hospital this morning," Robert told him.

With a look of determination, or exhaustion, Robert couldn't decide, Aaron handed him a piece of paper with a scribbled handwritten note, "I need to speak to this guy, Samuel. I pulled the bureau information on missing persons and murders and found a few things of interest. Look at this."

Putting on his readers, and squinting to bring the handwriting into focus, he read, half murmuring to himself, "Forty-three-year-old female. African American. Heart shape on chest, golf ball in throat, abdomen cut open, but intestines left in. Choked. DPD investigated."

"Whoa… What the? Wait… When was this?" Robert exclaimed, clearly shocked and now becoming worried.

Formulating his reply before speaking, he took his sunglasses off, allowing his eyes to adjust to the bright sunlight and addressed Robert, "Last year. Dallas Police Department investigated but couldn't find a suspect at all. It was an exceptionally clean kill. Same scenario as this. Same method. It matches."

Robert looked like a deer caught in the headlights. "What was the victim all about? Drug addict or respectable citizen?"

Aaron, unsure about how to answer, replied, "Dunno, but she was found in a motel. East Dallas, apparently. The address, anyway, is near Oak Cliff. It was left open. Nothing led to anyone."

Barely able to process the information, Robert looked up at the sun. Knowing that he now had a serial killer on his hands, he handed the paper back to Aaron.

74

Digging his phone out of his pocket, he scrolled through his contacts looking for Alison's number.

"Who are you calling, man?"

Hearing him speak, but not answering immediately, he pressed the call button and mouthed, "Alison."

Wanting to review the information further, he put his hand on Robert's arm and said, "Hang up. We need to speak to her in person. Nothing is done by phone unless it's a secure line." Aaron explained. "Where is she?"

Already realizing he knew the answer to his own question, Aaron slid the piece of paper back into his folder and closed the car door. Taking out a small steno notebook from his back pocket, he began to write. Pausing for a moment, he advised Robert, "We need to speak to 'Little Sammy', but I want to see him first. I also need to have a drug screen run on him."

Robert knew where to find 'Little Sammy'. Everyone knew where to find him. During the day, he could either be found mowing grass throughout town, or at the gas station, drinking a "pounder" of whatever beer was the least expensive. Probably the latter of the two, he suggested, "Let's go to the station. Ten-to-one he'll be there."

Both nodding in agreement, they got in the car. The town's only gas station was also a local hangout for high school kids. He could remember time and again driving up and down main street, patrolling on a Saturday night, only to focus his attention to the parking lot of Tripz Quick Stop. Packed with jacked up trucks and blacked out Mustangs, it was the place to be for any high schooler seeking a chat with one of their friends. Usually, it was a casual hang out spot, but other times it

75

could be a cesspool for cheap drug deals. He remembered seeing Tessie there a few times. Thinking about it now, he told Aaron, "Tessie used to hang out here as well, usually at night. It's popular for that crowd. For being such a small town, Fleetham sure has its problems with drugs, ya know?"

Not surprised, Aaron replied, "What else is there to do here besides get high and party in a field?"

Both men laughed as they drove the six blocks to the gas station. As they turned into the gas station's parking lot, they found what they were searching for. Sitting on the concrete curb was 'Little Sammy'. His drinking had begun earlier that morning, from the looks of him. Smoking a cigarette, almost to the nub, he took a large gulp from his can of beer. Wrapped in a brown paper bag, to hide the fact that he was drinking in public, he set it down beside him and lit another cigarette. His overalls too big, and his shirt too small, 'Little Sammy' stood up, grabbed his can of beer, and headed inside the gas station. After watching him for a few minutes from inside their car, the two men decided to talk to him. Walking into the gas station, 'Little Sammy' acknowledged Robert immediately. "Hey, there, old man, how's it hanging?"

Robert, who was still unsure about everyone else's accusations, but wondered all the same, took off his sunglasses and replied, "Hey, Sam, this is one of my colleagues. We want to talk to you down at the station. Can you come now?"

Belching from all the carbonated beer he'd consumed, and with his eyes on Aaron, 'Little Sammy' scoffed, "You're not from these parts are ya, boy?"

Grinning, unsure how to reply without sounding like a pompous prick, Aaron extended his arm to shake

76

hands with 'Little Sammy'. He greeted him with, "I'm Aaron, one of the detectives working on the Tessie Johanan murder case. Just routine, you understand. We're interviewing everyone in town."

Neither Robert nor Aaron were sure if he'd understood what was said to him. Sammy looked at both men, opened his mouth to speak, then abruptly walked past them. Stepping out of the gas station and assuming his position on the curb again, he lit another cigarette. Looking up at both of them, he asked, "Who done it? Why have you got to talk to me? I, uh, know about Tessie, sure. She was my pal for a while."

As he spoke, Aaron wrote in his notebook, *History of alco. Low intellig. Check history with Tessie*

Robert, knowing that 'Little Sammy' might shut down and not speak to him, sat on the curb as well. Multiple thoughts raced through Robert's mind. He kept thinking, *Could he have done this? Is he smart enough to not get caught?*

Robert, who had never handled or been involved in such a high-profile case, lacked the experience and interviewing skills of Aaron or Alison. Both were used to interrogating suspects, dragging the truth out of them, whereas Robert relied on his one skill—persuasion.

"Sammy, look. We've got to talk to you about this. You were seen on the security footage, close to the motel. It'll be a hell of a lot easier for you if you agree. If ya don't, well… it'll look funny. You understand, right?" Robert said, in the most guarded, yet suave tone he could muster. It took a lot of *oomph,* as Robert's mother would say, but he did it. 'Little Sammy' looked at Robert with those cerulean eyes, but unable to focus, "I ain't got nothing to hide. I'll prove it to you."

77

Aaron moved closer to Robert and Sammy, listening with an open ear. He was trying to pick up on something that would make him believe Sammy but hadn't heard anything yet.

Sammy kept glaring at Aaron, making it very evident that he had zero faith in him.

Attempting to gain his trust, Aaron reached out his hand, offering it to 'Little Sammy', "Please let me help you up."

Scared, Sammy addressed Aaron, "You're putting me in a bad place. I'm not a bad person. I believe in Jesus. I don't kill."

With his experience in criminal profiling and ability to gain entry into a suspect's mind, his voice suddenly softer and deeper, Aaron said, "I believe you. I just need to do this to satisfy my office. Do you understand?"

This time, 'Little Sammy' stuck his arm out. Aaron grabbed it and pulled him up. Standing, well, swaying a bit, Sammy steadied himself with Aaron's arm. It was quite clear to both Robert and Aaron that Sammy was as drunk as a skunk. Aaron kept thinking, *He's so wasted, this will be easy.* Keeping his peaceful and trustful face, he escorted Sammy to their car. With step one complete, Aaron could begin the process of putting the pieces together with the rest of his team.

"Robert, I need you to drive. I've got to make a call and send a few messages."

Pulling out his phone, he found Alison's contact details. With determination and excitement surging through him, he sent a quick text,

Station now. It's time to begin.

With the poor cellular reception in the town, the message took longer than usual to send.

78

Once he heard the beep, he knew that he was good to go.

As they backed out of the gas station, Aaron knew that his job was about to begin. He'd seen the actual motel room, he'd spoken to the lead criminal investigator, Alison, and he'd seen the body—or photos of it anyway. Now, it was time to catch the killer. He always knew that he was meant to be a criminal profiler. From an early age, he'd had a knack with people. He was kind and sweet, or so he was told, but could also be fierce and brutal. One of his college buddies used to say, "You act like a killer yourself!"

Aaron knew he was capable of getting inside the man's head. He doubted himself briefly... but only for a moment. Taking his phone and going through his recent call log, he found the number he was looking for, *Psych MD*. In his phone, *Psych MD* was his partner at work and his right-hand man. When Aaron couldn't pierce the shell of a suspect, *Psych MD* could. His name was Javier. As the name suggested, one could only draw a mental image as to what he looked and sounded like. Javier, or Javi as the team called him, was from Brazil. He had a dark complexion, an accent that rivaled any foreign film star, and the ability to coerce a suspect into telling him exactly what he desired. He was a graduate of one of the top medical schools in the country, and quickly became one of the leading forensic psychiatrists.

With years of experience under his belt, Aaron knew that Javi was the man he needed now. Attempting to send an outgoing call to him, he thought about what he would say in front of an active suspect. Aaron had all the time in the world to think about what to say as his phone call wasn't connecting. "Are there any cell towers

79

out here that actually pick up a signal?" He asked Robert, clearly annoyed.

Robert may have answered him, but he couldn't be sure. He tuned the world out when he was on a mission. Rather than attempting another call and risking raising his irritation level further, he sent a quick text to Javi, *I need you if you are free today. Call me at the Fleetham Police Station. About to begin an interview with an active suspect in murder case.*

Chapter Thirteen

Grabbing her files and purse, Alison readied herself to head out to the police station. With Jim nearby, she told him, "I've got to run. I'll be back later. While I'm gone... wait... you know what? Why don't you come with me? Everyone needs to read and hear your autopsy report."

Alison had taken the words right out of his mouth. The second Jim heard she was leaving, he'd thought to himself, *I'll head down to the station as soon as I complete my report.* "Give me a bit more time. I've got to wrap things up here, and finish typing the report. It'll need to be sent to a few people before I'll be able to brief everyone. I'll see y'all shortly?"

Nodding, satisfied with his answer, Alison headed to the double doors leading to the hallway. She'd had time to focus. She'd had time to rest. She'd had time to clear her mind, if only briefly, of the intense stress that had been building up over the last few days. She'd forgotten how emotionally difficult it was to handle a murder. Let alone, what was basically a slaughter.

Walking down the hallway, listening to her heels clack on the floor, she heard one of the double doors bang against the wall. It was Seth jogging slowly in order to catch up with her. "Hey, wait a sec, will ya?" He called out. Pausing and looking at the approaching doctor, she wondered, *What does he want now. I've got shit to do.*

81

Alison was quite impressed by his physical agility. Granted, he was by no means attempting anything that was strenuous, but he wasn't suffering from shortness of breath. She made a mental note to sign up for yoga once she returned home.

Seth flashed his porcelain smile at her and asked, "Listen, do y'all need any help down at the station? I'm free this afternoon. I'm on call tonight, but if you need me, I'll be there."

Amazed at all the extra help she was being offered from civilians, Alison smiled, nodded and asked, "Are you sure you aren't too busy? I might need help going over my notes. I only scribbled them down, and don't fully understand the medical jargon."

Seth laughed, which made her smile. It was a boyish laugh. A laugh of someone who didn't have a care in the world. A laugh that she would have loved to hear every day. "Sure, here's my number. Just call me when you're ready. I'll help Jim finish up. Four hands get the job done quicker than two." With that comment, he winked at her. Turning around, he headed back to the double doors, paused, and looked back at her. She was walking to the elevator—a short distance, but to her, in the pit of sterility, it felt like an eternity. She paused, pushing the elevator call button, and briefly glanced to her left. Seeing him looking at her, she thought nothing of it. In fact, it gave her a bit of a chill… a chill that she hadn't felt since her last serious relationship.

Hearing the double doors click shut, she knew that Seth had returned to the morgue.

Disappearing from civilization and entering the chamber of death, as she liked to refer to it. The elevator had arrived. Stepping inside, she took out her phone. Knowing she wouldn't have service until she reached ground level, she quickly re-read Robert's text message to her. She knew she was right and that 'Little Sammy' had been the one who slaughtered Tessie. Rolling the thought over and over in her head, she began thinking aloud, "He's the one. He fits the mold. Every killer has a mold."

Alison's mobile battery was fine, but the service wasn't. *No service*, or so the little icon at the right hand of the screen read. She felt safe with her phone in her hand. It was her security blanket. Elevators always made her uneasy. Alison had a slight fear of being in enclosed spaces, so the cubicle hanging from wires certainly didn't help. When the elevator reached ground level, it alerted her with a ting overhead. Stepping out, her phone began to vibrate. Service had been resumed, and texts were now coming in, both of them from Jim.

I know you just left but call me.
Results received from both fibers.

Tension and excitement began to flood over her. Walking through the main lobby, she paused at reception. Seeing the morning shift receptionist, Olga, she said hello and good day. She didn't have time to wait for a reply, though she was happy with herself for not being overly direct. Sadly, it was a shortfall that she had acquired from living in the 'too busy syndrome' of adulthood.

Stepping outside, feeling the midday Texas heat on her face, she felt free. Free from stainless steel. Free from death, if only momentarily. And free from the arctic tundra inside. She was frozen solid, as well as cold-natured. Every boyfriend she ever had complained about it. While they were sweating, she would sit wrapped up in a blanket… comfortable and cozy. Warming her ice-

83

cold body, she took out her phone and called Jim. He answered before the first ring was complete. "I knew you'd call the second you got service again. Figured you'd be in the elevator," Jim said.

Alison couldn't restrain herself and in her usual, abrupt tone asked, "What were they? What animal? Where did that other fiber come from?"

Already acclimated to her personality and habits of both interrupting and being short when she spoke, Jim told her, "The brown fiber we haven't been able to identify yet. The hair was from a common rat. I have no idea how the rat hair ended up on her... but that's not my department."

Intrigued with this bit of information, Alison requested, "Email that report to me. I'll hand it over to my team so we can figure out where the brown fiber originated. Thanks! Bye!"

With that, she hung up. Clicking her disable alarm button, and stepping into her car, she sat there for a moment. Processing this huge bundle of news, she couldn't help but wonder where the rat hair came from. She made a mental note to call an exterminator and have the motel checked. Every room. She needed to see if the motel was infested and it was just a shedding issue, or if it was planted. Both were possible because both could happen. Theoretically, anyway. Backing out of the hospital parking lot, images of Seth kept popping into her mind. Seeing him standing over the autopsy table. Seeing him jogging down the hall to speak to her. Seeing him in the doorway when she first met him. She was curious. "Oh, Seth, what are you up to?" She said aloud.

Alison had better things to do than to involve herself with a local doctor. She had a murder investigation to deal with. But she couldn't help it. There

84

was something about him that made her giggle like a little girl. Her mind said, "That's silly." Her heart said, "Be careful." Her workaholic female mouth said, "Go for it." She had an interesting sense of humor. At times, she was awkward, socially. This was one of those moments. The thought going through her head now. *A noir film. Her being the poor, lonely stewardess on a European jumbo jet. Seth being the soldier returning home from war. They meet, fall in love, and live happily ever after.*

With this thought, Alison made herself laugh.

Arriving at the police station, thankfully, cleared her head of any thoughts of Seth.

Collecting her files and bag, she stepped out of the car, temporarily blinded by the blazing sun. Walking into the front of the station, she saw that it was totally deserted. *It's a small town, everyone went to lunch or to the bridge club, I guess,* Alison thought. Hearing voices in the back, she let herself in through a closed, glazed wooden door.

Stepping into the Fleetham Police Station was like stepping back in time. At any moment, she could see Andy or Barney walking through the front door. She smiled at her mental image and let herself into Robert's office.

Sitting at a round conference table in the back of the room, were Robert, Aaron, and Samuel. Each with a Styrofoam cup of what she assumed was coffee, all three of them turning around to greet her. Smiling at them, she walked over to the table, set her bag on the floor, placed her files on the table and stared at Aaron. Knowing her all too well, he understood her silent request to let her have his chair. He obliged and rolled Robert's desk chair over next to her. Turning to Sammy, she asked, "How

85

are you today? Thank you for coming in and letting us speak with you."

'Little Sammy' was clearly intimidated by her. Most were. He began to sweat and was incredibly flushed. Knowing this was perfectly normal for any human in this situation, Alison thought, *Too bad for you, boy.* Sammy was scared. He was certain that he hadn't done anything wrong, but throughout the entire car ride over, he kept asking himself, *Did I do it? I have the drinkin' sickness. So, did I?*

Alison could see that he was fully consumed by fear. With that, she pulled out her legal pad, popped the cap on her pen and began to write. Noting the date, time, location, and suspect at the top margin, she put her pen down on the table and began searching for her digital recorder. Alison was an old soul in a young body. She transcribed her notes by hand. Always, with a fountain pen. She'd written with fountain pens since childhood, and never understood why others would not follow suit.

Finding her recorder in the depths of her bag, she placed it on the table, pressed record and began to speak, "This is Alison Chaney, lead investigator in the death of Tessie Johanan. Present for this interrogation are Robert Binder, Sheriff of Fleetham, Aaron Duncan, criminal profiler with the Federal Bureau of Investigation, and suspect, Samuel Harper. The date is Wednesday, June fifteen, 14:02 hours. Interview will begin now."

With her pen back in her hand, she wrote a few notes that weren't relevant to her interview questions. Namely, appearance of 'Little Sammy', his demeanor sitting in the office and his criminal history—or lack thereof. She noted the odor of alcohol and added a sub-note to perform a tox screen. With Sammy at full attention, the interview began.

86

Alison, "Sammy, may I call you Sammy, or do you prefer Samuel?"

'Little Sammy', "Yeah, I don't care. I'll answer to whatever name you want to use, ma'am."

"Fabulous. I want to begin with your family history. Can you tell me a little about yourself?"

"Well, let me see. I was born here in Fleetham years ago. That's when babies were being born right here at the hospital. Dr. Starr, he's the one who brought me into this here world. My mama took sick when I was 'bout twelve, so I had to work so we wouldn't go hungry."

"That must have been quite difficult for you. A child having to support a family. Where was your father?"

"I dunno. Me and my sister... that's mama's other child, she passed on when I was a baby. But my daddy, we never got to meet him. Mama said he went to be with another woman before I was born. I guessed he left when Mama was on baby bed rest."

"You said your sister died? What happened?

"She took sick. Got pneumonia. We buried her by the river. Mama had no money back then for no funeral services. Hell, I don't have no money to this very day."

"I'm very sorry. After your sister died, did you continue to live at home?"

"Sometimes I did. Sometimes I hitchhiked places. Sometimes I slept outside. Whatever I wanted to do I did."

"Okay. Sammy, I'm going to ask you very detailed questions, so you need to really focus and think about your answer before you say something, okay?"

"Okay."

"How did you know Tessie Johanan?"

"Everyone knows her. I saw her at the fillin' station. And at my house. And at the motel lots of times."

"Were you intimate with her?"

"No, ma'am."

"Did she ever buy drugs, or did you ever buy drugs from her?"

"No, but I know she does them. She likes the stuff from her doctor, and I've seen her shoot up."

"Where were you the night she was killed?"

"I was at home, then went to sleep, then went to get some beer from the gas station."

"You were seen at the motel. Do you remember that?"

"I don't know what you saw, but I wasn't at the motel that night. You've got the wrong person."

"Okay. Will you give me a sample of DNA and take a drug test? You don't have to, but it would help matters."

"I don't have money for a lawyer."

"You don't need one now unless you want to retain one, but that's not what I asked. Would you give us a DNA sample, and would you take a drug test? Also, we need to take your fingerprints."

"Okay, but as long as I ain't in trouble, I will."

"Okay, great. I'll be right back."

"Sheriff, I'm so scared. I don't understand all of this. All I did was get high with her one night, but I don't have it in me to kill someone."

Robert immediately asked, "What did you say?"

"I said that we used to shoot up—well, once anyway. That was a while ago. She used to get her needles from the pharmacy across town. But I don't know who she bought her junk from."

88

Alison got up from the table, giving Robert a look of confusion, excitement, and concern as she went to leave the room. Instantly, Alison and Robert had been on the same wavelength throughout the discussion, however, they both wondered whether his account of events was truly reliable. Aaron began writing. He had been making notes during the entire process, but wanted to connect more with Sammy, so he'd stopped briefly to listen.

As Alison walked out of the room to locate a swab, she reflected on what she had just heard. "It's all circumstantial," she said aloud. At that moment, Aaron exited the room, intending to have a private word with Alison.

"Ali, look, we've got a problem here. Unless you have something physical, you've got nothing. That's your main problem. However, there's something about Sammy that does concern me. The way he speaks. He has yet to look me directly in the eye. He is fidgety. His record is clean, but that isn't always relevant, ya know?"

Nodding, understanding exactly what he meant, Alison turned around to rummage through a cabinet, in search of a swab. Locating a box of sterile swabs, she swirled around and said, "I'm going to do a polygraph. Maybe he'll agree. I'll have to word it in a way that he'll understand. Jesus. I've worked so hard. I need to search his house, as well. I'll drop by on him tomorrow morning."

The two headed back to the room where Sammy was waiting. After entering the room, Alison could see the expression on his face. Sitting at the table, Sammy looked terrified. He looked like someone who had lost his life. He looked like someone who was afraid of even saying one word to her. Alison strolled over to him and

89

handed him the swab. "You know what, I think it might be better if I swabbed your mouth. I want to get as accurate a specimen as possible," Alison informed Sammy. Taking the swab out of the protective packaging, she asked him to open his mouth. With his mouth agape, she could see the poor life that he had led. She could smell the aftereffects of a night's worth of binge drinking—or routine consumption, she wasn't sure. Nevertheless, she thought his mouth told a lot about him. Having obtained the swab, she placed it back in the tube, sealing it shut. Writing his name, date, and time of collection on the label, she pocketed it, knowing she had a fixed amount of time to deliver it to the lab. "Thank you, Sammy. Just to be sure I have enough DNA can we have one of your hairs? It will also help with a drug test as well. Your hair will show several weeks' worth of drug use, if any."

"I still don't get it, ma'am. You act like I did it. I ain't done nothin'!" he protested, becoming more agitated by the second. Shifting his weight in his chair, he reached in his pocket and pulled out a package of cigarettes. "I've got to smoke," he announced to the room. Lighting up and taking a long drag, he raised his other hand and grabbed a large chunk of his hair. Ripping out a handful, he handed it to Alison. His hands, sweaty and covered in dirt, reached out to Alison, and grasped her hand. He looked into her eyes and began to tear up. As he started to sob quietly, he whispered, "Help me, Jesus. Give me the strength for this. Amen."

Robert and Aaron looked at one another, then turned to Alison. Maintaining an expressionless persona, she said the two words that she had never been spoken to any suspect, "Be strong."

90

With Sammy's hand still holding hers, Alison tried to pull away as politely as she could. Eventually removing hers, she patted his hand and softly said, "I also think you need to do a polygraph. As much information as we can get will help everyone out."

Sammy felt defeated. He didn't look at anyone, just the Formica tabletop and simply nodded in response to her statement.

"I want you to come back to the station tomorrow morning, please. I'll have Robert pick you up around nine."

Feeling invisible and broken, he only had the inner strength to say, "Yeah."

Chapter Fourteen

The morgue appeared peaceful and quiet. Usually, Jim wasn't busy, but although he only had one case to deal with, he felt as if he had a hundred. Sitting at his desk, staring at his computer screen, he typed out his finalized autopsy report. With all the results from the lab and the tox screen back, he was now able to rule the death as an obvious homicide. Strangulation was the main cause of death, with added substantial narcotics in her system. *I hope she didn't suffer,* Jim thought to himself.

He kept thinking about Tessie. He didn't know her and couldn't remember ever seeing her around town. But the brutality of the murder confused him. When he moved to Fleetham, he never in his life would have imagined that he'd be performing an autopsy on a body that had been so mutilated. Jim felt that her body had been nothing more than a toy to the killer—like a gift from Christmas—played with once, then tossed aside.

Putting all thought of her out of his mind, he digitally signed his name and printed out the report. Gathering his manila file folder, full of documents related to the case, along with several crime photos, he added the multi-page document to the pile. The folder had been empty at one time. Now, it held over fifty sheets of paper. From detective interviews with the motel guests, to incredibly detailed descriptions of the room, to lab reports—it read like a best-selling crime novel.

With that, he flung the folder down, stood up, and walked out of his office; through the double doors leading to the mile-long hallway, Jim had never been so glad to see the elevator in his life.

Stepping in, he mentally dismissed his career... if only for a few hours until he returned.

Usually he kept to himself, busying himself with a book, newspaper, or medical journal when he was at home. He was a loner. But an educated one. If he wasn't at home reading during his off time, he could be found outside gardening. His books relaxed him. His garden taught him about hard work, dedication, and patience. Driving down Jim's street, one wouldn't think he was the man occupying the home. With a perfectly manicured lawn that resembled hunter green velvet, to the geometric shaped hedges, his house looked like a photograph from *Better Homes & Gardens*, and not that of a lonely, medical examiner. Liked by everyone in town, most found him odd—he wasn't the cookie cutter small-town man. Jim belonged in the city, but at the same time, thrived in this town of less than a thousand.

Knowing he didn't have to return to work until mid-morning, he decided to focus his attention and empty his mind with his latest book. One of his favorites, *Whatever Happened to Baby Jane*, could always be found on his coffee table. He always suggested the novel to anyone willing to accept a book recommendation. His usual statement to them was, "If you want something funny, yet dark, read this. It makes me laugh and feel sorry for the poor girl all at the same time."

He'd almost finished the book, and by this point in the novel, Jane and Blanche were on the beach enjoying an ice cream cone. He knew how the book ended. He could quote it line by line. Seeing the two

93

central characters in his head, he couldn't help but wonder if the killer, whomever it was, treated their victims as Jane did. Returning to his novel, he completed the last few pages, and placed it back on the table. He'd re-read it soon, so there wasn't a need to return it to its shelf. Standing, he walked into the kitchen to search for his phone. Knowing his goal was relaxation, he decided to make a quick work call. "Short and sweet," Jim said aloud as he called Alison, "Morning. I just wanted to see if you're coming to the hospital later today or if I'm to go to the station?"

Alison, who was barely functioning on her first cup of coffee, replied mid-yawn, "Yeah, whenever you're free. Bring the file. I need to keep it at the station since the autopsy report has been added. Did ya find anything else?"

Waiting a moment before he replied, as he was in the middle of making a pot of coffee, he heard Alison snap, "Hello? Are you still there? Ugh."

"Just a second, I'm making coffee," Jim snarled back. "And no, I didn't find anything else. No additional hairs or fibers. No other trauma or wounds to the body. I finished my report with the conclusion of obvious homicide primarily by strangulation. The abdominal incision and removal of skin from the chest were all performed postmortem."

Alison, who was famous for multi-tasking was typing on her laptop. Jim could hear the clickety-clack of her nails against the plastic keys. "You're sure going to town on that computer there," he chuckled. Continuing to wait for her reply, he added, "Who is your main suspect? I can't remember if you had released that yet?"

94

"Didn't I tell you? I guess not… sorry, it's been so chaotic. The main suspect, so far… the only one for that matter is Sammy Harper. Everything is circumstantial now. I have him scheduled for a poly today. After that's finished, I'll search his home. Still waiting on a few more things to come back from the lab to give us some more information."

Jim knew Alison had dedicated her life to the service of others, in the form of being an investigator. The exhaustion in her voice was so obvious. "You're so determined. I admire that."

Sucking down the scorching caffeine, he told her, "I'm going to jump off here. I'll see you at the station later today."

As usual for Alison, she hung up without saying goodbye. Cutting people off was a hallmark for her. She was a professional at cutting people off, both personally and professionally.

Heading back to his bedroom, Jim stepped into the shower to get ready for the day. He knew he had a lot to do—a lot of thinking, anyway. Going over and over the day's plans, started to give him a headache. Standing in the shower, momentarily zoning out from the world around him, he thought of nothing. A black hole. The silence was perfect. Jim loved silence. He loved people, but he loved when they were silent as well. A world of aloneness is what he thrived on.

An introvert. A loner.

With the water beating down on his back, he said to himself, "Where did the narcotics come from?"

95

Chapter Fifteen

The eight o'clock hour had snuck up on her. Alison had slept last night, but not well. Since she arrived in town, she had gone to bed thinking about Tessie. She had woken up thinking about Tessie. She couldn't get her out of her mind.

Pouring herself a cup of coffee, *subpar at best*, she thought, as she missed her local barista back home, she tried to prepare her mind for the day. She knew today was the polygraph test. She knew she had to search 'Little Sammy's home... wherever it was located. She knew she needed to check with the lab.

"The lab," she said aloud. Grabbing her phone from the bedside table, she called Robert.

"Morning. Do you have the fingerprint results? What about matching the fingerprints on the syringe? Did anything show up?" Alison belted out. Not quite alert and functioning, she sounded more direct than usual. She loathed the morning, usually.

It was apparent that Robert had just awoken, by the sound of his voice, anyway. He replied with a thick and nasally voice, as if he were still lying down, "First of all, do you realize what time it is? And no, I haven't. These folks aren't even at their office yet. It's entirely too early to worry about this. Call them around nine-ish."

This wasn't the answer that Alison wanted. Though an excellent detective, she had a very short temper, and patience was a problem for her. Typically, when she asked for something, she wanted it yesterday. Scoffing to herself at his reply, she said, "I guess I'll have to wait then. I'm going down to the station to get things going. The polygraph examiner will be getting into town soon."

Hearing the spew and drip of a coffee pot through the phone, Alison realized that Robert was just beginning his day. In between slurps of hot, black coffee, he advised her, "I'll be down there in a bit. Just gotta get ready. I also need to go get 'Little Sammy'."

Ready to begin her day, she did her usual and hung up without saying goodbye. Her bag, sitting on the side chair, held her notebook. Much like her phone, her notebook was the lifeline of her career. It was nothing fancy—just a college ruled spiral, but to her, it was equivalent to the Bible. Inside were notes that weren't disclosed in her report. They were notes that were only pertinent to her, but at the same time, relevant to the investigation. It was her diary—for work.

As she finished getting ready for the day, her phone buzzed with a text message from Robert. Thinking he was about to tell her that he was already at the office, instead his message read, *Call Seth. He said he needs to talk to u.*

Hitting reply, she typed her reply, but was wary of sending it. After deleting it in its entirety, she wrote, *I will when I get to the office. What did he want?*

Waiting for his reply, she wondered what he wanted and why he didn't text or call her directly. *Did I even give him my card?* She thought. Not having much luck in the relationship department, this wasn't her strong point.

Alison was a career woman.

Didn't say. See u later ali!

97

Leaving her just as clueless as when she started the conversation via text with Robert, she put it out of her mind, located her keys and headed out the door. On the drive over to the police station, she went over the events that needed to occur today in her head. With the polygraph examiner conducting the interview, she knew that was one less thing she needed worry about. Her main focus, she thought, was to search 'Little Sammy's' home.

Pulling into the parking lot—well, in front of the police station, she saw a man sitting in his black SUV. It wasn't someone she knew—she knew everyone from the field. "Morning, I'm Alison. And you are?" She called over as she stepped out of the car.

Rolling down his window, he peered over his sunglasses and said, "Hey, how's it going? I'm Ross Anderson. I'll be doing the polygraph interview today."

Happy that the plans in her head were running smoothly, thus far, she smiled at Ross and handed him one of her cards. As she did, he began to open the door, stepping out to greet her properly. "I'm sorry, I'm usually far more gentlemanly than this. I was lost in thought going over today's questioning." Ross added.

Alison was impressed. It wasn't every day that a man decided to be a gentleman. She'd run into so many assholes over the years, which was her usual word to describe them. Oddly enough, she sometimes imagined that she might inadvertently find the man of her dreams whilst leading a case. However, so far. it had never happened.

As he was shaking her hand, having completed his greeting, Robert's car pulled in next to hers. "Hope I'm not disturbing nothing here," he said with an odd grin. Introducing himself to Ross, the two men shook hands, and dived into a quick conversation about the town and its citizens—namely, 'Little Sammy'.

As Ross gathered the remaining items he needed from his car, he gestured for them to go inside. As the two walked into the empty police station, Alison led them into the sheriff's office, where the interview would be conducted. "Before we begin, I need to set some ground rules here," Ross began. "First of all, I will be the only one to speak. You're welcome to take notes, but you mustn't ask any questions. The two of you will sit behind the interviewee, facing me. If it's changed in any way, I'll stop the interview and ask the two of you to step out. Understood?"

Alison and Robert both glanced at one another, then at Ross, and nodded. As Ross was setting his polygraph machine and notepad up, Alison was busying herself with preparing her area. Dumping a pile of folders and her notebook on the table, she turned to a clean sheet of paper and began writing.

Robert picked up his cup of coffee, and in a foggy morning voice announced, "I'm going to go get Sam. Be right back. Don't do anything I wouldn't do."

With that, he slapped his cap on, grabbed his sunglasses and headed out the door. With Robert gone, and only minutes until the suspect arrived, Alison had a few moments to chat with Ross. Knowing what his job entailed, she wasn't interested in the technicalities of the machine or what he planned to do. She was curious, however, about him. She wanted to know if he ever doubted the people he interviewed. She wanted to know if he ever wished he had gone into another career. She wanted to ask so many questions but knew she couldn't. *I'd look like a damn moron,* she thought to herself.

Alison appeared to be strong. But little did everyone know, she was also very weak. She had confidence but lacked self-esteem. Those very close to her knew, but to a stranger, she looked like the woman holding the title of, "The Bitch."

Chapter Sixteen

Sitting alone in his office at the clinic, Seth played a mindless game on his phone. Having finished killing the last monster in the game, he swiped it away and turned his attention to his internet browser. With his thumbs that were almost too large to accurately type, he performed an internet search, looking for *Serial killer traits.*

Pulling up 2,070,000 results, he had hours of reading to do if he wanted to make even a dent in the amount of information.

"Jesus. Are there that many crazies in the world?" he said aloud. Clicking on a random link provided by his search, he scanned the page of typed words for anything that sounded familiar.

Realizing he had clicked on the FBI page, he read the excerpt, *"Serial killers differ in many ways, including their motivations for killing and their behavior at the crime scene. However, attendees did identify certain traits common to some serial murderers, including sensation seeking, a lack of remorse or guilt, impulsivity, the need for control, and predatory behavior."*

Taking a deep breath, he read the paragraph again. During all his years studying medicine, he hadn't focused on the psychiatric realm at all… though it interested him, he was more equipped for family medicine and emergent situations. His ability to calm a hectic emergency room down was his forte. He had been

101

told that he was great with children. Having no children of his own, let alone a stable relationship, he was always quite shocked by that comment.

He'd had a girlfriend before. Only one. Liza. He met her online, living in a neighboring town. She was younger than he was, but as experienced as a fifty-year-old. He quickly fell in love with her—after their second date, but it was clear she had no interest in a long-term relationship. She ended the very brief encounter only a month after they met. She told him to move on and forget about her.

He'd always said, "She just wanted a bit of fun."

Now, Liza was almost insignificant to him. He'd moved on, but the memory of her still lingered. During their third of fourth date, he wasn't exactly sure, he had given her a ruby necklace. His birthstone was ruby, and he thought it would be a sweet memento to remember him by.

Talking to himself between laughs, he said, "She missed out."

Pulling his phone out, he sent Robert a text, *I searched for serial killer signs. I think you have the right dude. He fits the mold. What r u up 2 later?*

He threw his phone back on his desk and reclined in his chair. Closing his eyes, his mind drifted back a few days. His thoughts turned to Alison and what he remembered when he first saw her. She'd caught him staring at her, but he stared at all the pretty girls. That was nothing new. "I think she saw something in me that no one else has seen," he murmured.

Seth's phone pinged as Robert's reply came sooner than he had thought it would have.

Busy all day sorry bud.

He was disappointed as he wanted to ask him for a beer tonight, but he'd have to make alternative plans. Going back to his thoughts about Alison, he wondered what she'd say if he asked her for a date.

He'd have to formulate the exact thing to say to get her to say yes.

"Just wait, Miss Ali—I'll have you back at my place before you can say investigator." He said in his full, robust voice.

Chapter Seventeen

Robert left to pick up 'Little Sammy' from his house, which was about a ten-minute drive from the police station. Sammy lived outside of town, across the tracks. Many years ago, this was the home to all the African Americans.

The term *Across the tracks* truly did apply here. Before segregation had ceased, most, if not all African Americans lived in this area. Today, you could still see the remains of an era that had long since died. A single church remained amongst the dilapidated houses. The church, which Robert had attended a few times, looked like it was from a picture postcard. Its white steeple dominated the street. Robert wasn't a very religious man, but attending this church, the few times he had, gave him an extra 'oomph' that didn't exist in the Baptist or Methodist churches.

Driving down the street, past the church, Robert passed the remains of what looked like a store. As many years as he's lived in the town, he never quite knew what this building actually was. To him, it was history. To everyone else, including Alison, if he had shown her, it would be junk.

Sammy's house was at the end of the street. Originally, belonging to the minister of the African Methodist Episcopal church, it now sat empty—until Sammy decided to live there. Robert knew that Sammy didn't own the house, let alone pay rent—he was a squatter. When people would bitch about the fact he was living there for free, he's always reply with, "Who is he hurting? Leave him alone, and he'll leave you alone."

As he pulled into the driveway, his car spraying clouds of dust in the air to announce his arrival, he saw Sammy sitting on the steps of the front porch. With a can of beer in his hand and a cigarette dangling from the corner of his mouth, he waved. The look in his eyes—if Robert could ever remember anything in his life, it would be the baleful look in Sammy's eyes.

It frightened him. It upset him. His eyes looked like a defeated warrior readying himself to die on the battlefield. His head hung down, his face devoid of all emotion, and he looked and smelled dirtier than he ever had. As Robert slowly crept up the sidewalk, he thought to himself, *How absolutely pitiful.*

He could smell the alcohol on him before he even spoke a single word. When he did look up into his eyes, Robert could see the shear sadness that engulfed Sammy. His eyes were swollen and puffy—bloodshot, as if he had been on a three-day drinking binge. Unkempt and unshaven from the looks of it.

"Morning, sir. I hope you're good." Robert greeted him.

As Sammy stood up, stumbling in the process, he hiccupped and answered, "Yup, all is well that ends well, they always say. Don't ya think, sir?"

Standing next to him, Robert could see his face even clearer. He was so pale. It was only then that he realized the extent of his drinking problem and overall physical appearance. He'd seen Sammy in town all his life, but usually just nodded in passing—not giving him a second thought. Today, he actually saw him.

Taking his hand and placing it on Sammy's shoulder, he asked, "Do you need anything before we leave or are you good?"

Sammy, though worried about the day, and having drunk enough alcohol to hide his emotions, looked up, and smiled. It was a smile that Robert had only seen as a child. His grandmother had the same smile. It was the smile of love and compassion. A smile only given by someone who truly appreciated every action, no matter how large or small. It was a smile of gratitude. He spat as he spoke to Robert, "No, uh, I don't think so, but do you mind if I take the drink with me? I've got to have something."

Nodding, Robert understood. If 'Little Sammy' was in fact, the man who committed these crimes, he would have no problem with him having a sip on the way to the station. "Sure, but the can stays in the car once we arrive—you ain't taking that inside."

Pinching his lips shut, he nodded and sat back down. "I've got to take my medicine. I don't feel too hot today."

Robert's patience was beginning to thin, but he remained calm. "Do you need help or are you all set up with what you need to take?"

Sammy pulled himself back to a standing position and began to walk back inside his house. Taken aback by the odor, Robert had to breathe through his mouth for a few moments. He'd never seen anything so filthy in his life. Trash was the first thing he saw. Piled nearly to the ceiling, it ranged from beer cans to egg cartons to paper plates. Watching every step he took, he trod on something that cracked underfoot. "Jesus Christ, Sammy! How in the hell can you live like this?"

106

Sammy, busying himself in the kitchen, began to dig around in the refrigerator. Making his way through another room, which was originally the dining room, Robert could see Sammy through the doorway. Leaning against the door to the refrigerator, he began wiping his left thigh with an alcohol wipe. Curious, he quietly walked closer to the kitchen entrance. Inserting the syringe into a tiny vial, he pulled back, filling his syringe with a clear liquid. Jabbing the syringe into his thigh, he tilted his head back and took a long, deep breath. A breath that Robert had seen many times before when making a drug arrest. A look of pure bliss. A look of contentment. A look of pleasure. As Sammy finished injecting himself with the syringe, he reached for his phone, hands slightly shaking, and sent Alison a text, *Getting Sam now. He has syringes and some form of med. I'll check it out.*

"Sammy, what are you up to?" Robert asked, confused and curious as to what he just saw.

Throwing his syringe into the sink, Robert walked over to where he was standing. The sink was full of alcohol wipe packets, orange syringe caps, and more syringes than Robert had ever seen. He had a sick feeling in the pit of his stomach. He no longer wanted to be in this situation—this job—this life—this town. The harmless man who walked all over town, buying cigars with pennies, and mowing grass, was indeed, a killer. Robert's brain was racing. He kept thinking to himself, *Sammy. Did you really do this?*

Sammy, knowing how it must look to an outsider, especially with his history, simply said, "It's insulin. I got the sugar from my mama's side of the family. Twice a day every day until I die."

107

Leading him out of the kitchen with his hand on his shoulder, Robert escorted him to the front living room and out the door. Still unsure if he was being truthful about the insulin, he wished that he had the results of the drug screen back. Alison had written it down, but when was it ordered? *Was it even ordered,* he thought?

As they walked out of the front living room, Robert was relieved that fresh air was in abundance, but the stench from the house remained in his nostrils and on his clothes. He felt slightly nauseated, but he wasn't sure if it was from the filth of the house, or his nerves. Robert walked side by side with Sammy to the police cruiser. Opening the back door, he held out his hand as an invitation to take a seat. Realizing the terror that he must be feeling, he quickly closed the back door before Sammy had a chance to get in. He opened the front door thinking it would be less stressful if he sat in the front seat. As Sammy climbed in the front, spilling his beer on the floor as he adjusted himself in the seat, he mumbled, "I'm sorry."

Robert scoffed and asked, "Can you give me a minute, go ahead and get in the car. I've got to make a quick call." Stepping away from the car to where he wouldn't be overheard, he dialed Alison. It rang once, before she answered with an abrupt, "What?"

Not in the mood for Alison's usual behavior, he kept his conversation short and sweet. "We need to speak to Sam's doctor. If it's Seth, see if he'll talk to you. I'll see you soon." Hanging up, he thought for a moment. *If Sammy does have a clean criminal history, and his medical file checks out, then he's free to go.*

Nearing his cruiser, he got in and turned to Sammy. Like a child would pray at the dining table, with his hands folded and head bowed, Sammy was silent in his own world. Robert had never seen a grown man pray like that. He felt sorry for Sammy. Robert whispered, "This isn't right."

Sammy remained quiet for the few minutes they were in the car driving. A solemn moment for the two men, as they were both thinking about the day ahead. Nearing the police station, Sammy, with tears in his eyes, turned to Robert and asked, "Do you believe me?"

The feelings that hung in the car were plentiful. They could both feel the fear and pain. The thick, heavy air that surrounded them made it hard to breathe. Robert shrugged his shoulders, knowing that he really shouldn't voice his opinion. He looked straight ahead, not daring to look at Sammy. He wanted to keep the emotional barrier clear from himself, but at the same time, it was utterly impossible. He asked Sammy a question. "Do you believe yourself?"

No one said a word for a few moments. The police cruiser pulled into the station. Neither of them had the energy or desire to step out of the car, but the day had to move on. Robert, unbuckling his seatbelt and opening the door, broke the silence. "My heart says yeah I believe ya. My head says no you're the one who did this."

Sammy got out of the car, chugging the rest of his now tepid beer, and threw the can on the sidewalk. Digging into his filthy pants, he pulled out his pack of cigarettes, and a lighter. "I've got to smoke a bit before I go in. Watch me if you want or go in that there door." He was unaware of how he sounded. His voice cracked after every word. But he didn't care. Sammy knew he was innocent, but no one believed him. Dropping his cigarette butt on the ground, he headed to the door of the station. During his smoke break, or prayer—Robert was

109

unsure which, it was apparent to him that Sammy had gained an enormous amount of courage, conviction and strength, and walked to the door of the station, alone. Pulling it open, he stepped inside and took a seat in a nearby chair. Sammy thought to himself, *No one knows me but me. If they did know the truth I's wouldn't be here. Mmhmm.*

Robert walked past him, leaving him to his thoughts. Heading to his office where everyone was waiting, he paused at the coffee machine that sat behind the front reception desk. Pouring himself two cups, he offered one to Sammy, as he approached his chair. Sammy accepted and took a sip from the steaming cup. "You're a good man, Sheriff." His face, now looking more relaxed, had a smile. His eyes gleamed and he had an expression of contentment. Where it came from, Robert had no clue.

"Thanks. I'll see ya in a minute when we're ready for you. And... Sammy? I'm not as good of a person as you think I am." Robert replied. Turning around, he headed into his office.

Sitting at the table, usually covered with boxes of donuts and file folders, sat Alison and Ross, who stood up, and shook his hand. After explaining his polygraph test and procedure to him, Robert sat down next to Alison, who was filling up her fountain pen. Dipping the tip of the pen in the blue-black bottle of ink, she twisted the top. A jet of liquid rushed into the chamber, darkening the clear tube. Wiping the pen with a tissue she had stuffed in her pocket, she began to write, ignoring Robert as he sat next to her.

Robert, feeling a bit alone, asked Alison, "What do you think?

110

Alison, finishing her sentence on her notepad, capped her pen and looked over at him. "What do I think? About what? I assume you're asking about the case?"

Robert chuckled. He had always thought Alison was a tough cookie, "Yeah, I guess... or everything in general."

Alison rolled her eyes, looking away. Standing up and walking to the window that looked west towards the bank, she twirled around and said, "I think lots of things. I think that this 'Little Sammy' guy is guilty. I think that this town has nothing to offer anyone. I think that you're the most disgusting man I've ever met... you took advantage of this poor girl, Robert. I think that no one in this town has a clue about everyday life. That's what I think." Turning back around, she continued to look out the window, clearly avoiding further conversation with Robert. In the distance, she heard a man coughing violently. The wet, hacking cough of a smoker reminded Alison that Sammy had arrived. "Well, as our little criminal is here from the sound of it. Should I send him in, Ross?"

Not hearing his name, and involved in setting up the polygraph machine, he ignored her.

Alison snapped her fingers twice and repeated her question, "Should I send him in, Ross. Are you ready?"

Looking startled by the volume of her voice, Ross nodded and motioned for her to come back to the table. "Remember, you're to remain quiet. Don't speak or make a sound. I'll be recording this for the profiler to review later today. But one word, and the two of you will be asked to leave. Do I make myself perfectly clear?"

111

Alison rolled her eyes and replied, "Aye-aye, sir." Robert nodded and stood up. Heading to the door leading into the lobby, he could see Sammy sitting alone. *He looks like a child*, Robert thought to himself. Sammy was sitting on the blue, plastic chair, rocking back and forth. His eyes staring into a place that Robert couldn't see. No one could see, actually. Sammy was in a place all of his own, and at that moment, he questioned whether or not Sammy was even mentally able to understand the questions he would be asked. Dismissing the thought very quickly, as he was sure that the interviewer would word them at his level, he left his office and strolled towards him. Sammy looked up and gave a slight smile. "Are you ready, my man?" Robert asked.

Sammy, standing now, walked past Robert towards his office. Stopping at the threshold, he turned and said, "Ready as I'll ever be. Come on."

Chapter Eighteen

As promised, Alison sat quietly at the table, uninvolved. She opened her laptop to quickly check her emails. Sitting in her inbox, was a message from her crime lab, with the title, 'Result'.

Feeling a surge of excitement, she opened the email. Everything from the bureau was encrypted, so after entering her password, the attachment began to load. The email contained the fingerprint analysis, and the lab results for the brown fiber. Wishing that the interview could be postponed so she could deal with this, she quickly reviewed the scanned image. Staring her in the face was the answer that she needed and one she wished she'd had days ago.

The fingerprint analysis was now the most condemning evidence the case had received.

No longer was this a case of purely circumstantial evidence—it now had some solidity. The investigator at the lab had written in his report that, after dusting an area near the top of the syringe it had revealed a partial print. After conducting analysis and comparison, they found the match in their database. Samuel Harper. As she read further, she felt in the depths of her stomach that she had been right all along. At the motel, the night she arrived in town, she had told Robert she was going to catch the killer, "And by God, I have." She had accidently whispered something, lost in her own thoughts. Knowing that Ross would immediately

113

remove her from this interview, she lowered her head and continued to read.

The brown fiber that was found on the body was determined to be from an item of clothing. Specifically, a pair of dark brown, Workman's Delight overalls. With this information in hand, she knew she had to search his house as soon as the interview was over. Sending the file to the printer would be a challenge since she didn't have access to their firewall. She saved the file and closed her laptop. Taking out her phone, she scrolled through the thousands of contacts and found Aaron's number.

As soon as this interview is over, I want to search his house. Come to the station now and wait.

Alison was in no mood to obtain a warrant for a property search, and it would make the already fragile Sammy shut down. Instead, she devised a plan in her head, one she hoped would work.

As Sammy sat down at the table, all eyes were on him. Robert and Alison were seated behind Sammy, peering at his black, greasy head. The shirt he'd chosen to wear today had a month's worth of crusted filth on it, or so Alison thought. The sweater covering his button-down shirt was equally as dirty. Multiple holes or rips covered the back. As she sat down, disgusted at the sight of this helpless, pitiful man, her phone fell off her lap. Reaching under the table to pick it up, her eyes fixed on something straight ahead. Sitting in front of her was Sammy, but what she saw under the table made her skin crawl. His feet were flat on the floor, encased in muddy, scuffed boots, and more significantly, thick, brown grease-stained, overalls covered his legs. The thoughts in Alison's head began racing between everything from danger to excitement, to fear, to sadness. But what she

114

kept returning to was the thought that she was sitting behind a killer.

The interview began, "This is Ross Anderson, lead polygraph interviewer. The interview today will be conducted with Samuel Harper. Others in attendance are Alison Chaney, and Richard Binder. This will be recorded for court and legal purposes. Mr. Harper, I will explain the process. Please acknowledge that you understand the rules, okay? I will ask you a series of questions. Reply with yes or no. Do not turn around and try to limit the movement of your arms and body. Do you completely understand?"

Nodding, Sammy replied, "Yeah, I do, sir."

Alison wanted to get Robert's attention so badly. She wanted to show him the pants she saw under the table, but that would have to wait. Rather than focusing her attention on Sammy, she watched the interviewer. He was so stoic and full of zero emotion. *He must block everything out before he starts*, she thought. As the digital tape recorder was adjusted and placed between the two men sitting at the table, the interview continued.

"Is your name Samuel Harper?"

"Yes."

"Do you live in Fleetham?"

"Yes."

"Do you know Tessie Johanan?"

"Yes."

"Did you kill Tessie?"

"No."

Each time, Ross would listen to the answer and add a dot or a checkmark next to the printout.

The polygraph machine, which continually scribbled red ink on a white sheet of paper, was one of Sammy's main defense assistants. This determined if he

115

was lying or not. But as many have proved, a polygraph exam isn't always accurate. Robert hoped it would be.

"Did you give Tessie pain pills or a tranquilizer?"

"No."

"Did you strangle Tessie?"

"No."

"This interview has ended. Thank you, Sammy, for agreeing to take part."

As Robert wasn't aware of the forensic results that had been sent to Alison from the lab, he was blindly unaware that the man in front of him could possibly have killed Tessie. Listening to Ross' questions, and Sammy's simple replies, he wondered if he was telling the truth. *His voice sounded strong but was his heart in the right place? Or was he trying get out of a situation?"* he thought.

With each answer that Sammy gave, Ross looked at Robert and nodded 'yes'. There weren't any 'no' shakes of the head, which indicated that Sammy's answers were truthful. Alison sat fuming in her chair, standing up as soon as Ross had stopped speaking, and stormed out the door with her laptop and phone. Perched on the receptionist's desk, she opened her laptop and read the email attachment again. Wanting to ensure that she'd read the information correctly, she scanned the words until she came to the section regarding the brown fiber. She was certain she'd read that correctly, but just to make sure, she read it again for good measure. Seeing a notation she'd missed, *Rattus norvegicus,* she was curious to know what was being implied here. With an internet search at the ready, she typed in the two foreign words getting 891,909 results. With two beady, black eyes, staring her in the face, was a common rat. "I'll be damned. Latin for a common rat," she said aloud. Her

116

curiosity peaked as she kept looking at the vermin. "I wonder," escaped her lips, in a low whisper.

Closing her computer and tucking it under her arm, she marched back into Robert's office. Standing behind Ross, she was able to lock eyes with Sammy. "Thank you, Mr. Harper for allowing us to conduct the interview. We want to make sure we have all our ducks in a row, you understand. Also, would you allow us to search your home? We wouldn't want to skip a step and have something tragic happen to you, of course," Alison asked, her eyes locked onto his. The tone in her voice wasn't one of determination, but rather a need to win. At all costs.

She was determined to have this man arrested. Her intuition was rarely wrong.

Sammy didn't understand. He had answered the questions correctly, or so he thought. "Why do you need to go in my home. That there is my home. Where I sleep. There ain't nothin' to see. Do I have to let you?"

The last sentence made her smile, with each side of her grin curling up towards her cheeks. "No, of course, you don't have to, but realize that by saying no, and refusing to let us, you're adding another nail to the coffin. I'm trying to help you, you know?"

Nodding in response to her reply, he looked over at Robert, who nodded back. Turning his attention to Alison, Sammy replied, "Okay, fine, do what you need to do."

With full permission to search his home, Alison headed back to the lobby where she could use the telephone in peace. Dialing Aaron, she prepared herself for the conversation. Not yet aware of the bountiful supply of syringes that awaited her, she was intent on finding the brown fiber.

Answering without a greeting, Aaron advised her, "I'm on my way to the station now. I have a few ques..."

Cutting him off, she said, "He's agreed to the search. You'll ride with me to his house. Robert will join us."

Hanging up the phone, without realizing she had cut him off again, she walked to the front door of the police station. In her head, she was having a complete conversation with herself, *If this goes well, I will find what I need to have him arrested. This could go straight to trial. Easy in, easy out.* Something wasn't right, though. The thought sounded great in her head, but in her heart something was amiss. She knew the fingerprint was on the syringe—snapping her head up, she realized that was what she forgot to tell Robert.

"Robert, come here a minute, I've got to show you something." Alison called, hearing the scraping of metal as the chair was scooted back from the table. With her laptop open and the attachment loading, she slid her laptop over to him. Taking his readers out of his shirt pocket, he slid them on to read the fate of the man sitting in the next room. He'd passed his polygraph test. Robert was more positive than negative now, but at the same time, there was the issue about the syringes.

"When I picked him up this morning, there was a sink full of syringes. You'll see them today when you go and search his house. He told me that he's a diabetic and needs insulin. Has anyone verified that yet?" Robert scrolled through the rest of the attachment, reading the tidbit about rats, and then craned his head back towards his office.

"I'll be goddamned," he muttered, trying to see what Sammy was wearing. "The pants. I didn't even pay

118

attention to what he had on today. But if you would have seen his house, you'd understand why the rat hair makes sense. You've never seen anything as nasty in your life, Ali."

With her elbow on the table, Alison propped her head up with her hand, looking at him. She was grinning yet rolling her eyes at the same time. "Now, do you see why I always thought it was him? From the clothes to the hair, to the syringe. It all makes sense!" Pointing and tapping her manicured fingernail on the computer screen, Robert nodded in agreement.

As Robert continued to look blankly at the screen, not reading its contents, but rather, lost in his own mindless thoughts, Aaron walked in through the front door. Carrying his leather binder and a cup of coffee, he made his way to the front desk. "Morning, y'all!"

"Aren't you a big bundle of sunshine this morning, buddy?" Alison said as she walked over to shake his hand. Aaron nodded to Robert, in a typical "man-style" greeting, and opened his binder. He had his notes from the autopsy results, the crime scene, and those he had made when speaking to all those who were involved. His last task, well, second to last was to interview Sammy one last time and conduct a full search of his home.

As the three discussed their plans, the interviewer walked out of Robert's office and handed Robert and Alison each a copy of the transcript of the polygraph test. "You'll have my full report later today, but graphing showed no issues in his responses. I'm sorry, guys, you'll have to find another way to figure this out," Ross said to all of them.

Aaron asked if he could have a copy of the recording, after explaining who he was and what his role

119

was in the case. Nodding, Ross answered, "I'll e-email the report to you, Alison, as soon as I've completed it. Shouldn't take long—it was a pretty straightforward interview with straightforward answers. Y'all have a good one." Grabbing his bag, he walked out of the front door, with a smile on his face. He'd done his job. Sammy had done his job. He'd make sure his report reflected that as clearly as possible.

Realizing that Sammy was alone in his office, Robert trekked back and sat down at the table.

"You okay, buddy?" He'd obviously been crying. His eyes were puffier than usual and wet.

Looking at him, he nodded, and said, "Yeah, I think so. God told me that I'm goin' to be okay. That I will have pain, but once they see the real truth, I'll be a free man."

Re-wording the entire sentence so Robert could understand, he smiled, patted him on the shoulder, and handed him a silver flask from his top desk drawer. Winking at him, he said, "I'll be back in an hour to take you home. Sit here and relax, okay?" With that, he walked out of the office and closed the door.

Aaron and Alison were waiting in the same spot Robert had left them in. Waiting to go dig through this house of 'Little Sammy' to see what could be found. "Y'all ready?" Robert asked.

Holding the door open, the three walked to his cruiser. The summer heat was at full force, and it wasn't even noon. As they backed out, Robert couldn't help but wonder why he suddenly had so much empathy for someone. Robert's background wasn't that of an empathetic, caring person. He'd slept with, well, forcefully slept with Tessie. Was a heavy drinker. Questioned his beliefs in faith and religion at times. And

120

typically, only cared for himself. The thought made him feel good about himself. It made him feel whole. At the same time, the emptiness that came over him was overwhelming.

Chapter Nineteen

Turning right off Main Street, Robert drove his car down through town. With the bank's thermometer reading ninety-eight degrees, and a 'Have a great weekend' message following it, Robert said, "Welcome to life in a small town, folks."

Passing the small gas station, full of jacked up trucks and a few long-haul trucks, he turned left. The Fleetham Cemetery greeted them as he crossed the formidable railroad tracks. "Ever heard the saying, 'across the tracks', well, here ya go." Robert announced. The houses that were left had mostly collapsed, leaving only a memory of a world that had long since expired. Robert used to think about what life was like in a time when the world was divided. Then he would always say, "We still live in that world."

As the car slowed for a dog trotting across the street, he turned right. Waiting for them ahead, was the remains, of what Alison thought was an abandoned shack. The house, which Robert had visited many times before, was Sammy's. The front porch, covered in boxes of discarded trash, was the focal point of the view. Stacked nearly five feet high, they were held up by the grace of God. An old swamp cooler hung in the front room window, supported by the usual chains attached to the eaves of the roof. A cracked window completed the ensemble—an addition that was only enhanced by a strip of fading duct tape.

As he parked the car, Robert could hear the other two chatting in the back. "How on earth could anyone live like this?" Alison asked Aaron. Wanting to have some form of sympathy for Sammy, Robert turned and simply glared at both of them. Robert, while brusque and callous, did have a heart—though, he was too scared to show it. It was obvious that he truly cared about Samuel Harper.

With the trio walking up the rotting steps, they stepped inside the unlocked front door. Waiting for them as they walked in, was an odor that was hard to describe. It reminded Robert of his childhood, cleaning out the horse pens at his parent's farm, mixed with the odor of decomposing roadkill. Making his eyes water, he covered his mouth with his hand and turned around to see Alison and Aaron. Aaron, breathed through his mouth, trying to not inhale, while Alison stepped outside and began to gag. Hearing her outside, Robert followed behind, attempting to be of assistance. "I just need a minute. I'm good." Alison explained.

After a few moments of fresh air, she headed back inside. Robert, trailing behind her, left the front door open in the hope of allowing a breeze to circulate the room. Alison had a plan in her head—a plan to convict this man. Her list included samples of fibers and searching for any clues that might make the case one hundred percent watertight rather than circumstantial.

Everyone was full of determination and ready to work. Alison began explaining her plan to the two men.

"Okay, so first thing, we need to make a quick once over through the entire... house... and see if anything stands out. Then, I'll need samples of each carpet in each room. And see if you can find any signs of vermin. I'm sure it won't be difficult in this barn."

123

Her last sentence made Robert laugh. He knew she was serious but tried to make light of what she'd just said. Opening her bag, Alison handed each a pair of gloves and a mask. "Use it well, boys," she said, as she saluted each one.

As the three went their separate ways, Robert was reminded of why he was helping. He knew that he had a job to do, yet at the same time, he felt that it was wrong. Robert had been thinking earlier that there was something about 'Little Sammy'. Repeatedly, in his head, he kept asking himself, *Are we absolutely sure?* Pushing that thought out of his mind, and wanting to start the task at hand, he began his search in the dining room. Immediately to the right of the front entranceway was a room that only a hoarder would be envious of. A card table stood in the center of the room, one of the legs buckled and bent under the weight of what the table held. Sitting on the tabletop and spilling onto the floor, were bags upon bags of birdseed. One of the bags, Robert thought, had been either chewed by mice, or had burst from the additional weight of the bags on top of it. On the floor, directly under the table, sat the pile of birdseed sat.

Sporadically scattered around the perimeter of the seed were tiny ovals of black pills.

"Rat shit," Robert said to himself. He knew exactly what it was. He'd been raised on a farm where barn rats were plentiful. Walking past the table, another pungent odor hit him. Sitting in a huge box on the floor, directly underneath a large, picture window, were rotting peaches. The smell, a combination of wine and garbage, was probably the most nauseating stench he'd encountered—more so that the reek of filth as he entered his house. Clouds of gnats and flies buzzed around the box of sludge. Beating on the window, in an attempt to escape the prison of horrors, were two honeybees.

As Robert continued through the entrance to the kitchen, he met Alison and Aaron peering into the refrigerator. Walking over to them, he fell, tripping over an old rug that had begun to bunch up in the center. The other two yelled at the sudden shock of him falling, however, no one offered him a hand of assistance. Pushing himself up with both arms, Robert was able to see the floor. They were standing on what Alison had been coveting. The brown rug. Interestingly, it was the typical, low-pile kitchen carpet that homes of a vintage era had—rather, this carpet was what he had had as a child. Thick, heavy pile carpet. Originally, it used to be a dark chocolate brown, but over time and heavy usage, it had faded to the color they were seeing today. Alison realized that Robert had found something but wasn't sure what. The main clue was staring her in the face—being too focused on throwing 'Little Sammy' in prison, she'd completely missed the main reason for her visit to the house. She squatted down next to Robert to have a closer look. "It's absolutely disgusting. Feel how sticky it is over here," Alison told Robert.

As the two of them finished surveying the pile of the carpet, Alison took her tweezers and plucked a few fibers and hairs from the rug. Dropping them into a clear, sealed bag, she pocketed them for safe keeping.

Robert felt quite proud of himself for finding such an important item. It wasn't every day in Fleetham that he found a possible answer to a crime. Now that Alison had achieved her goal, he thought, *Maybe he did it. Everything is right here. How could he be innocent now?*

125

"Boxes of insulin bottles. This thing doesn't even work. I thought it needed to be kept cold?" Alison asked. As she gazed inside the refrigerator, not knowing what she'd find, her head whipped back, calling for Robert.

Looking inside, he knew what he'd find—what he'd smell first, but he wanted to block it out of his mind if possible. Sitting on the shelf, next to a jug of curdled milk, sat about ten boxes of bottled insulin. Plucking one of the boxes from the shelf, leaving a trail of sticky goo that had formed on the bottom, he took it out to examine. The insulin had since expired and was an odd shade of eggshell. He knew that insulin wasn't supposed to resemble milky water, so he was certain this wasn't what it appeared to be. "I need to have this sent out for analysis. Insulin isn't supposed to look this murky... especially when it's labeled as 'Regular' insulin." Robert told the other two.

Taking an evidence bag out of her backpack, Alison opened it, while box after box was placed inside. Sealing it, she returned it to the depths of her bag. With the refrigerator finished, they turned their attention to the sink. Inside, as Robert had seen earlier, were hundreds of used needles. "Well, well, what do we have here? Robert, you might want to re-think things. I can see the expression on your face—I know what you're thinking," Alison snickered.

Reaching into her front pocket, where all her field items were, she pulled out a pair of tweezers and her pint size, red bio-hazard bottle. Picking up a lid and five syringes, she pushed them through the top slot. She didn't have to be a medical professional to know about the dangers that came with a used needed—she'd seen the damage done in her career. She had lost count of the

126

number of bodies that were diagnosed with HIV—*probably from a dirty needle*, she always thought.

"We'll send these for analysis as soon as we leave. I don't want to wait forever like we did on that damned hair sample," Alison demanded. Robert had had enough of the whole process, so he left the kitchen and went down the hallway. Carefully, he tiptoed around trash, bottles, and boxes. About three feet along the hallway, resided the bathroom. He didn't realize how small the house was until he stepped inside. The door had permanently been jammed in place by all the trash on the floor, so he squeezed inside. The sink, full of brown, liquid sludge, which steadily dripped water on the floor. It was as if the house had been vacant for thirty years. The bathroom smelled musty, reminding him of a basement that hadn't seen sunlight in a decade. The second he stepped over the threshold of the hallway his foot accidently kicked a beer bottle into the neighboring baseboard. A rat squealed and ran into a hole under the sink. Walking farther into the bathroom, he noticed that the toilet had long since been unusable. Filled to the brim with raw sewage, he was rather surprised that there wasn't an odor coming from it.

Terrified that any form of additional movement could cause a shift in the floor, he slowly turned and walked back into the hall. Alison and Aaron met him at the doorway, as he slid out. Aaron, with his notebook in his hand, continuing to write, told them, "He's anti-social, a hoarder, and probably has a personality disorder. I think he has a fear of everyone and a need to keep meaningless things close to him. Things matter to him. Collecting things, protecting things… but his OCD—as evidenced by his hoarding, could have stemmed from a traumatic event as a child. It usually does."

Nodding at this bit of information, Robert opened his mouth to speak, but Alison cut him off.

"We need to finish. Move".

The three of them continued walking down the hallway, ending up at the door to the bedroom. This was the last door down the long hall, but this was where they wanted to spend the most time. "In a 'typical' home, your innermost secrets and most valued items are here," Aaron said. Stepping over empty beer bottles and crunching on, Alison wasn't sure what, they made their way into the room. There wasn't a bed, or if there were, it was hidden beneath twenty years' worth of clothes and trash. A single broom was propped up against the wall.

"How ironic, "Alison laughed.

In a pile on the floor, were a pair of brown overalls. The same clothing that Alison had seen during the interview. Taking her tweezers and a tiny, plastic Ziploc bag, she plucked a few fibers from the fabric in the leg. Sealing the bag, she shoved it in a side pocket of her backpack. "I've got to get out of here, Ali. I truly do think we have enough evidence. The pants and the rat droppings are sufficient," Aaron stated, his eyes beginning to water as the stench was too much. Without saying a word, he turned around, and walked out the door. By the time he reached the front room, Alison and Robert could hear him heaving. The odor was getting to them all. Robert was beginning to feel queasy, and Alison had already had her bout of stomach trouble when they first arrived.

"He's right, Robert. Let's go. There's enough here to prove a case. He won't argue, you know. He's mentally challenged anyway. Let's go, I want to run this

128

stuff to the lab," Alison told Robert, looking at his watering eyes.

The pair turned and began their journey to the front door. They must have missed it on the way in, but sitting on the floor, next to what appeared to be a pillow—yellowed with age and rot was a box of condoms. Snapping his fingers at Alison, they walked over to them. They both quickly realized this was his sleeping area. Grabbing another evidence bag, she snatched up the condom box and added it to her stash. Alison straightened up and gave Robert the most curious look. It was a look of pride, but it was also a look of defeat, as well.

"I'm tired, Robert. I'm tired of doing this, yet I continue. Isn't it funny in a way? There's something about Tessie that pulls on my heart. I try and try to not get involved emotionally, but there are those cases that you just can't block out. This is one of them. Don't you think?"

He knew exactly what she meant, but at the same time, he had the same feelings towards Sammy. He nodded and raised his hand in a follow me gesture through the door.

Chapter Twenty

As they exited the house, Aaron was leaning against the cruiser, puffing on a cigarette. "Sorry, y'all, but I had to step away for a minute. I haven't smoked in years, but it was just something that I felt I had to do."

Robert halfway wished he'd smoke in his cruiser. The odor still lingered on their clothes and in their noses from their time spent in the house. Cracking the windows, they headed back to the station. Waiting for them, was a Porsche. Seth's car. Pulling the cruiser next to the luxury sports car, they were all curious why he'd decided to show up. His services weren't required, and they were all sure he was needed at the clinic. "Hey, y'all. No one was inside so I thought I'd just wait and see." Seth called out. Opening his car door, he stepped out. Wearing, what appeared to Alison, to be black, designer jeans, Italian made shoes, and a skin-tight, white button-down shirt, he ran his fingers through his shaggy, feathered hair, and strutted over to their window. Rapping his index finger on Alison's window, he squatted down to be at eye level with her. Raising his eyeglasses and resting them atop his head, he flashed his porcelain smile. His smile, Alison remembered, was the only thing she truly found attractive about him.

Giving her chills, she shuddered, but remained as composed as she could. "Hi, Dr. Binder. We only just finished."

He began to laugh. She could smell something minty, which she assumed was gum or a mint. "Told ya to call me Seth. You're Ali. I'm Seth. Understood?" He said in a smooth and buttery tone

That's another thing I like, she thought to herself.

Robert climbed out of the car first, walked over to Seth and shook his hand. Clearly on a mission to deliver the items collected in Sammy's house to the lab, he left rather quickly. Leaving Aaron and Alison alone to entertain the doctor. Aaron greeted Seth with, "What's up, man? What are you doing out of the hospital these days?"

Seth looked at Aaron and smiled. Returning his gaze to Alison, he opened her door and extended his hand to her, hoping she'd grasp it. Instead, she turned her head, bent down, and picked up her purse. Aaron burst out laughing in the backseat, while Seth, his hand still outstretched, glared at him. Aaron had immediate chills, squinted his eyes, and tried to figure out what Seth was up to. Alison and Aaron worked well together—Aaron was good looking—Aaron had the appeal that Seth possessed. But he wasn't remotely interested in her. He had a long-time girlfriend and was only seeking advancement in his career and a lower mortgage.

Seth withdrew his hand, realizing that she wasn't going to comply, and stepped away, in order to give her additional room. Getting out of the car, purse on one shoulder, her arms full of files, she pulled her sunglasses down from the top of her head and stepped up the curb. Aaron followed suit, intentionally lagging behind, in an attempt to watch Seth. It was clear to Aaron what Seth was doing as Alison was walking in front of him. Any man with a brain cell could figure that one out. Seth had a look of desire, but also something that Aaron couldn't

131

quite place. *I'd like to get to know you and your brain a bit better,* he thought.

As Aaron stepped onto the curb, hearing the door close in front of him, he was alone outside. From where he stood, he could see into the entire police station. Sitting on a metal chair, talking to the receptionist, was Sammy. Standing unusually close to Alison, was Seth who was leaning against an old, wooden counter, his left hand in his pants pocket, and his right hand rubbing his chin. Robert stood in front of the reception desk, chatting to Sammy.

Aaron thought it looked like a scene from a movie. "The entire town is screwed up," he said to himself. Alone, without the distractions of Alison barking chores at everyone around her, or Robert complaining about something, or Sammy whining—he was able to think. After seeing the house, he was able piece together a description of a highly organized, yet mentally unstable killer. By the same token, he could also see where he was incredibly sloppy. He answered his questions during the polygraph interview without hesitation and had zero false answers. Aaron always wanted to fight with the courts because they loved to discard his interview results on the premise that, "Sometimes, they can be inaccurate."

"Bullshit," he said to himself. Thinking about all the times that he's saved innocent men from being sent to jail, he knew his results were accurate. Typically, in small towns, the useless citizens, for lack of better words, were the ones who took the heat—such was the case now.

He remembered the items found in Sammy's house. The carpet fibers. He didn't care about the syringes, but it was the fibers. Fibers can only be found

132

in certain areas. *It's not like everyone has the same brown carpet. This isn't a coincidence*, he thought. Recalling the state of the house, he wondered if there was more to it than they had seen.

Not wishing to obsess about it all day, he wanted to run through the case files, to see if he could find anything that was missed, in the description of the body or the interviews. Walking back inside, he went straight to where Sammy was sitting. "Hey there, bud, are you still doing okay?"

He didn't reply. After a few second of waiting for him to answer, Sammy let out a loud snore.

"Asleep," Aaron said to the room. Leaving Sammy to rest, he found Alison's pile of folders. Knowing they contained all the information pertaining to the case, he sat down at the nearest desk and began to read. Beginning with the discovery of the body, he scanned each line. From there to the presentation of the body, to the trophy removal from the body—it read, to the crime enthusiast, like stereo instructions. Truly, this was why he decided to get into this field—he loved a good puzzle, and this was as good a puzzle as any. As a profiler, he was able to immerse himself in a world of death, deceit, and destruction. He got to delve into other's lives and figure out why they did what they did. Regretfully, he always wished, especially at this moment that he had attended medical school. At this point in his life, it was, of course, too late, but nevertheless, he could use the assistance of a psychiatrist. Finishing the first few pages, he closed the file, stood up, and walked over to Sammy. Alison, Seth, and Robert watched him walk—rather quickly, and shrug his shoulders. "Go home, buddy. You're done here. You need to rest, and we'll see you tomorrow," Aaron gleefully told Sammy.

133

Shaken and half awake, Sammy looked up at him and said, "Oh, uh, sorry, I fell asleep. Do I get to go home now? Am I a free man now?"

Offering Sammy a hand to stand up, he accepted and pulled himself to his feet. The seat was damp where he had been sitting there all day. As he walked towards the door, Aaron had a feeling why it was so wet—but he'd clean it off later. What was important now, was for him to talk to Sammy by himself. Announcing to no one in particular, "I'll be back in a while," he walked out the door with 'Little Sammy'.

"I want to talk to you alone, if that's okay?" he asked. Sammy nodded and went with Aaron, stopping in front of the police station. Digging in his pocket, he pulled out his packet of cigarettes. Flicking his lighter, he took a long inhalation, coughing mid-drag. Attempting another long, relaxing puff, he held his breath for a minute, savoring the taste, as the nicotine flowed through his bloodstream. Aaron sat down on the curb, motioning for Sammy to follow suit. As Sammy sat next to Aaron, he began to speak, "You know, I didn't do nothing. I answered all of the questions and I know I don't tell stories. My mama taught me that a sin is a sin."

Aaron was listening but his mind began to wander to the murder—not only the murder of Tessie, but the murder that was brought to light the other day in Dallas. "Sam, I usually don't talk to the suspects, unless it's a highly unusual case. My job is to dig around the crime scene, look over a body, things like that. This— what I'm doing now, is not normal. I'm not a good person to do this, but I need to. I might lose my job, but I don't care. I want to know the truth. The real truth— not the truth that's been made from a few pieces of trash picked up at your house. So, can I ask you a few things?"

134

Sammy flipped his cigarette out into the street and lit another. He didn't say a word in reply to Aaron's question, but between the two men, the silence spoke louder than anything. Sammy knew that he was in trouble, but he hadn't figured out why. He knew that Aaron was a good man, but he didn't know why he was trying to help him. Sammy stretched out both legs, crossed them, and gave his silent approval to begin speaking.

"Tell me about when you were a kid. I'm curious."

"We were a poor family but good people. Mama worked for a family across town cleanin' and runnin' errands. Daddy left Mama when we were just babies, so Mama brought us kids up all by herself. I had two brothers who both passed years ago."

"Were you ever married? Do you have kids?"

"No, I ain't got kids, but I loved someone once. She was the daughter of a woman Mama worked for. She never knew. I didn't think it was right for someone like me to love someone with money like she had. She was a good woman and is happy now."

"Where do you work?"

"Here and there. I mow grass and help around. I get government money cuz' I got the sugar and need shots. I don't see well neither."

"Do you drive?"

"Yes, but not anymore. I don't have a car and can't see good at night."

"So, at night, you usually stay home?"

"Yeah, I like to piddle around and collect things."

"That's good to know. You've taught me a lot about yourself."

135

Aaron felt relieved with the replies he received, but at the same time, he knew that Sammy would have difficulty in court. From the syringes found at his house, to the fingerprint left on the syringe at the crime scene, it was going to be hell for him. Sammy stood up, and walked around a few cars, returning to where they were sitting. "Can you take me back to my place? I want to be by myself," he said. Aaron, knowing that he must be exhausted, agreed. "Let me check and see if Robert needs anything else—if not, I'll run you back home. I'll be right back, buddy."

Aaron stood up, put his hand on Sammy's shoulder, and gave him a comforting pat. Walking back into the police station, he found Alison and Robert digging through file folders. Clearly absorbed int their work and not paying attention to him, he turned around and walked back out the door. Unlocking his car with his remote, he motioned for Sammy to follow him. Aaron opened the front passenger door and let Sammy in. Closing the door behind him, he walked around to the back of the car and stopped for a moment. Looking up into the sky, he closed his eyes and said, "God, it's been a while. I'm not sure you're even there but give us all strength. Amen." Making the sign of the cross on his chest as he was taught as a young child, he raised his hand and smiled. Getting in the front seat, he backed out and headed to Sammy's house.

Chapter Twenty-One

"You know, we still don't know about the medicine. Can you hand me that file, please?" Alison asked Robert.

The files, stacked a foot high on the table, held every single detail of the investigation. Going through each one, he realized that she'd labeled each folder in accordance with timeframe and location. When he found "motel" he figured that was the correct file. Opening it, he was welcomed by the postmortem photos of Tessie. Her eyes, lost in a transition between life and death, stared him in the face.

To the right of the body, sitting on the bedside table, was a bottle of pills. The bottle was circled with red permanent marker, in an attempt to not lose the image. Alison had written notes while she was at the motel, which were paper clipped to the back of the photo. He found her handwritten notes from that night and read, Hydrocodone/Acetaminophen. From what saw, it was a full bottle with no pills missing. Filled at Fleetham Drug by his son, Dr. Seth Binder only a few days before the murder.

Of course, Seth wouldn't have disclosed the names of the patients he treated, but he wondered why he didn't say anything to them. Robert thought to himself, *I guess he treats so many, he didn't think about it?*

Alison was buried in the glare of her laptop, reading an email from her office, not paying Robert any attention. Sliding the folder over to her, hoping to awaken her sense of alertness, he said, "Here. Seth wrote the prescription a few days before she was killed. See? They're your notes."

Looking away from her screen, she pulled the folder closer and read her notes again. Picking up her phone, she dialed the clinic. Introducing herself to the operator, she asked to speak to Dr. Binder immediately. Elevator music played on the phone—something that was meant to induce calmness in a patient, but to Alison it only added irritation. After a few moments, Seth connected with her on the other line.

"This is Dr. Binder. How may I help you?"

"Seth, this is Alison. We need to speak to you at the police station. Can you head over now? It's rather important, and we don't conduct our interviews over the phone," she explained.

The tone in her voice suggested not only irritation, but an intense level of seriousness—almost threatening, Robert thought.

"Yeah, I have a few more patients to see, then I'll drive over. It'll be about two hours or so, though. Will that be okay?"

Nodding to herself, knowing Seth couldn't see, she replied with, "Okay, thanks," and hung up. Having completed the phone call, which she found quite odd, given this missing piece of information, she looked at Robert but said nothing. Alison was sure they were both thinking the same thing—*why?*

"I'll have a subpoena issued to review the actual medical records," Robert added, hoping to relieve some of their newfound anxiety over the case.

Going through the file again, she re-read her notes from that night. Mumbling to herself, she read the initial description of the room, the position of the body, the medicine and syringe at the bedside, and the amount of blood on the bed. Written at the very bottom of the paper, was an entry she'd forgotten about, *check her background.*

"I can't believe I forgot something so crucial to the investigation. See, this is how I get when I'm stressed—forgetting something like this just makes me want to..." Alison said, but didn't finish her sentence. Logging on to her background history portal, she typed Tessie's name and date of birth into the search engine. After a few moments of scanning millions of internet records, her background results appeared. Moving the computer over so Robert could read as well, they both searched for anything important. Her database, which surpassed that of a common background check, would show them the internet accounts associated with someone, social networking accounts, last known address, the car they owned, and the usual criminal history. Reading through the information, they saw nothing that was pertinent to the case. The last known address was that of her parents, whom Robert confirmed had since died. No car was listed, although Robert did think she had one—but couldn't remember clearly. "Well... that's a bust," Alison said as she slammed the lid of her computer closed.

Robert stood up, stretched, and walked over to the coffee station, pouring himself a cup of black, scorched coffee. "Want any?" he asked Alison. She shook her head and walked over to the front window. Going over the investigation in her head, detail by detail, she was confident that she didn't need any more information to make an arrest. But at the same time, she doubted everything she did. Something didn't feel right to her. This was a new feeling. She'd always been so sure of herself during any investigation she had led.

"You know, I think this is enough. Everything matches. The fingerprints, the syringes, the fibers, everything. The one missing puzzle piece is the medicine. That's what I don't understand. How did Sammy get the Versed?"

Sipping his hot coffee, Robert walked back over to the desk and sat down. Picking up the photographs again, he began to think about the night he spent with Tessie. A lot had changed over the years with him. A lot had changed over the last few days with him.

The night he spent with Tessie was a memorable one, but one that he truly regretted now. He'd seen her standing around the edge of the gas station, smoking and attempting to get a few bucks pulling a trick. Robert knew that there were a few girls who did it as a means to get drug money, but he let it slide, thinking, *who are they hurting?*

He knew Tessie had nothing to her name, so he pulled up and began to chat about what her plans were that night. He knew she'd accept any offer—most people of that caliber did. What he didn't know was what awaited him once the transaction took place. Taking her back to his house, he gave her a drink—enough to loosen her up and not be so nervous. He thought she shouldn't be so jumpy, seeing as how this was a normal thing—but since he was a sheriff and all—that was the justification he used. After she'd finished her whiskey and cola, he took her in the bedroom. Not giving her the chance to set the ground rules, he knowingly took advantage of the situation. Shoving her on the bed, he did what any heartless male would do. His task was pleasure. That's all he cared about—not Tessie. Not if she was safe—but his own satisfaction.

He'd had his way with her, then telling her the next time he caught her in possession of drugs he'd bust her ass, he threw her out the door. He had no intention of taking her back to the gas station. "Get out of here, you little slut," he remembered telling her, as she gathered her jacket and walked out the door.

That was the last time he saw her, with the exception of the discovery of her corpse. Before he'd seen her mutilated body, he was a very callous, heartless, cold man. Today—if he'd had met himself on the street, he wouldn't have recognized himself. "Death changes everyone, don't ya think, Ali?"

Alison didn't answer. She didn't know what to say. She knew that she had to speak to Seth about the prescription, but it was almost a moot point now. The fingerprint and fiber confirmation sealed the deal, for her. "I'll talk to Seth, but I want an arrest after he leaves. I have enough evidence to have Sammy arrested. This will go to court, and once everything is presented by the prosecution, defense won't have a leg to stand on."

Chapter Twenty-Two

It had been about two hours since Seth received the call from Alison. Signing off the chart of his last patient, he walked back to his office. Logging into his computer, he pulled up his electronic medical record documentation program. Adding his credentials and passcode to the login screen, he waited as everything loaded. It was the main irritation of his job—his server was always slow at retrieving his EMR file. He wished, at times that he still used pen and paper to write his progress notes.

As he waited for his system to load, he opened the drawer to his desk and pulled out a bottle of pills. Feeling anxious and stressed from the day, he tipped out one of his anxiolytic tablets and swallowed it dry. Hoping the pill, highly coveted by any drug addict, would take effect soon, he opened Tessie Johanan's chart. He'd figured out, without being told, what they needed. He knew he'd prescribed her a class 2 narcotic but didn't find it relevant during the initial investigation.

I see hundreds of patients a week—this isn't uncommon, he thought to himself.

Printing out the progress note, knowing he was breaking patient-physician confidentiality privileges, he folded it and shoved it in the depths of his scrubs' pocket.

Buzzing the front desk, he informed the receptionist that he needed to cancel all remaining afternoon appointments and reschedule them for tomorrow. Grabbing his bag and cup of coffee, he headed towards the entrance to the lobby. Pausing a moment, gathering his thoughts, he wondered if this would be an issue with Alison—he'd clearly withheld information, but didn't feel it relevant to the case at the time.

Walking out the front door of the clinic, he caught his reflection in the tinted glass. He had goosepimples all over his arms, at the sight of himself. He knew he was handsome and had a feeling others did as well. Smiling at his own reflection, he walked out into the Texas heat and headed for his car.

Driving to the neighboring town took about half an hour—depending on the number of highway patrolmen sitting around, and the weather. This area of Texas was known for rough winters and blistering hot and windy summers… all of which wreaked havoc on any driver. Cranking his stereo up, he relaxed to the sounds of Bach. Classical music always interested him. It soothed him. Growing up, while his dad blasted the latest country tunes, he zoned out with an aria or a slow sonata.

During his drive, he often thought about the events that occurred during the last few hours—but today, his mind went back to his childhood. Growing up, he was alone. Seth was the child who his parents had forgotten. He was left without a boy's best friend, his father, and the nurturing, loving nature of a mother. His parents didn't intentionally forget him—life just got in the way. From his father's sheriff role, to his mother's constant doting on her students, Seth felt like the world evolved around anyone but himself.

Left to his own devices, he quickly involved himself in academia. He taught himself to love and deeply admire classic literature, as well as science and classical music. That love of studying drove him to attend medical school later on. With his passion for science, came a love of anatomy. Living in a small town with little to do, he found solace in studying animal behavior, and watching God's creations living in his own backyard.

Since Seth was an avid reader, he often took that as an excuse to dismiss himself from any social outing. He was the "loser" in his school. Granted, he was utterly brilliant academically, his social skills were less than optimal. Unable to make friends, he became mischievous, often finding refuge in the teasing of others.

As Seth drove down the highway, his mind went back to his senior year. He knew he was the top student in his class, yet at the same time, he yearned for the brotherly bond of friendship his peers had. With only a 4.0 grade point average to use as a weapon, he went out on a limb and asked the most popular cheerleader, his seatmate in biology, to the prom. "Why would I want to go with you? You're such a freak of nature." Her name was Elizabeth. "Lizzy" to her friends.

Seth wasn't quite sure why she'd said no, but nevertheless, the rejection formed yet another wall around him.

After graduation, his freshman year of college had begun. A new environment. A new group of students. A new life. Seth was adamant to make friends, at all costs. Joining as many study groups as he could, he forced himself to become more social. This wasn't natural for him and he often felt as if people were staring at him. His tendency to remain quiet during discussions or his ability, or lack thereof, to engage in regular human interaction quickly became the downfall of his efforts.

Again, he relied on his education to pull him through this time of his life. Graduating college and attending medical school, he lived a life all his own.

His life was Seth. He always thought that he'd been raised as a loner. He'd failed at any social normalcy. His devotion to medicine became his outlet and love.

Speaking aloud to himself, Seth declared, "If they only knew what I went through to get where I am today. I'll never fail, nor will I ever be broken."

Chapter Twenty-Three

Passing the cut-off road to the cemetery, Seth knew he was almost into town. The gas station was on the right, full of local high schoolers socializing with their friends. Trucks packed full of kids, blasting their country music, Seth rolled his eyes and thought, *What a waste of time. This isn't real life.*

While Seth was slowing down to avoid hitting his bumper on the many potholes that littered the streets, he passed the grocery store. Walking out was a woman he'd never seen before with a very dark complexion—*Hispanic*, he thought. Carrying a bag of groceries in one hand, and a cigarette in the other, she placed the bag on top of the car and finished the last few drags of her cigarette. He'd pulled over to watch her. Losing himself in his observations, Seth's mind wandered. He had thought about Tessie a lot today but couldn't understand why. She'd been on his mind since he'd awoken that morning.

As he sat in his car, his eyes locked on the Hispanic woman, who happened to look towards the road. She smiled at Seth, thinking he'd probably pulled over to check his navigation—or something equally as innocent. Seth gave her his million-dollar porcelain smile and slowly drove on.

Seth realized what he'd just done. "What the hell?" He said to himself. Running his fingers through his hair, he picked up the pace of his driving speed. He whipped his car left and turned onto the street where the police station awaited him. Robert's car was parked in front of the building, as well as Alison's. Turning into the parking area, he intentionally parked at the end of the curb, so as not to accidentally scratch his Porsche. Stepping out, he leaned against the car for a moment to collect his thoughts. He was looking at absolutely nothing, but at the same time, was seeing a different world in front of him. In his mind, he saw a hospital that carried his name. He saw a clinic that bore his wife's name. He saw a pharmacy that housed pharmacists he'd personally picked. He saw nothing. Looking down at the concrete street, he began to laugh. His laugh wasn't one of humor, but of awkward embarrassment for his hometown. "If only they knew what I could do for them. If only they truly knew," Seth whispered. With that, he straightened his shoulders, adjusted his shirt, and walked up to the building. He could see his father and Alison sitting around the table in the front office of the police station, obviously elbow deep in something. Strolling in casually, yet very confidently, he said, "Sorry, I got tied up at the clinic. What's up, Dad?"

His sudden appearance startled them both. Jumping slightly, Alison glanced up, smiled at Seth, and said, "Oh, hello. I'm so glad you were able to come down. We just want to talk to you for a minute, please."

This made Seth grin from ear to ear. Thoughts began to race. Thoughts such as, *She's glad I came? What does that mean, I wonder?*

Sliding the photograph of the body over to him, Seth looked at the image, expressionless.

Alison had assumed Seth would show some form of emotion, but he just sat there. Alison began her usual

147

form of direct questioning to Seth, "Do you see what bothers us about this photograph? See the bottle?"

Truly not paying attention to the details of the image, he was solely focusing on the body. Seeing her splayed in this position with her abdomen gaping open, he opened his mouth to speak, but nothing came out. He closed his eyes for a moment, taking a deep breath in an attempt to relax.

"I know, Son, I know. I felt the same way and I didn't even see her during the autopsy. I know this is something that you don't see every day, but we do need your help," Robert said, the exhaustion evident in his voice. Robert pointed to the bottle with the notes written by Alison. "See—the name of the medicine was… wait a minute, I have it down here somewhere… oh, yeah, hydrocodone. The doctor who prescribed it was you."

"It's hydrocodone, just to clarify. And yes, I did prescribe it to her. I brought the progress note of her visit. I'm sorry, I didn't even realize that it would have been pertinent. I see hundreds of patients a week, and don't think about them after they've been discharged from my care," Seth told his father. Alison, looking at him from across the table, felt uneasy about his answer. She thought to herself, *How did he not think about this? No one is that busy… are they?* Chewing on her bottom lip, Seth caught her staring. She quickly averted her eyes back to her laptop and began to type.

Robert stood up, feeling a little tense around Alison, and walked over to the coffee pot. Pouring his son a cup of coffee, he turned and asked him, "Why didn't you tell us? I don't understand. You obviously knew she was—you know what? It's all bullshit, anyway. I want to ask you something, though?"

148

Nodding, Seth gave him his answer without saying a word.

"Did she happen to say anything to you? Anything that would have caused you to be concerned for her safety? Anything like that?"

Seth began to tap a ballpoint pen on the table to break the silence after Robert spoke. He looked his father straight in the eyes and explained the day of her visit, as best as he could remember: "I don't recall exactly what she said during her visit, but I do know she came in for complaints of chronic back pain. I knew she was a drug user—you could easily look at her and tell. I was unaware that she could have potentially been in danger. She said absolutely nothing about that to me, or to the nurse. The nurse, by the way, accompanies me in the room with all female patients. I have no desire for some soccer mom to accuse me of raping her. So, I take my own protection. But to answer your question and the Queen of Sheba's question over there, no. Nothing was said. Nothing was observed. It was a usual exam with no abnormal findings."

Alison wasn't satisfied with his answer, but it was very clear that Seth was adamant about not adding more information. She continued to take notes, transcribing his conversation to her notepad. She looked up and caught him staring at her. His eyes. Her thoughts drifted to his eyes. She always found him attractive, but knew he was entirely too pompous to pursue—apart from that, "she didn't date co-workers" she'd always said. Granted, he wasn't a true colleague, but he was Robert's son. Her cheeks began to flush from him continuing to glare at her. Turning around, she told Robert she needed to speak to the rest of the investigation team that afternoon. "I believe I have

149

enough physical evidence to issue a warrant. The problem will be the jury. I don't want the defense to downplay his level of intelligence and his history of nothing in this town. That's the problem. He has a history of doing nothing wrong. He's a model citizen—as model as he can be, anyway."

Seth opened his mouth to speak, but before he was able to do so, Robert asked them both a question. "Are we truly sure, Ali? I mean, are we absolutely certain? At first, it was very iffy. We have evidence, but are we positive?"

Seth looked as his dad. His expression was that of someone who was not only confused but taken aback by Robert's level of sincerity. Seth began to laugh, and asked his father, "What the hell has happened to you, Dad? Why are you suddenly so saintly? Last time my dad was around, he didn't give a shit about anyone. Now look at ya. Baptist preacher next week?"

Seth continued to laugh at his comment. Looking at Alison, her face was as blank as an empty chalkboard. She said nothing to Seth in response to his remark. Robert walked back to the table, looking at Alison and smiled. He put his right hand over his heart and told her, "You don't know me, Alison. Seth does, and he's right. Something happened in the last few days, and it's something that I like. You only know me now. You didn't know me back then—and what I was truly like. You'd be ashamed, and I'm sure you wouldn't have a positive thought about me whatsoever. The point is I done changed. And it feels good."

Alison had to wipe a tear away from her cheek. She wasn't an emotional person at all but hearing him—hearing that Robert... the man who had "won the west" actually did care. She knew this, but always thought he'd

150

hidden it to protect his image. "Death changes people, Robert. It changed me. You don't know me either, ya know. I used to be a lot sweeter than I am now. Now, I'm all work and no play. Death changed me to the point of having a permanent wall around my heart. Death was good to you, but death was horrible to me." The second she finished her sentence, she stood up and walked out the door to the restroom.

I need a break, she thought.

Robert and Seth remained at the table. As they sat in silence, Seth asked his dad the most curious of questions. "How old is she? Alison, I mean. She's someone who I'd love to know better. What's her story?"

Robert had an immense amount of respect for his colleagues, especially Alison. He'd grown to truly like her. She was much younger than he was, and his fatherly instincts kicked in—more so than they did with Seth. "No, she's not for you. I don't want you trying to date someone that I work with. Just find someone at the hospital. Why not a nice nurse?"

Immediately feeling frustrated by his father's lack of attention towards his desires, he pursed his upper lip—a habit when he was upset—and told his father, "You never truly cared. I don' know why I asked. Good luck on this dead girl situation you've got here. Hopefully, you'll find the person who hacked her up… if not, I hope they don't force you into early retirement. You haven't lost your touch, have you?"

Standing up and slamming his chair back under the table, he walked to the front door. He heard the bathroom door open the second he began to leave. Turning around, he gave Alison a smile and told her goodbye. Walking to his car, he began to whistle *Moonlight Sonata* by Beethoven. A melody that induced

151

relaxation during the most stressful of times. A melody that he intended to play for Alison after one of their future dates.

Chapter Twenty-Four

Aaron found driving with Sammy to be quite an experience. He had to avert his attention to something else, otherwise the odor from the filth and urine would have made him gag. Sammy sat in the car, looking out the window not saying a word. Aaron broke the awkward silence by asking him something he'd never asked anyone. "Do you want me to pray with you? I am not very good—I question a lot of things, but since I've been in town, I've learned a lot about myself. I'd be happy to do so if you'd allow me to."

Sammy turned his head and looked at him. The expression on his face and his teary eyes gave him the answer he sought. As they turned down Sammy's street and pulled into the driveway, Aaron grabbed Sammy's hand tightly, and bowed his head. "Father, I'm asking you to keep Sammy safe, keep him alert, and help him to make the right decisions when and if has to go to court. He's your child, so protect him. Give us all strength to handle whatever may lie ahead. In Jesus name we pray. Amen."

Sammy whispered, "Amen," after Aaron.

"I don't think any livin' soul has ever done that for me. You have no idea how much it meant. Thank you," Sammy said, his voice breaking at the end of his sentence.

Aaron smiled at him. He had an attraction to Sammy—not in a sexual way, of course, but spiritually.

153

Aaron had thought this for some time, especially after he first was introduced to him.

Aaron released his hand and told Sammy to close his eyes for a moment. "Do you remember when you were a child? Think back to that time. Try and remember a happy memory but make it a strong one. The happiest memory you have. Do you have it?"

Sammy nodded his head. "Okay, great. Now, take that memory and how you felt, and use that feeling to make yourself happy now. Remember, you can choose to be happy just as you can choose to be sad. Today, choose happiness. Okay?"

Sammy nodded again and said "Okay."

Aaron couldn't believe what had just happened. He honestly hadn't ever said anything that personal to someone, let alone someone who was the main suspect in a murder investigation. He'd promised himself that he wouldn't stop even if he were fired for his actions. Today was a new day. Today was the beginning of a new life for himself.

Sammy left the vehicle first, tottering down the overgrown front yard to his front porch. Aaron, slightly jogging behind him, called out to him, "Wait a minute, I noticed earlier that your door was open. Didn't you lock it?"

"No, sir, I don't lock my doors at all. They don't shut anyhow. Who would want to come in here anyway?" He told Aaron, as he pushed the front door slightly to squeeze through.

Aaron didn't enter the house. He wasn't afraid... despite the stench that he knew would welcome him. He'd seen the crime scene. He'd seen the body. He'd seen the autopsy report. But sitting there with Sammy, and speaking with him, he wasn't sure Alison had the

154

right person. As a profiler his job was to delve into the twisted mind of a killer. He had been unable to do that with Sammy.

"I'll be right in, I just want to sit here and think for a minute, okay?" Aaron yelled inside to Sammy. Sitting on the front steps of the porch, he looked down at the ground and closed his eyes. His mind went back to the night he arrived in Fleetham. The first night he arrived in town was the night he saw the pictures of the body. He'd never forget the way she'd been positioned. The precision of the abdominal cut. The perfect shaped heart on her chest. The severe aggression of her body in general. Thinking about that image and comparing it to Sammy—*there isn't a comparison. He doesn't have the mentation and the steadiness to do that,* he thought.

His phone was vibrating in his pocket. A text from Alison, *Come to the station now*

"What does she want now," he said to himself. Standing and putting his thoughts out of his mind, he walked into the house to find Sammy throwing birdseed on the floor. With each wave of his hand, thousands of tiny seeds scattered the floor. The absolute second the seeds bounced on the filthy carpet, several small mice came scurrying out from under a side desk, devouring the free food. "I've got to run. Are you good, Sam?"

Sammy didn't answer, only turned and smiled. Nodding once, he indicated that he was content with his current surroundings and wished to be left alone—at least that's what Aaron understood he meant.

Replying to her text, he headed back to the station. He was determined to tell her his thoughts, but first, he needed to speak to the rest of the investigation team. He'd prefer to do this as a group, so he wouldn't have to repeat the story a hundred times. As he turned

155

back onto the main road, a Porsche raced down the highway. Traveling at top speed, it was a blur as the car headed out of town. He recognized the car as Seth's and wasn't surprised by his driving behavior. Aaron had noticed his arrogant attitude, as well as his need for everyone's approval and attention. "What a prick," Aaron said aloud.

The police station was busier than usual today—ten cars were lined up in front of the curb. Mostly law enforcement vehicles of some sort, and definitely not local, he'd deduced that Alison had called everyone in for a meeting. Probably, the same meeting referenced in his text messages.

Stepping out of the car and onto the curb, he took a deep breath and prepared himself for the biggest debate of his career. Smiling to himself, and thinking, *The biggest debate in the smallest of towns. Pitiful, but in a funny way.*

As he walked into the police station, all eyes were on him. Fifteen men and women were sitting around the desk, each with their faces buried in a pile of papers. Each member of the team had the same look of concentration. As he walked into the office, Aaron looked at Alison, who was busying herself with her phone. She glanced back at Aaron, motioned for him to sit down, and began to speak to the group.

"Okay, so since our profiler has arrived, we can begin. We are all here to discuss the evidence and potential arrest of Samuel Harper. In front of each of you, you'll find a folder containing all the evidence and my report. Please review, and we can discuss shortly."

Aaron pulled Alison aside, grabbing the evidence folder as she got up, and began his debate. "Look, I need to talk to the entire group before we make this arrest. I don't think we have the right guy. It doesn't make sense to me, Ali. I spent some time with him, and he's not the guy. I'm telling you."

Alison, squinting through her tired eyes, turned, and looked at the group. With everyone catching up on the information in front of them, they paid her no attention. Turning back to Aaron, she said, "Have you spoken to Robert about this?"

Robert heard his name in the silence. Walking over to the quiet corner where Alison and Aaron were standing, he said, "What's up? I heard my name."

Aaron, full of a burning desire to save someone whom he believed was innocent, nodded, and began to speak. "I was telling Alison that I think 'Little Sammy' is innocent. I spent time with him today. He's not the one, man. He doesn't have it in him. He's borderline retarded for Christ sake."

Alison chucked at that comment, raised her hand and placed it on his shoulder saying, "Calm down. I have the physical evidence. Remember, you just talked to him. You know the old saying, 'You never truly know someone.' Never forget that."

Robert realized that this conversation would quickly become redundant between the two of them, so he returned to the table and began thumbing through his phone. *Is Alison right?* Robert wondered. Not wanting to overthink, the thought left just as quickly as it came.

Alison returned to the table, with Aaron standing in his original position. She picked up her computer and began to read the summary of the investigation to the team. Detailing all information, she stated, "I believe we have enough if you'll read my conclusion. Samuel Harper fits the profile, the fingerprint matches the one we found on the syringe, and his image was captured on closed circuit television. This is no longer an investigation based solely on circumstantial evidence…"

Mid-sentence, Aaron interrupted her. "Yes, what Alison said is true, but… I spent a few hours with him, and I have additional information. The information I would like to present is not physical, but it's based on my expertise as a profiler."

Every person sitting at the table turned and looked at Aaron. Intrigued by what he'd just said, Alison replied with, "This isn't really important to the arrest, but if you feel you must add something, by all means."

Aaron took out his phone where he'd written a few key points and began to read. "First of all, now that I actually took the time to do this, his demeanor doesn't suggest that of a killer, let alone a serial killer. For one thing, he doesn't drive. Secondly, his mentation is maybe at a ten-year-old level?" He felt his face flush and the blood rush from his hands and feet, leaving them ice cold. He knew he'd struck a nerve when he rebutted the leader of the pack.

Alison glared at him, hoping he'd finish quickly so she could do her job. As Alison listened to what Aaron was presenting to the group, Robert raised his head from his pile of information laid in front of him and glanced at Aaron. The look on Aaron's face, Robert noticed, was that of someone who had just discovered water in an ocean. Robert had never seen someone so sure of himself and pleased, all at the same time.

Robert stood, and paced across the room, asking Aaron a question, he was sure everyone had on their mind. "What makes you so sure about this? How can you negate physical evidence? Evidence that was presented and discovered with you present most of the time? I'm not saying you're right and she's wrong or nothing like

158

that, but the fact remains that the evidence is in your hand. Right now."

Nodding, Aaron agreed with what Robert had said. As he turned around, staring out the window at the town, looking at nothing really, he replied to the group. "He's right. Alison's right. But I'm also right. I've thought this through. I don't normally interview the suspects. I look at everything else. I'm glad I went out of my 'scope of practice' to dig deeper into this. Everyone turn to page three of the investigation packet, please."

The room was filled with the scooting of chairs in an attempt to ready themselves for the task ahead. As the file folders simultaneously flipped to the third page, the image of Tessie haunted them all. "Now, look at the picture closely. Tell me what you see? Does anyone see something that's curious?"

Everyone scanned the image, including Alison, attempting to find something that was curious about the photo. "Curious," Robert said, not realizing he'd spoken aloud.

"What was that, Robert?" Aaron asked him interested in what he might say.

Robert looked up, holding the photograph in front of his face, and said, "Your question is absolutely ridiculous. Look at this picture. Of course, it's unique. Look at the body. What the hell are we supposed to be looking at? This isn't a 'find the image' game here, ya know."

A few people laughed at his comment, knowing he was right. Alison interjected and in her usual, direct voice, asked Aaron, "This is a waste of time. Instead of playing games, why not get straight to the point. What exactly are we supposed to be looking at here?"

159

Aaron took his pen and pointed at the incision to the abdomen and to the heart shaped cut-out on the chest. "This, my friends, is what you should be focusing on. If you haven't yet met Sammy, you wouldn't understand. He's an alcoholic, and a very bad one at that. He shakes, and barely stands up when he walks. And the door to his house doesn't even lock. Anyone could have walked in and planted these items in the motel room."

Alison glared at him the entire time he continued to speak. Clearly confused, she held her hand up in an attempt to interject. "And your point would be? Because, I've yet to see it. Let's remember that this isn't a genius we are dealing with, either."

Aaron, clearly frustrated and feeling as if Alison and the rest of the room were undermining his professional opinion, began to raise his voice slightly. "Am I the only one with a brain here? Jesus. I'm trying to tell you that there's no way he could have made such a perfect cut on the chest and the abdomen. Look at it. It's perfectly straight. If Sammy would have been the killer, Tessie would have looked like a gutted deer."

Some of the people at the table nodded and agreed—primarily women, the ones not in agreement, were the men. Clearly supporters of Alison and Robert, the men were silent, signifying their disagreeing opinions. A small bead of sweat formed on Aaron's forehead as he leaned against the window, facing the group. "Do you all understand where I'm going with this? Someone killed her, yes, but it wasn't Sammy."

Chapter Twenty-Five

Alison resumed her seat at the table, having listened to Aaron's speech. "Okay, we need to move on here. While I understand exactly what Aaron's saying, we can't deny what's staring us in the face. If everyone agrees with the physical evidence in your hands, then I say we obtain the arrest warrant and handle this now. Are there any objections?"

After a few short moments of mumbling amongst themselves, a solid "yes" was given by everyone, with the exception of Aaron. After the decision was made to make the arrest, Aaron walked out of the police station and sat on the curb. His thoughts were all over the place, primarily on Sammy. He had read about cases where the wrong man was behind bars, but never knew he'd be involved in such an incident. "The courts will screw him over," he whispered to himself. He'd met a man a few days ago that he was certain was the killer. He'd also met a man yesterday whom he knew was innocent. Both assessments he thought were correct, yet at the same time, they were both wrong.

A blast of cold air hit him on the back of the neck. The door had just opened, with Robert coming outside. "I just stepped outside for a sec. It's getting too tense for me in there. Everyone keeps repeating the same things over and over. I wish they'd just bury this shit just like they buried Tessie."

Robert sat down on the curb with Aaron and handed him a cigarette. Declining, Aaron said, "No, thanks, but if it were something stronger, I might not say no."

Robert laughed at his comment, knowing how upset he was with the decision to move ahead with the arrest. "Ya know, buddy, I've been there, too. Several years ago, there was a drug problem going on here in own. I arrested the gal who had all the evidence. Turns out, she was freed after all. This isn't for us to decide. He's still gotta survive the jury and 'ole Judge Rosenburg. Don't worry about it now."

Aaron said nothing, instead, he hung his head down, and was lost in thought. Robert sensed he wanted to be alone, so he patted him on the shoulder and stood up. Flicking his half-smoked cigarette out into the street, he went back inside to the discussions that awaited him.

Replaying the last few days in his head repeatedly, Aaron felt that he was missing something, but he wasn't sure what exactly. Standing up, he quickly walked inside, and grabbed his pile of folders sitting on the end of the conference table. Sending a military salute/wave combination to the table, he walked to the back of the lobby and disappeared into an empty office. Sitting Indian style on the floor, he spread out the folders, organizing them by timeline. His job description was about to begin. *I will re-invent my job as a profiler and add an extra element to make my point clear to everyone,* he thought.

Chapter Twenty-Six

As the discussion at the table ended, Alison called her central office to give a brief synopsis of the day's events. After finishing her conversation with, "It'll be completed today," she turned to Robert and winked.

"We can leave the judge out of the arrest until it's time for court. There's probable cause here. Let's do it. I'll come with you. Ladies and gentlemen, thank you for all your efforts. You're free to go."

The room cleared quicker than she anticipated, leaving Robert alone with her. Aaron remained in the back office, *wasting time*, Alison thought. "He doesn't need a babysitter to play martyr, let's go get our man."

Alison and Robert straightened their stacks of papers, and gathered the necessary paperwork needed to bring Sammy in. "What time do you want to head over there? The sooner the better, don't you think?" Alison asked.

Nodding, Robert reached in his desk drawer and pulled out his revolver, holster, and handcuffs. "Shit, it's been years since I've worn these things. I never thought I'd actually need them in a town like this, ya know?"

Alison, with her sunglasses on and phone in her hand, was delayed by Robert's nostalgic thoughts. "Hurry up, what's the problem?" She asked, the frustration rising in her voice.

163

Robert stood up, handing her the cuffs to carry. "You're doing this, just so ya know. You have as much power in this town as I do. This is your baby."

Alison had a grin bigger than Russia on her face. Her cheeks filled with blood and her neck became splotchy. Her appearance was that of someone who had just completed a ten-mile race. The excitement on her face was echoed in her voice when she gushed, "I knew you'd finally agree with me. Let's get this done. I'm ready to go back to the city and resume my normal life."

As she finished boosting herself with her own zeal, the two walked out the door, heading towards his cruiser. The heat from the day made the short walk almost unbearable, with Robert breaking out in an immediate sweat. "You know, there are people who live in this town and actually don't have air-conditioning! I done quit trying to figure out how they function. I'm sweating like a whore in church during a Sunday evening revival."

Alison needed a laugh. As ecstatic as she was, she was equally as somber about the entire ordeal. She relished her days of arresting people for crimes they'd committed, but all the same, she knew the destruction it would cause in their lives. Turning to Robert, she began to speak, but the words wouldn't form.

He looked at her and knew she was in deep thought. "Whatcha thinking over there?"

Alison stared straight ahead as they drove to Sammy's house. In a quiet voice, she told him, "I'm happy we made this decision, I mean, it was staring us in the face, basically, but I do feel sorry for him. I really do. But at the same time, he knows the consequences of things, don't you think?"

164

Robert nodded, but had a concerned look on his face. "It sounds like you're doubting your decision, honey. Are you?"

Alison didn't reply.

Crossing the railroad tracks, Alison anticipated the distinct bump of the car that was looming. Crossing railroad tracks was a phobia of hers. Her fear, to this day, was that a train would turn the corner unseen, and end her life. Today was no different. She held her breath until they were safely across.

Sammy's house looked no different today than it had the first time she saw it. The trash in the house still remained, spilling out into the yard, the door was still half-closed, and to Alison, it looked as if another window had been broken. "I just don't know how anyone can live like this. I don't think it matters if you're like Sammy or not. It's disgusting." Alison commented as they turned into the driveway and parked.

Stepping out of the car, the odor immediately hit her. She didn't remember smelling it when she first toured the house, but thought it was because she had other things on her mind at the time. Now, standing on the threshold of the driveway and yard, she was able to take in the full image of his estate.

She thought the stench was just from the trash. She didn't give it much thought until she started walking up the front steps. With Robert trailing behind her, she knocked on the door. As the two stood outside on the front porch, the odor Alison had smelled earlier became even more intense. Snapping her fingers at Robert, in an attempt to get his attention, she pointed to the front door, half ajar, and said, "What do you smell? Is it familiar?"

Robert had been busy looking around at the piles of trash on the porch, not really paying attention to what

165

Alison was doing. He was used to her, ever since he'd known her, she typically went her own way.

Sniffing in the air, he knew the smell was familiar. Closing his eyes, he tried digging into his memory. His mind drifted back once more to when he was a child and went hunting with his father. A few days after the hunt, and the meat had been cleaned, the odor would start. It was the smell of death and decay.

Turning to Alison, he said, "Something is rotten. It's probably all of this shit outside."

She knocked on the door, softly at first, then realized she couldn't be heard. Pounding on the door, it swung open from the force of her knock. Inside, the view hadn't changed. There were still boxes piled to the ceiling, and a heap of birdseed and assorted empty containers littered the floor.

"Sammy, are you here? It's Robert and Alison. We want to talk to ya for a minute." Robert called out.

Silence greeted them. Robert stumbled over an empty whiskey bottle lying in the floor. As he kicked it out of the way, a pale, white image caught his attention. "Hey, do you have any gloves in your bag? Or did you bring your bag with you?" He asked Alison.

As she shook her head, he told her, "I'll be right back." Jogging back to his cruiser, he hunted through his first aid kit, digging out a pair of powdered latex gloves. By the time he'd closed the trunk of the car, Alison had appeared on the porch. Completely confused by his urgency, she had her phone in her hand, ready to call her team and ask them to return. "What in the hell is wrong? What did you see besides a liquor bottle?"

When the last glove snapped against his wrist, he bent over, peeling a dried-out condom off the grimy

166

floor, The backside of the condom had a layer of grease that had adhered it to the carpet—what once was carpet.

Robert took his pen from his pocket and carefully lifted the rubber prophylactic rim. Inside, long since deteriorated, was a grayish black piece of something. Motioning for Alison to come closer, he asked, "Turn your phone light on. There's something in here and I don't think it's the after party of a fun night."

Alison swiped up, and her mobile phone light glared ahead. Inside, the black substance had a few strands of hair attached to it. Along the sides of the condom were dried smears and drops of a blackish substance. From experience, Alison recognized the coloring of dried blood, and instantly had a wave of chills. "This is it. We are in the home of a serial killer. I need to have my team search this house again. Clearly, this was missed."

Robert took off one of the gloves and slid the condom inside to protect it. The other glove, he left on. Why, he wasn't sure, but felt it wasn't important at the time to remove it. He knew Alison was right. He knew he had to make the arrest—or someone did, anyway. "Ya know, I've known him all my life. How many people has he killed? Who's to say he didn't venture to other towns and do this, too? But the question is... how?"

Alison shook her head. Her brain in a million places with a million different thoughts, the thing that was most important was this arrest. She had to get him off the streets. She had to offer some protection to the town. To her, the protection that she'd offer would be to send the threat to jail. Collecting herself, she motioned for Robert to follow her. Walking through the kitchen, the view was the same as before. Trash everywhere. That

167

odor that reminded them of decaying flesh lingered in their noses.

Nearing the back bedroom, a sound broke through the silence. Asleep on a pile of dirty clothes was Sammy. He was softly purring as he slept, a sound that reminded Alison of a very contented puppy enjoying an afternoon nap. Sammy had four whiskey bottles littered around his sleeping mat. *He must have passed out or drank himself into a stupor,* she thought.

The two were standing directly over Sammy. As they looked down, the reality hit them. "We are going to have to see if he's even competent to stand trial," Robert told Alison. Nodding in agreement, she took her foot and nudged Sammy on the back, sending him into a snorting fit. He turned over and opened his eyes.

"Oh, hey, sir. I didn't know you were coming by. What can I do ya for? I was just taking a nap."

Alison remembered her soft heart earlier in the car, but it was quickly replaced by disgust and hatred. The stench from his breath was overwhelming. It was a mixture of alcohol and a filthy mouth, making her eyes water from the nausea building in the pit of her stomach. "Ugh," she said under her breath, not really caring if Sammy overheard her or not.

Sammy sat up and began to have a coughing fit. Years of smoking had taken its toll on his once strong lungs. The wet, raspy cough was followed by a series of spitting into a dirty shirt laying on the floor.

Realizing that Alison was with Robert, he quickly stood to his feet, steadying himself against the neighboring wall. "Oh, I'm sorry, ma'am, I didn't see you standing there. Can I help you with somethin'?"

Alison cleared her throat and began to read the words she'd said so many times before. They were

168

second nature to her, but she still felt having a printout gave her an added amount of security. Standing in front of him, Sammy was a pitiful sight, she thought. He wasn't going to fully comprehend what she said, but regardless of that, she had a job to do. So, she began, "Samuel Harper, you're under arrest for the murder of Tessie Johanan. You have the right to remain silent and to refuse to answer questions. Anything you say may be used against you in a court of law. You have the right to an attorney before speaking to the police and to have an attorney present during questioning now or in the future. If you cannot afford an attorney, one will be appointed for you before any questioning if you wish. If you decide to answer questions now without an attorney present, you will still have the right to stop answering at any time until you talk to an attorney. Please turn around with your hands behind your back."

Sammy looked at both of them as if he'd been hit by a truck. He didn't understand what she'd just told him and began to sob quietly. Sputtering his words, he asked Alison, "Ma'am, I don't understand what you just said. I didn't do nothing to Tessie. I told you that the other day. You remember, right?"

Robert put his hand on his shoulder and attempted to comfort him, in a way that only a father would know. "Sam, we have evidence that leads to you. Fingerprints and the camera image. I don't know another way out of this. But until the courts decide if you're guilty or not, you'll have to come with us. You'll be in my jail, so I'll look after you. Okay?"

Alison began to speak in response to Robert consoling Sammy but felt it best to keep her mouth shut. Thinking to herself, she said, "I never understood why

169

people console a criminal or have an ounce of sympathy, but I guess, to each their own."

Alison handed Robert the handcuffs, and he clicked them in place on Sammy's wrists. Not following protocol, and as Sammy wasn't violent at the moment, he cuffed him with his hands in front of his body. This was the least threatening method, he thought, and considering his mental state, thought he would respond better this way.

Sammy lowered his head, sobbing silently, all the while murmuring something that resembled a prayer, or so Robert thought. Alison led the way out of the room, as Robert ushered Sammy through the doorway. With his hand on his shoulder, he guided him to the front of the house and out the front door. By the time the two men had reached the front porch, Alison had already opened the back door of the police cruiser, waiting for her assailant. Sammy shoved his shoulders away from Robert as he was trying to help him into the car, and said, "I can do it. I can do anything. I'm finished needing any man's help."

Alison closed the door and instantly felt an enormous load of stress drift away. "I did it. That son of a bitch won't touch another living soul ever again," she said to Robert.

Walking to the passenger side of the car, she slipped inside and pulled out her phone. Scrolling through the list of contacts, she found her lead criminal supervisor at the office and typed, *It's done. Arrest made. Headed to jail now.*

Chapter Twenty-Seven

Sitting alone in his living room, Seth pulled out his phone and called his dad. After multiple rings, Robert's voicemail began, *This is Sheriff Robert Binder. Leave a message and I'll call ya back."*

With a tone of irritation in his voice, he left his dad a voicemail. "Hey, Dad, call me when you have minute, I need to talk to you about something."

After ending the call, his mind went back to his few encounters with Alison. He knew she was busy with the investigation, but he longed to be near her. With the image of Alison in his head, he thought, *If only I could take her out somewhere. She would love everything about me."*

Grinning from ear to ear, he stood up and went to the kitchen. Finding his favorite bottle of vodka and pouring a coffee mug full, he returned to the couch and began to scroll through his social media account. Typing in her name under the search bar, he found Alison's account. Set to private, as most pages were, he was, however, able to see a few of her photos.

Scrolling through her images, taken through the years, he began to become aroused by the mere sight of her. Biting his bottom lip, his thoughts raced to not only dating her, but becoming intimate with her as well. With a whispering voice, he began to speak, "I can't wait to take you in my arms and smell your hair. Your hair and your eyes were the things that drew me to you. Oh, Alison. I might call you Ali. I like that better."

During his whispering to his phone screen and her image, he began to rub the right side of her cheek with his thumb. Fantasizing that it was her face, his eyes had squinted, and his face began to flush.

His phone began to vibrate during his fantasy session with an incoming call. It was his dad. Answering rather quickly, he greeted his father, "Hey, I have a question and need your help with something. Are you busy?"

Robert and Alison were almost to the police station, where they'd book Sammy and place him in a jail cell. He had limited time to talk but spoke to his son in his usual, fatherly tone. "I'm swamped, what's up? Is it an emergency?"

Seth felt an ounce of hope with this, as he assumed Alison was probably nearby. With a grin on his face, he said, "No, not an emergency, but I need a favor. I want to speak to Alison and take her out to dinner or something. I might come over to the station later today. Will she be there?"

Robert looked at Alison as he heard his son ask the questions. Hoping she didn't overhear, he replied, "I'll have to call you back later, is that okay?"

Seth ended the call without saying goodbye. Throwing his phone across the room, hearing the glass shatter, he began to scream. "He never cared. The bastard never cared about me. It was always work, work, work."

Walking into the kitchen, he took his bottle of vodka and began to drink. About a cup of the icy, clear liquid was left, and in one gulp, the bottle was empty. Throwing the bottle on the floor—the Russian bottle of

172

security, as Seth usually referred to it—it shattered into a million pieces. Shards of glass sprayed across the room. The cabinet adjacent to the refrigerator had been left open when he grabbed his cup earlier. Staring him in the face was his bottle of anxiolytics.

Feeling anxious after the telephone call with his father, he flipped the lid open and stuck his tongue into the depths of the bottle. Unsure how many tablets had stuck to the wet surface, he swallowed them dry.

He loved his pills. He began taking them at an early age to control his anxiety and aggression, something that he continued to suffer from to this day. His psychiatrist had labelled him as someone who had antisocial behavior, obsessive compulsive disorder, and manic depression. Sitting on the black leather couch of his "head doctor" as Seth called him, he could remember years of therapy. Years of a quack physicians telling him to talk about his feelings or think about this or that. He hated psychiatrists, which is why he chose internal medicine. His passion of diagnosing, treating and fixing illnesses far surpassed that of trying to dig into people's heads.

The memory of his years of psychiatric treatment lingered. Seth began to have such agitation with the mere memory of his childhood that he rammed his fist onto the kitchen counter. Made of granite, it didn't give way. Immediately oozing blood, he looked down and was expressionless. All his knuckles instantly began to swell, and a slow trickle of blood continued to pool on the brown granite. Taking his other hand, he dipped his forefinger into the small puddle of blood and began to write on the countertop. Fading from top to bottom, the letters eventually formed Alison.

173

Seth knew that if anyone walked into his house, he would have been, not only embarrassed, but more than likely his father would have known that his psychiatric problems were no longer stable. In the gleam of the granite, he could see his reflection. Running his bloody hands through his hair, he combed it back, as he often did. Liking the appearance of the windblown, feathered look, he smiled, which accentuated his beady eyes.

"Bedroom eyes," he whispered to himself. Seth had been told he was stellar in the intimacy department, and always yearned for more.

Thinking to himself, he said, "I miss dating. I miss everything."

Seth's history of relationships was few and far between. His previous and only real relationship, for that matter, ended very quickly, as Liza felt he was becoming too serious and that wasn't what she wanted. Although she was very gracious in receiving the ruby necklace he had given her to remember him by, Seth felt that she had zero interest in the gift.

What Liza wasn't aware of was his true personality. He was always very possessive, requiring constant attention, and quite the jealous type. The relationship ended with Seth's emotions crushed, which added to his behavior of pursuing women incessantly.

During medical school, he was frequently told to 'back off' by many girls—in fact, he had had two restraining orders by the time he was twenty-three. His frequent calling and stalking of his potential girlfriends always drove them away.

Seth thought about Alison again. *This time, it will be different. I will be a different man. I'll be the man she needs. She will see. I saw how she looked at me.*

174

Bandaging his hand in the bathroom, he changed clothes and spritzed himself with his favorite cologne. Taking a bottle of pheromones out of the medicine cabinet, he dabbed a small amount in the nape of his neck. His hair received another feathering from his hand, and he straightened his collar. Walking out the door, he grabbed his shattered phone, hoping that he could at least place a call. As he slid into the front seat of his Porsche, he slapped it in gear and screeched down the street. Determined to get an answer to the question that was driving him mad, he sped towards Fleetham, with only Alison on his mind.

Chapter Twenty-Eight

Arriving at the police station, Alison stepped out of the cruiser; her pride having grown during the short drive over. *I can't believe I made the arrest in such a short time,* she thought.

Standing at the rear passenger door, she waited for Robert, who walked around the car, stopping directly alongside Alison. Opening the door, he offered Sammy his hand to steady himself. Alison swatted his hand away, stating, "He doesn't need help. Do stop helping him, Robert."

As Sammy stepped out of the car, teetering slightly to the left, he looked directly at Alison and said, "Ma'am, I'm going to pray for you."

Robert led Sammy into the police station and directed him to the back office. "Please stand in front of the screen, we need to take your picture."

Sammy hobbled over to the green screen and stood facing Robert. He could see Robert adjusting the camera, in order to get it in focus. To his left, was a large ruler, he assumed would be used to measure his height. Sammy glanced over, completely confused by the events that had taken place. "I don't understand, sir," Sammy told Robert.

Standing motionless, the blinding white flash came to life. "Okay, now turn to your right," Robert instructed him. Doing as he was told, Sammy turned to his right, staring at the cinderblock wall of the interior of the building.

"Turn to your left," Robert added. Shifting his weight from one foot to the other, he turned to face the other way. This time, Sammy could see a pile of boxes stacked in the corner. "More free men in those boxes," Sammy snickered as the white flash momentarily blinded him.

"Sammy, I have all the pictures I need, I think. I've got to get your fingerprints again… ya know, for the files. Come here."

Walking over, Sammy stepped on his shoelaces, causing him to lose his balance. He caught himself on the edge of a metal framed desk that was in front of the green photo screen. Leaning against the desk for stability, he looked at Robert. Neither man needed to utter a word at this very moment as the message was clear. The look Robert saw, was one that he'd never forget. He knew that the mistrust and hatred Sammy felt for him was strong, but until that moment, he wasn't sure of the intensity.

"Sir, which finger do you need? I've got ten of them," Sammy said, smiling in a way that wasn't meant to be funny.

Robert began rubbing Sammy's right thumb in the pad of ink laying in front of the two. Pressing it from side to side, to capture all the patterns of his fingerprint, he filled up the card, one digit at a times. He chose not to reply to Sammy, as he felt that silence would benefit them both. After his last finger had been added to the card, Alison tapped her fingernails on the door and let herself through.

"Okay, so I've got to finish my report, but I need to speak to Sammy after you're finished. I'll speak to him in his jail cell for added security," Alison announced. As she finished speaking, she looked Sammy up and down with piercing eyes.

My God, this poor man, Alison thought. Her feelings weren't that of empathy, but rather distaste. She'd prided herself on her appearance, as well as her character, so, to see a man with this type of moral turpitude made her think how lucky she had been in life.

Robert caught her glaring at Sammy, so she quickly averted her eyes and gave a nod in his direction. Backing out of the room, her eyes reverted to her latest criminal arrest. Pursing her lips, she closed the door and walked back to the front office.

Robert closed the lid to the ink pad and tucked the fingerprint card inside a manila filing folder, sitting on the desk. "Okay, buddy, we're finished. If you want something to eat or drink, I can get that for you. Are you good?"

At first, Sammy didn't answer, instead he picked up the folder and threw it on the floor. By now, he was sweating profusely as he hadn't had a drink in quite a while, so his cravings were starting. Robert realized that Sammy's agitation at this moment wasn't because of his arrest. "Sit down for a minute, I'll be right back," he concluded.

Stepping out of the room, he quickly made his way to his office. Opening the top, left drawer, hiding under a stack of triplicate traffic tickets, was his own 'highway to heaven'. His flask. Used during very stressful days, or a typical Tuesday, he always kept it handy. Pocketing the ice-cold stainless-steel container, he returned to the booking room, finding 'Little Sammy' in the same position that he'd left him in. Handing the flask to Sammy, he nodded and sat down at the desk,

178

allowing him to relax for a minute. Sammy unscrewed the cap and swallowed the entire contents. Smacking his lips and turning to Robert, he laughed saying, "That there is some damn good whiskey, sir. Thanks, that took the edge right off."

Robert took the flask as he handed it to him and slipped it back in his pocket. *The last damn thing I need is to have Alison see me with this,* he thought. Nodding towards the door, he and Sammy walked out of the room. As he left the booking room, Sammy was immediately disoriented by his surroundings. Awaiting him on the other side of the threshold were the rows of jail cells.

"You'll be in cell number three. Let me open it up for ya," Robert told him, attempting to keep his voice calm.

Sammy trotted behind Robert like a submissive pup, stopping and pausing whenever his 'master' did. When they arrived at the entrance of the cell, the feeling was that of death and despair. Sammy had never experienced jail before. The sights and smells were by no means familiar to him.

Sammy stepped inside the cell, pausing to make a complete mental image of his surroundings. Sitting to the immediate left of the door, was a tiny sink, with an automatic faucet. Seeing only a blue dot on the handle, he assumed that hot water wasn't something a prisoner was privileged to. The sink, by his standards was quite clean, however, it did have a layer of black, slimy grime covering the surface. Next to the sink was a very tiny stainless-steel toilet. Not having a lid, was something that Sammy hadn't ever seen before. "I'll be goddamned, how am I going to use this pisser without a seat to sit on?" He said to himself.

179

As he turned around, he was confronted by the bed. The platform, a painted, slate grey sheet of metal, was covered with holes. Lying atop the metal sheet was a very thin mattress. Rubbing his head, the thought of a restful night's sleep quickly vanished. The mattress that he would be using until he was moved was made from what Sammy thought looked like blue, pin-striped overalls.

"You know, sir, I have overalls that same color," Sammy told Robert, who was busying himself with the door lock.

The pin-striped mattress had several cigarette burns, and a very large dark yellow stain in the center. "I will sleep here tonight and try to rest," telling no one in particular. As he glanced back at Robert, he pulled his sagging pants up and sat down on the bed. Surprisingly comfortable, he leaned back and told Robert, "I'll take a nap. Are you through yet, sir?"

The lock finally gave way and slid into place. Pocketing the master set of keys, Robert nodded and said, "No, sir, I have everything I need. Detective Chaney will be here in a bit, she wants to talk to you some more. By the way, do you need me to call your lawyer. You'll need one, ya know."

Sammy didn't answer. He took both shoes off and kicked them on the floor. Robert stood in front of the cell door, watching his every move. "Sir, you go back to work. This free man is okay."

Sammy waved Robert off, as he turned over on the metal bed, facing the white cinder block walls. Taking his thumb and touching the bumpy concrete, his mind drifted to a childhood memory.

His childhood hadn't been a particularly memorable one, however, he did have a few happy memories. Sitting in the basement as a young teenager, playing with baseball cards, and wishing that he'd make it to the pros. Escaping his life and entering one all of his own, especially with a real memory, was his coping mechanism.

Apart from drinking, his very few happy childhood memories kept him from withering away into a world that he knew nothing about. This world, as he so often thought, was not a happy place. This world was full of crime, punishment, sadness, loneliness, and deceit. This world, sadly, Sammy thought, was happening right now.

Chapter Twenty-Nine

As Seth continued the drive to Fleetham, his thoughts alternated from aggression to compassion to lust. He thought only of Alison and what he'd do with her once he got her alone. His plan was to take her to dinner, then have his way with her, at his house.

This could go either way, he thought.

Cranking up his car stereo, he let his mind drift. The effects of his pills had kicked in a while back, so his reactions were slower than normal. Being a habitual user of pills and alcohol, he was accustomed to the aftereffects of both. Having practiced medicine for several years, mostly under the influence of either drugs or alcohol, he had become a master liar and manipulator of the truth—adjusting his demeanor to appear normal.

He could see the rusty water tower straight ahead, indicating that he had almost arrived in town. The speed limit had changed, so he adjusted his speed accordingly. With the Fleetham Cemetery sign just to his right, he slowed his car almost to a stop, and veered left, turning onto the street.

"Before they lock him up forever, I want to see his house one last time," Seth said to himself.

His car slung gravel as he drove down the street. Weaving back and forth in an attempt to avoid the notorious potholes that riddled the town's streets, he finally arrived at the crossroads of the area everyone called, "across the tracks".

182

His mind was an open vector to reminiscing now—one of the side effects he loved when he decided to over-indulge on his prescription meds. Taking his memory all the way back to adolescence, he was reminded of the many nights he spent in this part of town.

His parents would have grounded him for an entire year if they'd known. Seeing the vacant houses, he could remember each girl that he'd had the immense pleasure of 'visiting' as he called it. His visits entailed a quick dinner, and a trip back to his place.

"They thought they were going to have a nice evening—little did they know," he spoke quietly to himself.

Opening the glove compartment in his car, mementos of each girl rested in a cloth bag. The bag, given to him by his mother during elementary school, served as a bookbag, until he discovered a more appropriate usage for it. Covered with several compartments with zippered closures, he quickly learned that he could hide almost anything, without fear of being found out.

His first attempt at concealing his life was his freshman year of high school. Having been rejected multiple times for dates, he decided to take matters into his own hands and steal something special from one of the girls who had turned him down.

During physical education class, he was a frequent visitor to the girls' locker room. Knowing the girls were out on the basketball courts practicing their drills, the locker-room would be completely empty. Slipping inside, he'd rummage through all the gym bags, merely curious as to what he'd find.

183

However, this particular day was special. Inside, wrapped in a paper towel, forgotten by the girl, was a used tampon. More than likely she'd meant to discard it in the trash bin. However, it managed to make it into Seth's hands.

Fearing he'd be caught in a room that was completely off limits to any male student, he pocketed the contraband and slipped back into his section of the gym.

Resting in the uppermost zippered pocket was his prize. This continued for many years, into his formal education during medical school.

Overhead, a crow called out to his mate, snapping his mind back into present day. Seeing Sammy Harper's dilapidated house made him feel as if he were, in a way, back home. In his youth, he'd visited this house many times before, unbeknown to its inhabitants. His visits weren't to converse with its occupants but to lead girls astray.

"If Dad only knew. If Alison only knew. Hell, if Mom only knew," he said, with a grin.

"Today's not the day, though. I have to focus. Today, I get to see my girl. Today, I get to see the woman I've dreamed about my entire life." His mind alternated between lust and emotional happiness, and he wasn't sure if he could distinguish the two apart. His therapist had told him many times that he had a warped sense of reality.

184

Chapter Thirty

Sammy had counted sixty-four ceiling tiles while resting on the metal bed. He'd counted them twice to ensure that he'd been correct. On the floor, he'd counted six roaches making their way across the cell floor, heading to the main hallway of the jail.

He'd been in his cell a little over an hour but had already seen so much. While the images were devoid of any form of excitement, his mind had made up the difference.

"I'm gonna get me out of here and go home. I just know it." Speaking to himself, he thought a word of encouragement would help him through the misery of his present predicament. In the distance, a door opened, followed by a series of footsteps.

Slapping a metal chair against the ice-cold concrete, created a sound that reverberated through the entire building. Sitting down was Alison, behind her, Robert and Aaron. Alison said nothing for a moment, only looking, through the cell's bars at Sammy. As Sammy sat up in his bed, he smiled and asked, "Do you need something, ma'am?"

Alison waved her hand behind her left shoulder, with the intention of having Robert and Aaron leave her to question him alone. Her pen was already uncapped and writing by the time Sammy walked over to the bars and peered out. He sat on the floor in front of the cell door, as there wasn't a chair for him to sit on. As he sat, a roach crawled over his hand, sending a tickling sensation through his entire body.

He wasn't afraid of bugs or vermin, as his house had a plethora of socially unwanted visitors. Sammy called them 'his friends'.

Shaking the bug off his hand, he rubbed his hair out of his eyes, and looked at Alison.

As she sat in her chair, looking down at him, the feeling of dominance took over her. She usually felt superior to most people, and today was no exception. From this angle, she could see Sammy and what he stood for—in her opinion, it was trouble.

"Sammy, what I need to talk to you about, is, well… it might be unpleasant for you to hear. You see, when we arrested you, we found something in your house. I'd like you to explain it to me, please. As it's now considered criminal evidence, photos have been taken, which I will show you now. Do you understand?"

Nodding, he remained silent.

Taking three photos out of her file folder, she explained each one in detail to him.

"Ya see, I wasn't sure what this was at first. Then, after I truly saw it, it hit me. It seems there's a pattern here, doesn't it? See, the first picture here, it's a bit difficult to distinguish exactly what it is, don't ya think?"

Handing him the black and white photo between the bars, he looked at it carefully. His eyes were squinting, in an effort to bring the image into focus. He handed the photo back. "Ma'am, I don't know where you found that rubber, but it ain't mine. I'm a good Christian."

A very quiet laugh escaped her mouth. "That's lovely, but we did find it in your house. It had apparently

186

been there for quite some time. The rubber had stuck to the carpet and the grime that is layered on it, but what's inside is what interested us. Take a look at this picture, please."

The second photo was passed through the bars of the cell, and Sammy grabbed it with his hand.

"What's in there? I just saw something black."

The image was given back to Alison, who slid it into her file folder.

"Precisely. It's rather difficult to fully see what's inside, let me show you this picture. Hopefully, it will spark some shred of memory you might have forgotten."

The third photo was taken out of the folder and this time, slid under the door. Sammy had to scoot back about a foot in order to keep it from wedging itself under his pants. As he picked it up, he couldn't understand why the detective would show him this. The image staring him in his face, was a black heart—or he thought it was black.

"What is this? It's a dark heart. Black or sumthin'."

"It's interesting that you immediately recognized it as a heart. I had some difficulty at first. Thank you for being able to identify it so quickly. What I want to know is…"

Interrupting her, he said, "I don't mean to be rude or nothing, but it's totally clear that there is a heart. Hell, even a little babe could tell that."

"If you'll excuse me, I'd like to finish what I was trying to tell you when you interrupted me. As I was saying, what I want to know is, why was it in your house? Where did you get it? Well, the question I should ask is… who did you cut it off?

187

Sammy was speechless, unable to answer straight away. Pulling himself up with the assistance of the cell bars, he walked over to his bed and sat down. "I want to speak to the sheriff, ma'am. You are trying to tell me I did something, but I ain't done nothing wrong." His voice elevated by the time he finished his sentence, and his emotions running high, he lowered his head and stopped speaking.

Sitting in her chair, her back beginning to ache from her unnatural posture, she stood up and walked to the exit door. Knocking twice, Robert opened the door. "You rang?"

"He wants to talk to you. He's refusing to answer any more questions from me."

Alison stormed out of the jail into the booking room and sat waiting for her cue to return. Pulling out her phone, she typed into her search engine, *Fleetham, TX history.*

Robert sat down on the same chair that Alison had used for her interrogation session and stared into the cell. Sammy sat on the bed, head lowered, sobbing.

"Buddy, what's up? Alison said you done sent for me. What can I do for ya?"

Sammy looked at Robert, his eyes puffed and red from crying. Blowing his nose on his shirt sleeve and wiping his eyes, he stood and walked dramatically to the cell door. "This ain't right. I ain't done nothing, and this woman is makin' me sound like I'm the devil. She showed me this picture of a used rubber with a heart of something inside and said I did something to someone else."

Robert nodded and leaned forward into his chair, resting his head between two bars of the door. "We found this in your house, on the floor. It had been there for quite

188

a while. Everything was dried up inside. I'm sure you saw that in the picture. Look, she's trying to do her job, but she can only do half of it. You have to do the other half. Can't you help us out? Can't you tell us who and why? Mainly why?"

Sammy looked into Robert's eyes. He knew that he cared, or he wouldn't have taken the time to sit down like an equal and talk to him. He knew the sheriff had been someone you didn't want to mess with, but under that exterior was a man who cared.

"There ain't no why. There ain't nothing to tell. Test me again. Give me a lie test. I'll pass it with flying colors just like I did the last one."

Taking a deep breath and exhaling slowly, Robert stood and stuck his hand through the bars. "Shake my hand, Sam. I want you to tell me something, then I'll leave you alone, okay?"

Sammy slowly walked back over to the door and grabbed his hand. Expecting a forceful handshake, as only a true southern gentleman would give, he was surprised. Robert took his hand in his and held it. "Sammy, listen to me, and listen carefully. This is your life here. I ain't shitting you when I say this. This is your goddamn life I'm holding in my hands. I need to know if you killed Tessie or anyone else. You'll be asked by the judge, the jury, and every lawyer in the area. Now is the time to fess up. If not, then it's your problem and no longer mine. I've helped you, but now my job is done. Understand?"

Sammy squeezed his hand tightly—his gesture by way of showing that he understood what he'd said. Simply nodding in response to his question, he released Robert's hand and walked back to this bed. "Say, Sheriff? Thank you."

189

Robert nodded once and smiled, leaving Sammy alone in the jail. The door shut, with a metal clang echoing in the background. Alone, Sammy said a prayer, "Lord Jesus, give me strength again. Help me. I need you now. Amen."

Chapter Thirty-One

Sitting in the booking room, Alison read the results of her internet search, seeing over 10,000 results. She wasn't remotely interested in most of them; however, a few caught her eye. Multiple stories about a drug arrest, dog fighting circles and petty theft were listed, but an article from the local newspaper stood out.

"Local Man Found Dead Inside House. Authorities Baffled."

Clicking on the link, a microfilm version of the newspaper article appeared on her screen.

Scrolling through the article from the *Fleetham Times Journal*, dated September 1, 1991, she read through the highlights, then went back to absorb it in its entirety.

Phillip Yanez, 54, was found inside his home at 430 NE 1ˢᵗ Street on August 30, 1991. Authorities are unsure of the details. However, it was released to the public that he was found gagged, bound to the bed and disemboweled. Lead detective for the case, Lt. Daniel F. Smithson, declined further comment, stating that this was the worst crime the town had ever seen. "I live in a city. This doesn't happen in small towns. Whoever committed this crime will be caught and charged. Any information you might have, please contact Fleetham Police Department."

Having read the quotation twice, Alison didn't understand why she hadn't heard about the case earlier.

191

Perhaps, since it was so long ago, it wasn't relevant to this case? She thought.

As Robert locked the door behind him, keys jangling on the side of his pants, he made his way to the table where Alison was sitting. The look of concern and worry bothered him. "What's wrong? You look like you done seen a ghost."

"I was just reading this article about a murder that took place several years ago. Why wasn't it mentioned when I arrived? I'd like to see the case file. It sounds very similar to this one, doesn't it?"

Adjusting his gun belt, which he'd now taken to wearing again, he groaned and sat down, "Yup, I remember that day very well. I had only been in office a couple of years when it happened. Worst thing that ever happened here until Tessie's murder. I guess I'd filed it away at the back of my mind. I don't remember exactly what the body looked like, but I know it was as bad as Tessie's mess."

Returning to her search engine, she typed in: *Fleetham, Tx murder 1991*

Forty-six results popped up, ranging from newspaper articles, interviews, and a summary of the court transcription, which had been released by a local television station. "Can you go and get that file for me? It's probably in a back file since it was so long ago. I'll wait here."

"I guess that's my cue to leave. I'll be right back, but don't overthink this. The case was closed but unresolved. We all thought it was a transient person passing through. Nothing was found that led us to anyone."

Alison nodded at what he said but wasn't truly listening. As she continued to scroll through the results, she clicked on an article written by an independent journalist for the *Dallas Evening News*. Dated a few days after the *Fleetham Times Journal* article, the Dallas article was much more detailed and opinionated. Written as an editorial, she could only imagine the remarks the public might have made.

Following the investigation of the murder of Phillip Yanaz, the entire state would like to know who did it and why this incident occurred. Texas prides itself on the safety and security of its citizens, granted, there are a few bad apples here and there, Overall, those who reside in this wonderful state, feel safe and secure. Now, following the death and murder of this innocent man, tensions are running high.

Locking doors, adding additional porch lights, and feeling an overall sense of anxiety about their daily lives, the residents of Fleetham are demanding action. As I write this editorial, it appears that the investigation has ceased, or at best, "been brushed under the carpet." When will it end?

Anxious and nervous, Alison scooted her chair back and walked to the front of the police station. She couldn't stand to sit in the concrete room alone anymore. *It feels like a basement prison*, she thought.

Finding Robert rummaging through the desk in his office, the thoughts of the murder twenty-plus years ago wouldn't go away. "Do the family still live in town? I'd like to speak to them."

The question caught him off guard. Snapping his head up, "I wouldn't advise that. They're a bit different. Every day after the murder they did everything they could to find the killer."

"Well, wouldn't you want to find the person who murdered your son? That's a dumb reply, Robert. I need

193

to speak with them and will after I've finished reviewing the case file. By the way, where did Aaron go?"

Shrugging his shoulders, he answered silently and continued to dig in his desk drawer. Pulling out a six-inch-thick folder with a rotten rubber band holding the cover closed, he handed the folder to Alison. "Jesus Christ, this file is thick. I'd forgotten how much information there was. But here ya go. Have fun. I've got to call the county attorney's office or someone to find a public defender for Sammy. If I have to run down to the courthouse, I shouldn't be too long."

She squinted at the tiny typed print. "Where's Aaron? I need him. Has he called you yet? He was just sitting in the back office before we went to pick up Sammy, wasn't he?"

Throwing on his vest and adjusting his badge, Robert cleared his throat and coughed. "Yeah, and his car is gone. Who knows? I'll call him in a bit. I'm out. Catch ya later. Call me if you need anything. Happy reading."

Taking out her phone, which desperately needed to be charged, she thumbed through the contacts, until she got to Aaron. Typing a text message, she wrote, *Where are you? I have new developments!!!*

The message was immediately tagged as "read". She knew that he'd had his phone in his hand and wasn't engaged in something that would prevent him from replying. Rather than sending a reply via text message, he called.

"What's up, I'm just next door. I was reading something. Do you need me?"

Alison wasn't sure how to begin the conversation about yet another murder that happened in the town. "I'm in Robert's office."

194

Finishing her sentence, she ended the call and pocketed the phone. Stretching the rubber band to slip it off, it broke. "Like everything else in this town, you decide to rot, too," she grumbled, pulling the remaining bits of rotten rubber from underneath the folder.

Turning to the first page, revealed a photograph attached with a paperclip. Assuming it was Mr. Yanaz, she was now able to put a face to the name. He was older than he looked. "Worked outdoors," she said, continuing to study the picture. Fine lines graced his deep-set eyes below which he wore a crooked smile and a full beard.

At that moment, Aaron appeared, propping himself up with his arm against the doorway. "What's the rush, I was getting ready to finish my report and close up shop. I'm not needed until this thing goes to court. But you know Sammy isn't the problem. There's someone else in town who is hacking girls up. Don't ya think?"

Aaron's words went in one ear and out the other. Alison didn't honestly have a clue what he'd just said. Instead of listening to him, she yanked the picture from under the paperclip and passed it across the desk. "Don't ya think that's the face of an honest man?"

Aaron quickly glanced at the photo and flung it back on the desk, landing face up. "Yeah, I guess. Looks like a farmer. Who is that?"

Picking the picture up, Alison fixed her eyes on the victim. "His name was Phillip Yanaz. He was murdered in 1991, here in Fleetham. He was found in his home. Gagged, tied up and disemboweled. Sound familiar?"

"Holy Jesus. Why wasn't this mentioned? First Tessie, then that other gal a year back, now this? Are there any other murders that no one decided to mention?"

195

Aaron walked over to the desk and picked up the thick file. Licking his finger, he quickly thumbed through the pages, knowing what he needed to find.

"Here it is. Offender Profile report. Nine pages. Damn."

He wasn't talking to anyone in particular, just lost in his own world, reading the dictation.

"Back then, even though it was only 1991, these reports were dictated then transcribed. Lots of times, they were typed incorrectly, so who knows how many errors are here. But this guy, I took his place. He worked at the office thirty years or so. He was damned good, so I would assume this is smooth as silk."

His eyes were scanning left to right, picking out the information he thought important.

Assailant, more than likely antisocial, has dependency issues, either drug or alcohol, or both. He/she has a deep-rooted history of violence and/or destruction to objects, animals, and/or bullying. It is my opinion that he/she suffers from depression, anxiety, severe vanity issues, unresolved need for attention, and has an undiagnosed condition of psychotic behavior.

"This is almost identical to my report... or will be, anyway. Does this sound like Sammy? That's the question I kept asking myself when I first began looking at everything. See, it doesn't fit, don't ya agree?"

Alison nodded, continuing to dig through the pile of papers and photos. Stapled together in a bundle, she picked up the postmortem photographs. "The crime scene photos are almost identical to Tessie's. Same pose of the body, same abdominal incision, same everything. Although there isn't a bottle of pills, everything else is almost identical."

196

Beneath the postmortem photographs, the autopsy report awaited Alison's review. Typed in general format, the report read very much like Tessie's—with the exception of the narcotics found in her system.

A linear twenty-centimeter incision was made to the midline abdomen. Approximately sixteen inches of intestine had been removed from the body prior to autopsy, at the crime scene. Anal tissue was torn, as well as lacerations to the peri-rectum region. A golf ball was removed during excision of neck organs. Ligature marks are noted to the midline neck, horizontally. Bruising was noted to bilateral wrists and ankles—common with restraint and attempting forceful removal of restraint. Scleral hemorrhaging was noted to eyes, consistent with strangulation. Hyoid bone was crushed, consistent with strangulation... Probable cause of death: homicide via strangulation Secondary cause: disembowelment, severe blood loss.

Alison's voice cracked as she finished the last sentence. Her arms and back of her neck were covered in goosepimples. "I've never been so terrified reading a report in my life. I just don't get it. Why wasn't it disclosed to us? Robert said nothing had happened like this. Ever."

Aaron walked over to the desk, picked up the file folder, and began to scan the many pages. Tabs of sticky notes protruded from the sides of papers, creating a rainbow stairstep effect. Taking the macabre look away with the colors, he momentarily remembered something he'd learned in training from Robert D. Hare. "A psychopath can tell what you're thinking, but what they don't do is feel what you feel. These are people without a conscience."

197

"But speaking to Sammy, he fits the description. I think so anyway. He's an obvious addict. He's antisocial, he's everything that fits the profile. I stand by my decision." Alison stated, as she leaned back in her chair, attempting to move away from Aaron who she felt was invading her space by hovering over the desk.

"I'm not arguing about this and I wasn't even saying you're wrong. I was just making a point. What else is in here?"

Pages of interviews with citizens, newspaper clippings, random photographs of people lay aging in the folder. The smell from the disintegrating paper was making them both a bit nauseated. "I've got to get some air. I need a break." Alison stood up and walked out of the office.

She realized that people essentially worked when they wanted to there, hence why the receptionist had left early. Pouring herself a cup of coffee, she made the decision to go for a drive. "I'll be right back. I just want to run into town. I want to get out of the office and get a breath of fresh air and vitamin D. I'll be back in a while."

Where her destination was, she wasn't sure. What she did know was that she needed to think. For years, she was only able to think—to truly think, uninhibited thinking, when she was alone, by herself, in the solitude of silence. Her car offered just that.

Driving out of the parking lot, her car was the temperature of an oven. Blasting the air-conditioner at full force, she turned right, then left, then right again. She didn't know the town well, so her destination was a mystery. Passing the small post office, she saw the funeral home on her right.

At one time, the funeral home had been a private house, belonging to a very prominent family in town—

198

The Binder's. Not knowing that piece of information, she drove past, heading west.

Planted at the end of the street, the dark red building welcomed her with a sense of peace and comfort. *Fleetham Library and Records*.

Smiling and feeling a tinge of relaxation come over her, Alison pulled into the gravel parking lot. "God's with me today."

A lone brown truck was in the parking lot. The librarian's, or so she assumed. The building was a perfect rectangle, different than any other building in town. Gleaming in the afternoon sunlight was a historical marker on a steel post. Positioned at the base of the steps, it told its history to all who visited.

Built in 1883, the Fleetham Depot served north central Texas for eighty-one years, as one of the busiest train depots in the area. Designed by the North Star Rail Company, original wood parquet floors, imported stained glass windows, and ivory door handles grace this building. The additions were introduced in 1969 when the library was moved from its previous location. Upon completion of the library, the North Texas Historical Society classified this location as a marked historical site, protected herein, from demolition. Extensive renovations were completed in 1969, prior to the grand opening ceremony of the library.

Looking up at the large window with a span that Alison thought must be nearly ten feet, she could understand why the building was historically protected. The stained-glass window depicted a scene from the famous painting by Pieter Bruegel the Elder. Set in what looked like a million glass pieces, Alison could imagine each passenger seeing the image of the Biblical Tower of Babel, reaching to the heavens.

199

Wracking her brain, she tried to remember the story. From what she recalled, the painting suggested that God was angered by the building of the tower and decided to prevent it by scattering the people throughout the world, confusing their languages so that they were unable to return and continue from where they left off.

"Fitting for a train station," Alison chuckled, as she climbed the incredibly steep steps.

The front door was modern, consisting of a storm door and a regular, wooden front door. The building had settled, so she shoved her shoulder into the door, cracking it open. An overhead bell rang as she entered the front lobby of the library, which was a small museum.

Rows of glass cases displayed the town's historical items. Ranging from old newspapers, to quills and old Indian artifacts, it was a curiosity of sorts for passers-by.

Looking up, the division of old and new was apparent, by the slope leading into the front of the library. *The museum has been added later,* she thought. Walking up the incline to the main library, the ghosts of past travelers, almost visible, remained at the connecting terminal.

The scrubbed hardwood, which had seen two world wars, the Spanish influenza epidemic and many happy and sad moments, left an impression on all who walked across the floors. To Alison's left was an oak desk, which resembled an Edwardian period piece. Sitting behind the desk, head down in a book, was the librarian. Esther Van Clove, or so the nameplate read.

Alison pushed her sunglasses on top of her head and cleared her throat. "Excuse me, I'm Detective Alison

200

Chaney. I was wondering if you could take me to your microfilm room so I could look something up?"

Flashing her badge in front of the librarian, who exuded an air of superiority, otherwise unnoticed by a passing traveler to the historic building.

"Oh, hello, honey. What are you searching for exactly? I have thousands of newspapers on film. Are you looking for a specific year or event in town or across the state?"

Pulling her mobile phone out of her pants pocket, she swiped right, and her internet browser appeared. "I'm looking for information about a murder that took place about twenty years or so ago. I'm investigating another case but found this interesting and would like to read more."

"Sure, I'll take you down. Will you just sign your John Hancock here in the book, please? I like to keep a record of who is looking at my microfilm and why. You understand, I'm sure."

Alison took the cheap ballpoint pen in her hand, attached to the table with masking tape and nylon twine, and signed her name, along with, the date and time. *What an overbearing old biddy,* she thought. Chuckling slightly at her own thought, she began to follow Esther down another ramp, once she'd finished registering.

Finally, she caught up to her in another section of the building where the aesthetic of the building's history shone bright. Overhead, milk glass, globe lights hung from brass chains, illuminating the words of great authors. Protecting the literary farces and horror novels from above was a ceiling of pressed metal sheeting.

Alison had seen the sheeting before, in other older buildings but hadn't seen it as preserved as this. In an intricate design of ivy and lilies, it looked as if it were

201

only recently installed. "The ceiling is beautiful. When was it added?"

"Oh, mercy me, probably around the 1920s or so. I'm not entirely sure. I do know the station was damaged heavily during the 1942 tornado, but to my knowledge, it didn't destroy the ceiling tiles. They are somethin' to look at, huh?"

As the two descended farther into the library, rows upon rows of books cradled them. To Alison, it felt like a blanket. She was an avid reader, so losing herself in the comfort a novel's characters offered usually calmed her.

Nestled in the west corner of the library, underneath a sign that read "All Passengers Proceed Left for Tickets" sat a roll-top desk. On the desk was the massive microfilm computer. Larger than a traditional desktop, the green hued screen was asleep, awaiting the command to search a particular event or year.

Esther briefly educated her on the ins and outs of the system. "It's a bit crazy sometimes, so you have to use the light scanner slowly, otherwise, the images blur. If you need me, just holler. I'll be up at the front. I've still got a few things to do yet."

Nodding and smiling, Alison sat down, pulled out a pocket notebook, preparing herself for the information she may or may not find.

Chapter Thirty-Two

Seth's mind had drifted back to the present and the images that were before him. Walking back to his car, he turned his head and caught a glimpse of something out of the corner of his eye. It was Tessie.

"What the…" but the sentence ended abruptly. He stopped, turning around fully, and looked back at the house. There was nothing there. His heart racing and sweat forming on his brow, he took a long, deep breath and turned back to his car. As he opened the door and sat in the seat, he thought he saw something strange. On the front seat was a puddle of blood. He took his sunglasses off, in an attempt to verify properly, but as before, there was nothing there. "I've got to get out of here, this place is fucked."

Speeding down the road, gravel spraying behind him, he slowed towards the entrance to the cemetery. The chain had not yet been latched across the entrance. "Cemetery Closed at Dark" the sign overhead read.

Creeping his car slowly into the entrance to the cemetery, he paused as he saw the first tombstone. *Major Edward Wright.* Staring at the arched, marble stone, he closed his eyes and gave a thought of peace and comfort to the major.

Straight ahead, a one-hundred-year-old cottonwood tree shaded a quarter of the cemetery. Directly underneath the massive tree sat a marble bench. A lamb was affixed to the edge. The grave of a child.

Nearing the bench, he turned his car slightly to the left, onto the adjacent path, in order to see the grave clearly. *Teddy "Buster" Murphy.*

The sadness of a parent overcame him. His face flushed as he thought about how it had altered the parents' lives forever. Eternally grieving for their son, taken from them years before it was time.

A single tear trickled down his scruffy face, leaving a trail of emotion. Wiping it away, he made the sign of the cross and blew a kiss toward the sky. Continuing his turn, he nearly hit a five-foot-tall headstone. In the shape of a tree trunk, it read, *Marian Owens, Woodman of the World.*

He'd always been curious about the fraternal organizations around town. However, he had never been invited to join them. Seth resented his parents for isolating him from society so much and wished that he'd had the security of a close-knit family.

The headstone he had come to see was Tessie's. He wasn't sure but thought her family might have a small family plot. He knew she came from nothing, so he wasn't expecting to see a giant effigy. When he arrived at the freshly dug grave, the dirt piled in a perfect, curved rectangle next to the hole, there was nothing. Instead of a gravestone of any sort, a single, metal nameplate had been stuck in the ground, "I can't stay here for long, but just in case you can hear me, I always cared for you." The words came out softly, as if he were speaking to someone in mourning.

In the distance, he heard a crow calling again. Unsure of the significance, he merely thought it was a random occurrence of nature, but the more he thought, the more he thought it was a sign—from above or below—that someone was speaking to him. Not wanting

204

to focus on the negative emotions that he could feel building in the pit of his stomach, slowly rising to his brain, he turned back and walked to his car.

The afternoon sun was in full force, giving its heat to anything in its path. Dressed in attire fit for autumn, he shed his light jacket and threw it in the back of the car.

Driving faster than he had anticipated, he drove past the metal-framed entrance and headed back to town. The cemetery was roughly two miles from town, just a five-minute drive. Blasting Chopin from his speakers, he listened, yearning for the comfort that came from his collection of classical music. Passing the grain elevator, he knew he was nearly to the town's only flashing light. Pausing for a moment, not bothering to come to a complete stop, he drove down Main Street.

Unsure of where he would eventually end up, he turned right past the funeral home, the home of his antecedents. Smiling, knowing that his family was at the forefront of the town in which he resided, he remembered his father telling him how proud he should be to be a member of such a noble family.

This feeling, one that was instilled in him from an early age, followed him to the present day. He had a superior mindset. A mindset that would serve him well, and it was thanks to his family.

Passing the funeral home, he saw the library in the distance. A black car, *official looking,* he thought, was parked in the parking lot next to an old truck.

Swinging into the parking lot, his mind immediately went to Alison as he recognized the car. *Maybe this will be my chance to catch her alone and get her to go out with me.*

205

Opening the door, he paused, pulled down the visor mirror and ran his hand through his hair. Feathering his hair, the method he preferred, he straightened his collar and flashed his porcelain covered teeth in the mirror. "You're the sexiest man I've ever seen," he told his reflection, recalling his fantasy of Alison.

Stepping out of the car, he strutted up the steps, careful not to look too nervous. Walking into the library entrance, he saw the librarian sitting at the desk. A wave of dizziness swept over him, causing him to sway slightly. After steadying himself, and his balance adjusted, he focused his eyes on her. "Hey, there, haven't seen you in a while."

Esther's face had the most petrified expression from seeing him. "Oh, uh, hi, honey, what can I do for you?"

She spoke to Seth's back as he looked around the library, searching for Alison. He raised his head slightly and drew in a deep breath through his nose, "I'm just stopping by, thought I'd look for a new book. I've read everything else. I'll be back up here when I'm ready to check out."

"Mmhmm, take your time, hun."

Walking down the ramp that led to the lower half of the building, the books welcomed him. Going through medical school, he found solace in the words of scientists and physicians.

Walking down the Romance aisle, he casually looked at some of the titles. Assuming he was being following by Esther, he took a few books off the shelf at random and tucked them under his arm. Turning the corner, he ended up in the Biography section. Craning his head, he took a quiet, deep breath. The faint scent of perfume, not that of an older woman, but someone his

206

age would wear, was coming from the distance. Following the scent, he saw her sitting in the corner of the building. Her head was buried in the information projected onto the microfilm screen, oblivious of his presence.

"Ahem, uh, Alison? Is that you?"

The sudden interruption startled her. Jumping, she dropped her fountain pen, spraying ink on the scrubbed, hardwood floor. "Oh, shit, sorry, I didn't know anyone was here. I was lost in my newspaper. How are you, Seth?"

The thoughts racing through his head were raunchy and inappropriate, yet romantic—all at the same time. His body heat had risen immensely, as he was becoming aroused by the mere sight and smell of her. "*Imagine what she would be like outside this place.*" Grinning from ear to ear for longer than was necessary, his mind wouldn't stop fantasizing.

"Hey, Alison, I just stopped by to check out a few books. I didn't realize you were here. Whatcha reading? I guess everything is fine at the station with Dad?"

Unsure of what to say, and not wanting to give too much information to someone so unimportant to the investigation, Alison shrugged her shoulders and adjusted herself in the chair. "It's going well, busy but good. Robert's doing his thing. He ran an errand earlier today and will be back at the office this afternoon, he says. What are you up to today? I guess you're not busy at the clinic?"

Seth hadn't been to work today, having decided to take the day off and cancel all his appointments. He was getting less and less interested in work recently, partly because of his ever-growing dependence on alcohol.

207

Wishing he had a drink to get him through the conversation, he shifted his weight from side to side to distract his mind. "No, took the day off. I just needed a break, ya know? I'll go back home later and relax with a book. I'm glad that I ran into you. I wanted to talk to you about something."

Alison couldn't possibly think what he wanted to talk about, unless it was case related. Her brow furrowed, half in concentration, and half in curiosity. "Oh? What do you need to speak to me about? I can't discuss the investigation, you know. You already know about the autopsy, but most of the information is classified."

Seth knew she was confused about the conversation from the get-go. However, he knew he had to do this. He couldn't wait any longer. His fantasies had lasted long enough. "Listen, I know you're busy with the investigation, but when it's over, I would like to get to know you better. Would you like to meet me for one night? Since there's nothing here but a ratty café, I suggest I take you to this little Italian place, not too far from my house. How about it?"

Blushing, yet irritated by the question, she cleared her throat and adjusted her shirt—a nervous habit. She felt security and relief from stress by performing the ritual. "Well, yeah, um, maybe. I mean, I'm very busy with the case. I can't make it tonight, of course, but I'm sure I could free myself up for an evening. It would be nice to get away from the police station. How about tomorrow?"

Thankful she couldn't hear the thoughts buzzing through his head, he smiled and turned around for a brief second. The excitement on his face needed to be controlled. He couldn't wait for their dinner date. Finally, his dream was going to become a reality.

208

"Fantastic! The restaurant isn't far from where I live. I'll text you the address and time and meet you there. Plan on having a wonderful evening."

Swiveling the desk chair back to face the computer, she waved goodbye, "Sounds great, but I've got to finish this. See you later, Dr. Binder... Seth."

Walking back up the ramp toward the main section of the library, he handed Esther the stack of books he'd grabbed off the shelf. "I decided to read one of the books on my e-reader. I'll just leave these with you, if that's okay. Have a marvelous day!"

Esther took the books, confused by his sudden urgency to leave, and walked back down to the bookshelf to replace the books. Not paying attention to Alison, she began to hum one of her favorite hymns.

"Honey, are you okay over there?"

Staring at the computer screen, reading the headline of the paper, she hollered back, "I'm good, thanks."

The headline was what she was interested in, more so than Seth. The paper, dated 1989, focused on a series of deaths that had taken place in Fleetham. The curious thing was it wasn't the murder of human beings, but the slaughtering of horses.

June 12, 1989: Local rancher, Billy Walker, reported yesterday that a number of his stock horses had been killed. It was apparent that it was intentional, as the animals were found in front of his barn, chest and abdomen cut open and all internal organs removed. The heads of the animals were uninjured. Authorities are investigating the incident. However, the investigators would greatly appreciate any additional information. A reward of $5,000 will be given to anyone who comes

209

forward with information leading to the arrest of an individual(s).

Chapter Thirty-Three

Transcribing all the information she'd read into her notebook her vision began to blur.

Knowing that Esther would allow her to return any time she wanted, she shut down the microfilm machine and trekked up the ramp to the front of the building. "I'll be back tomorrow as I'm tired from all that reading. Thank you for letting me use your machine. I really do appreciate you taking time out to show me everything."

The compliment meant a lot to Esther. She usually didn't speak to her readers much, but she preferred it that way. An introvert by nature, she was happiest with a book spread out in front of her, absorbing the words of a past author. "Oh. That's sweet of ya, honey. You come back any time you want. Since you know where the microfilm is, you won't need my help. I've got this steamy romance novel I'm reading and simply can't put it down. I'm sure you understand, honey."

It was like listening to a story line on a television romance channel. "What you said about your book made me laugh. Thanks for that. Have a great day!"

The amount of work that awaited her back at the police station made her feel sick to her stomach. Pausing to look at the display of arrowheads, her plans for tomorrow popped into her head. *I really am going to dinner with Seth. It's just dinner. No big deal.*

Walking toward the door, she glanced out the window and spotted Seth's Porsche. He was sitting in the car, talking to himself. Alison didn't give it much thought, as nowadays most cars had some form of hands-free device. "Speaking to a patient," she murmured under her breath, embarrassing herself by talking aloud.

Pushing the door open, she walked down the steps to her car. As she opened the door, he lowered his window. "Don't forget about our dinner tomorrow. I can't wait. It'll be so much fun!"

To her, his voice sounded almost juvenile—like a high schooler asking a girl out on a date for the very first time. She didn't respond, only waved and smiled. Her uneasiness about tomorrow's plans were slowly creeping up on her. Putting the thought aside, she knew she needed to step away from the office and relax a bit.

Reversing, she saw him staring at her. Waving to him, she drove down the street, back to the police station. When she arrived, more cars were parked in front of the building than usual, but with an air of determination she walked inside.

Engrossed in the same file she'd left him with, Aaron sat at Robert's desk. He'd read a considerable number of pages, with the face-down pile much taller than it was when she left. "It looks like you've been busy. Find anything interesting?"

Looking up, his expression didn't require a verbal reply, but he gave one anyway. "There's a serial killer out there. He or she or it hasn't been caught. That's the bitch of it. The evidence found at the scene wasn't substantial... it's all circumstantial. Same thing here, until we had something physical to go on. The only difference between Tessie and this guy is that the victim didn't have hydrocodone or Versed in his system. He had dinoflagellate algae."

"And what the hell's that exactly?" Confused by his comment.

"I looked it up. I'd never heard of it before either. It's an algae that infects shellfish. Symptoms are just like Versed, except this stuff occurs naturally. The thing is the nearest coastal area is about twelve hours from here. See my problem with this?"

Sliding the autopsy report towards Alison, she briefly scanned it, trying to find the exact excerpt he was referencing. Highlighted with a strip of yellow adhesive paper, the sentence told its ugly truth. "So, was the victim given these algae before or after he died? Wait… where does it say it was found?"

Using his pen as a pointer, Aaron ran it down the page, stopping at the sentence that answered her question. "Duh, duh, duh, mmm, oh, here… It's just there. See? 'Toxin found in bloodstream'. So, he was alive when he was infected."

Thinking about the trip she took to Mexico a few years ago, and the killer shrimp cocktail at the oceanside café, she wondered if anyone could be a victim. "But wouldn't you know if you had eaten rotten fish? I mean, we've all had shrimp or scallops or some kind of seafood that tasted a bit strange. Haven't you?"

Chuckling during this serious moment, he replied, "Yeah, well, I looked that up, too. Freezing and cooking doesn't kill the algae. So, what I think happened was he was knowingly given whatever shellfish had been contaminated. The effects slowly took over, then he was savagely assaulted. What the autopsy doesn't give a clear answer to is the ligature marks. There's bruising, just like our case now—which would imply that it was done

213

while he was still alive. His hyoid bone was crushed—so he was strangled. But the report doesn't give that as the cause of death. However, I'm assuming... You know what the first three letters of assume spells. I'm just saying... The point is, he wasn't brutally killed before he was unconscious. That's a given fact, as per the autopsy report. The incision, just like Tessie's, was postmortem... there was minimal bleeding at the site."

Alison nodded, but was confused. "No, there are discrepancies here. Remember the amount of blood on the bed? That wasn't a postmortem thing at all. It happened when she was still alive."

"You're right. So, maybe they aren't related, but the cutting and disembowelment are almost identical. Coincidence? Maybe so, maybe not. It's just interesting to me that this case just went to sleep and was forgotten. What's even more interesting is why Robert didn't bring this up. Hell, he was the sheriff at that time, as well."

Boots clanking on the tile, announced to Alison and Aaron that Robert had arrived. Carrying a Styrofoam cup full of something, he walked into his office and sat down on the corner of the desk.

"What's happening, y'all? What did you find out about ole' farmer Joe here?" Alison rolled her eyes and walked to the door. "What I really don't understand is why you didn't tell us about this. Everything is so similar, yet different at the same time. The cuts and ligature marks, the toxins found in his blood. That's why I don't understand why we didn't know about it. Aaron thinks it's a serial killer situation."

The loud laugh almost rattled the windows. Spilling his drink from jiggling up and down, Robert snorted and leaned his head against the adjacent filing cabinet. "You city people. Everything is such a

214

goddamned emergency for you. Yes, I get that Tessie was murdered. I know it was terrible. But we all, even the city detective, thought this was a random killing perpetrated by someone passing through town. We thought whoever killed him did it for the thrill of it, as sick as that might sound."

Aaron wasn't pleased with his response. "How can you be so callous. You're the sheriff, for Christ sake. The least you could have done is *attempt* to get to the bottom of it. But no, you didn't. You shoved this case in the back of the drawer and called it a day."

Aaron was walking out of the room as he finished speaking, heading to the front door to take a breather. He paused when something caught his attention. Along the south wall of the police station, rows of pictures proudly displayed many years of the town's history—and family history, as well.

The picture that caught his attention was one of Robert and Seth. Seth was a small child, maybe five or six, standing on a large fishing boat, somewhere coastal. Holding a very large shark, a proud father shared a happy moment with his excited son. "Hey, Robert, could ya come here a minute?"

Alison and Robert both marched to the front of the police station. Alison's heels and Robert's boots were in unison, making a rhythmic rapping, lending a bit of life to the otherwise dead atmosphere.

"Yes, sir, what can I do ya for?"

Pointing to the wall of pictures, Aaron walked over to draw his attention to the fishing image. "I didn't know y'all liked to fish. I used to fish with my dad all the time."

Taking a swig of his beverage and letting out a large, belly deep belch, he smiled, and his eyes twinkled

215

as he looked at the picture. "Oh, yeah, the son and I used to go fishing every year. We both love the ocean. It's a place where we can completely relax and forget about the world."

Alison had no interest in this "man discussion", as she often called them, but let Aaron finish his thought. "Do you and Seth still take fishing trips?"

Downing another giant gulp of his drink, he coughed, choking on it. "Oh, yeah, I bought me a little cabin on stilts along the beach. We go sometimes, but mainly Seth goes by himself. It's his little vacation away from being a life-saving doctor."

Robert was now standing directly in front of Aaron. Veering slightly to the left, Aaron could see the corner of Alison's face. She had caught his gaze, the moment he moved his head. Aaron gave her a look, understanding that he couldn't speak openly about whatever was on his mind.

Chapter Thirty-Four

Driving down Main Street, after leaving the library, Seth couldn't stop thinking about tomorrow's plans. He had so much to prepare, so many items he needed, and so many things to rehearse. Needless to say, this was the most important date he'd been on.

He thought of her as someone he could marry. He thought of Alison as his soulmate. Granted he hardly knew her having only spoken to her for little more than five minutes, he thought she was the one who would complete his life. "Now, I have to get her to trust me. That's the hardest part, you know?" He said aloud, which was normal when he was anxious.

"Yes, I know, but you have to calm down, and you have to remember that she knows how to distinguish fact from fiction. Also, she can tell if you are full of shit." Another thing that happened when he was nervous or didn't have enough alcohol in his system to calm his brain down, was to answer to his verbal thoughts. The voices began when he was a child, which he had always attributed to a guardian angel.

"Everyone has one," he would always tell people, if he was overheard. He was careful to control his mind in public, knowing he shouldn't be heard talking to himself, let alone answering himself.

He was extremely cautious about many things. As soon as he arrived home today, in preparation for tomorrow, he needed to secure his belongings.

217

Nobody knew, but Seth had a very large collection of things. The things he'd collected, he'd had since he was a very young child. No one appreciated their value except him.

Passing the police station, he saw his dad's car parked in front. Not wanting to bother him with his work, he continued on the forty-five-minute drive to his house.

Seth loved living outside of Fleetham. He was close enough to the hospital in town, yet far enough away to escape the mundane life only a small town had to offer.

Driving down the lonely stretch of highway, the only landscape he passed was that of fields and farms. Growing up in a small town offered little excitement, most of which he created himself. Nearing a dirt road that led to another small farm, he turned, his car idling. Stepping out, his feet slid on the fine sand.

The memories flooding his mind of dirt road adventures when he was younger suddenly gave him a warm sense of nostalgia. It was down this very road that he'd experienced one of the biggest thrills of his life. A thrill that altered the town and its citizens.

His love of medicine and anatomy drove him to his adventures as a young boy. Seeing how the body functioned gave him an odd feeling—it was only later in life that he understood what that feeling was. His therapist called it ghoulish behavior. Seth called it pleasure. Either way, as he wasn't the most popular of boys in his class, his dominating personality gained him the advantage of getting his own way… most of the time.

Chapter Thirty-Five

Finishing their discussion about their fishing adventures and summer follies, Robert and Aaron retreated to his office. Sitting at the desk, side by side, the two thumbed through the files, trying to make a pattern of events that would link the two crimes. Alison remained in the front section of the police station, staring at the photographs. Seeing Seth next to his father, made her curious.

As a younger teenager, Seth had the look that any sixteen-year-old girl would swoon over. His square jaw and broad shoulders instilled a feeling of attraction in her, albeit only physical. The expression on each photo of Seth was both stimulating yet frightening. Ignoring the thought, she crept back to the office and stood in the doorway.

"When you two are finished, I'd like to leave. It's been a long week, and I'd like to relax for a while. I still have a lot of work to do tomorrow."

Robert, ignoring her, continued to speak quietly to Aaron about the events that happened twenty years ago.

Aaron looked at Alison and winked. "We're nearly finished. I'm going to dinner after I get out of here... wanna come?"

Thinking about it, she had a feeling he didn't want to just have dinner, but she accepted anyway. "Sure, it'll be a nice change from ordering take-out, anyway. I'll go on ahead then and go over to the café, so

219

I can get a few things written up. I don't exactly have a desk here to work at."

Her comment made Robert laugh, a loud, jovial belch erupting from his stomach. "Girl, you kill me. Little miss princess. I'll gladly move so you can work here, by all means, your highness."

Incredibly annoyed by his statement, she replied curtly. "I'm good, but thanks, anyway. I'm going to head out. Aaron, I'll see you in a bit. And, Robert, you have a great night."

Turning around, she headed to the round table she had sat at earlier. Grabbing her binder and bag, she hoisted everything over her shoulder, and stomped out the door. Not giving either of them a second glance, today she chose to leave her work at the office. But as ever, the temptation to work after she had left the police station proved to be too much for her. With a feeling of self-worth growing inside her, the thought that kept playing repeatedly in her head was, *Today, I turn over a new leaf. Today, I'm a new Alison.*

The drive to the café wasn't far… two blocks south, so she didn't have time to relax before she got there. Parking by the curb in front of the café, she was greeted by a few older men who had opted for an afternoon of coffee and gossip.

"Howdy, ma'am. Let me help you with the door." One of the men said as she stepped out of the car. Amazed by the kindness she'd experienced while visiting, she nodded and smiled, strolling into the restaurant.

The air was thick with grease and cigarette smoke; typical for an establishment such as this. No matter how nauseating the room was to her, the home-like atmosphere took it all away. Her childhood flashed

220

before her, and she was sitting in her grandparents' kitchen, helping cook Sunday supper.

Taking the booth in the far corner, to not be distracted by the loud patrons, she opened her laptop and began to type.

She was a quarter of the way finished with her investigation report, leaving space to attach the photos and autopsy report. Adding a page break underneath section three, it came time for her to type the criminal profile addition.

As she typed, in her mind she tried to envision how the killer had seen in her. *God, what kind of person could do this to her?*

The assailant is more than likely a person who finds pleasure in hurting others, whether it be human or animal. He/she has the ability to manipulate victims, to the point of total deception. The victim had no knowledge of the forthcoming incident, however, if she had, she played it off as a sexually deviant act.

Transferring Aaron's information to her report, she added an addendum to reference later. *Add newspaper information to compare, if relevant.*

Lying next to her laptop, her leather binder was open, exposing her yellow legal pad. Taking her fountain pen and adding a few random notes from today, she noticed something peculiar about one of the events that had transpired over the last few days. Remembering the images of Tessie's body, and those of the murder twenty years ago, she recalled that the previous case wasn't identical to Tessie's.

She had a heart-shaped cut-out on her chest. The prior murder didn't. Adding that information to her notes, she drew a line and added a sub-category.

Check fingerprints from prior murder.

221

Alison recalled the interview with 'Little Sammy' and how he continued to deny the incident. His expression seemed genuine. However, over the years, she'd seen many *genuine* people, a term she used loosely. Throughout her life, she'd known few who were truly wholesome. Moreover, the criminals who she had arrested lacked one particular feature. None of them had a conscience.

During her career she had determined that the key factor in any case was the lack of conscience in the criminal. Whether he or she had committed the murder, or were an accessory to the crime, in her professional opinion their conscience didn't exist. She'd had many criminal psychologists disagree with her, stating that the conscience is always present.

Meeting Sammy for the first time, she honestly didn't initially suspect him. However, with the physical evidence that came to light, her opinion quickly changed.

Closing her laptop and capping her pen, she whispered under her breath, "I'm done."

The menu sat propped up between the salt and pepper at the side of the table. Grabbing it, she opened the cover to scan through its contents. Her fingers stuck to the thick, laminated plastic. Years of grease and nicotine added a sticky tape like film, which she detested.

Living in a large city, she was primarily accustomed to food delivery services with exorbitant prices. Here, in this tiny town of less than a thousand, the prices were oddly inexpensive.

The waitress had seen her pick the menu up and hobbled over to her table. Alison soon learned that her name was Gertrude and she was sixty-eight years old.

222

"Honey, what would you like? Everything here is done cooked fresh back in the kitchen."

Checking the menu one last time, she placed her order. "A side salad with dressing on the side, a large iced tea, and a slice of chocolate pie."

Smiling and pulling her pencil from behind her ear, Gertrude added the order to her pad, "It'll be out in a sec, hun. Holler if you need anything else."

With that, the waitress smiled, flashing her ill-fitting dentures.

Smiling at her, Alison looked around at the occupants of the restaurant. Mainly consisting of older men in overalls, there were a few women and younger couples about. Looming directly above her, the head of a deer adorned her corner of the room. The décor of the restaurant was certainly not that of a Michelin rated restaurant in New York City, but it had a certain relaxing ambience. For the moment, at least, the stress of the case was tucked away in her binder. She assumed Aaron would want to discuss things further, so she didn't fully empty her mind of work, just yet.

Curious as to when he'd arrive, she pulled out her phone, seeing a few missed calls. The caller, from a number she didn't have saved in her phone, had left three voicemails. Flicking the voicemail app open, she pressed play.

Thursday, 6:01 p.m. Hey Alison, it's Seth. Just wanted to say I will see you tomorrow.

Thursday 6: 04 p.m. Hey, it's Seth again. I forgot to tell you that if you want to wear something casual that's fine. Bye for now.

Thursday 6:10 p.m. Alison, I was curious why you aren't picking up. Nothing important, just making sure you received my calls.

223

Unsure why he called her so much after already confirming their plans, she rolled her eyes and erased the messages. Escaping her lips in a whisper, "How did he even get my number?"

Gertrude arrived with her tea and a basket of glazed, homemade dinner rolls. Sitting on top of the steaming hot mounds was a pat of butter for each. "Oh, the carbs. Thank you so much!"

Gertrude smiled and handed her the iced tea and dinner rolls. "You're welcome, honey. The cook back there makes these every few hours, so you know they're fresh. It's his mama's recipe, I think. Your salad and pie will be out in a jiffy."

Taking her knife and splitting a roll, she added another pat of butter. The heat instantly melted the knob of butter, leaving a soggy piece of "goodness", as she called it.

Being a believer in only eating healthy foods, the occasional carb fest wouldn't hurt her. By the time her salad arrived about five minutes later, she'd already devoured two of the rolls.

The second Gertrude turned around, heading back to the kitchen, Aaron walked through the door. The chime above the door announcing his arrival.

Scanning the room, he spotted Alison and gave her an awkward overhead wave.

"Man, I'm glad I got out of there when I did. Robert can be a real pain at times. He continually went over this one report that wasn't even relevant to what we were doing,"

Sipping her tea, Alison handed him the menu. "You made it pretty obvious you wanted to meet me tonight. What's going on? Couldn't you have chatted back there?"

224

With the menu in front of him, he decided what he was going to order before pulling out his phone and clicking the vibrate button, so he wouldn't be disturbed. "No, I couldn't. I needed to get you out of Robert's earshot. I think there's something screwy going on here."

Her ears at attention and eyes suddenly wide, she opened her laptop to take notes. She was a fast typist, so transcribing his full conversation wasn't a challenge for her.

"Okay, so hear me out. I thought about something earlier today. Did you notice how Robert kept going through the file, page by page?"

Pausing from her typing, she looked directly into his eyes. "Aaron, we all were. Obviously, we were working. What are you getting at?"

As he was about to begin his detailed explanation, the waitress approached the table. "Excuse me. I'd just like a glass of soda—I don't care what kind."

Scribbling on her notepad, Gertrude took the order, and stuck her pencil behind her ear. Strands of sweaty hair had fallen from her French twist bun, leaving her face framed by a curtain of hair. "Yes, sir. I'll bring out more rolls. I done told the missus here that they're the best around. I'll be right back, honey."

Grabbing one of the two remaining rolls, he ripped off a huge chunk and began to chew. With a mouth full of bread, he cleared his throat, swallowed hard and began his speech.

"Okay, I've thought this through. I know things that you aren't aware of… at least, I don't think you are. While you were out earlier, I did my own form of investigating. I've stepped way out of my boundaries… just so you know."

225

The clatter of plastic hitting the tabletop announced to both of them, that Alison's salad had been delivered. Full of mealy tomatoes and wilted lettuce, it was anything but appealing. Pouring on the portion of dressing that could serve another four people, she took a bite to ease the sudden load of tension. "Okay, this is really my investigation, but I'm open to other opinions. What do you know?"

Tucked in the pocket of his jeans, he pulled out a photograph of Tessie. She was obviously younger and much less weathered looking. "Where did that come from? It doesn't even look like the same girl."

"That's the bitch of it. When Robert and I were sitting in his office, he had the top drawer full of random papers. I was actually looking for a notepad and happened to find this picture. If looks could kill... let me tell ya. The look on his face gave me chills."

Just as she bit into a forkful of lettuce, Gertrude walked over to the table and handed her another glass of iced tea. "Honey, are ya doing okay? Need anything else?" They both shook their heads.

"So, anyway, I just flat out asked him why he had the picture. He told me that years ago he had taken advantage of her. He slept with her, Alison. From his version of things, she was going to be arrested, or had been. Needless to say, he completely took control of the situation."

Alison's face was blank, her mouth hanging open. "This changes everything. But what? But why would..."

Aaron nodded in response to her inability to finish her sentence. "Exactly. I already know what you're going to say. I asked myself the same thing. But what's interesting about all of this is that he showed zero

226

emotion. He was almost proud of what he had done. Ya know?"

Alison's fingers were typing faster than she'd ever typed before. Her Word program had already filled two pages of notes, solely from Aaron's words. "What else did he tell you? Did he see her again after that?"

"He didn't say. He did say that she'd dropped out of high school a few weeks before this happened, but he didn't say he'd seen her after the fact."

She snapped her head up and slammed the laptop closed. "What did you say? She had just dropped out of school? That means she was underage."

"Exactly. Motive. Am I right, or am I right?"

Chapter Thirty-Six

Robert decided to work later than usual today, partly because he needed to clean up the mess that Aaron had made of his desk, and partly because he wanted to talk to Sammy a bit more. As he tapped the handful of papers to line them all up, he added the thick file and slid it back in his desk drawer.

He turned the lights out in his office and limped over to the booking room that led into the main jail. His back was hurting, so his limp was more pronounced on his left side. Years of being slightly overweight and having a sedentary lifestyle had wreaked havoc on his lower back. "Thank God I'm not working for the highway department," he'd always tell people.

The booking room was dark, but he didn't need a light on to navigate. He knew the layout of the police station so well that he could walk around blindfolded and not have a problem. Turning the doorknob to the entrance of the jail, the rush of stale air took his breath away. Since the jail wasn't used often, it wasn't aired out properly. With a mixture of musty mildew and stale cigarette smoke from the former inmates, it reminded him of the adult video stores he frequented when he visited Austin.

His boots made a sound that reverberated off the concrete block walls, breaking the dark silence. He quietly neared the cell where Sammy was being housed, so as not to disturb him. Not sure if he would be sleeping or not—or sleeping off his alcohol, he crept up to the cell door.

Sammy sat on the floor, staring ahead at nothing. When he saw Robert standing over him, he stood up quickly. The sudden change in position caused him to stumble backwards. Catching himself on the bed, he sat there a moment to equalize his blood pressure.

"Sir, I'm sorry, I didn't see you there. Am I going to go home now?"

Robert looked at Sammy for a few moments without saying a word. He wasn't sure exactly what he wanted to say, but knew he had to tell him something. "I was just checking on ya. How ya doing?"

Sammy's hand was busy scratching a scab off his arm. Flicking it on the ground, the wound began to trickle a small, yet steady stream of blood. "I'm good, but ready to go. I told ya I'm not the right man here."

Tipping his hat towards him, Robert turned around without saying another word and exited through the metal door. Slamming it shut with a resounding clang, the lock clicked into place with a turn of his key. "I just don't know anymore. I just don't know." The words spilled out. He knew no one could hear him but it felt good to get some of his emotions out.

Chapter Thirty-Seven

The café was unusually busy this evening. As the special happened to be liver and onions, Alison assumed that the entire town craved organ meat on a Thursday.

"As much as I want to think this is plausible, I just can't, Aaron. He's the sheriff. You and I have both been around him. I mean, you know? This is your thing though. You profile these cases."

Tilting his glass up to get the last few morsels of ice, he set the cup down on the edge of the table. He'd hoped the waitress would understand the universal signal for a refill, but in this town, he doubted it. "The whole family is weird, even Seth. He seems eccentric to me. But let me finish. If you think about it, it makes sense. What if Robert planted all that shit in Sammy's house? What if he let himself into the house? I mean, it's not hard, as Sammy's door is always unlocked and open. There are all sorts of possibilities here."

"Aaron, listen to me. I'm not saying you're wrong, but again, why?"

Aaron's phone began to vibrate on the table, distracting him momentarily. Checking it, to ensure it wasn't something important, he went back to his conversation. "That's easy, Ali. She was underage. All the motive in the world. Maybe someone found out about it and threatened him? Oh... I forgot something about Sammy. What if Sammy was just there at the right time and the right moment? He's always so drunk, he wanders all over the place."

She finished her salad and buttered the last remaining roll. Now cold, but tasty all the same, she began to eat her third one. "Well, it makes sense I guess, but I've never given it any thought. I figured we'd ruled everyone out who was a suspect, but never thought of adding Robert to the mix."

"Although, I do think he should take a polygraph test. Just to make sure and rule him out. I can have Ross come back to town, and I'm certain he'd be able to make it tomorrow."

Speaking round a mouth full of bread, she uttered, "You're sure about all of this, aren't you? I guess you know what you're talking about, but Robert?"

"I know it's crazy, but I need to, even if I'm wrong, just to ease my mind. I've already called Ross, anyway. He'll be here in the morning."

Her eyes rolled in response to him having already called the polygraph examiner. "Of course, you did. Okay, do your test. I'll stand by Robert the entire time. I'll give you anything in the world if you are right. If you'll do the same for me. Deal?"

He stuck out his hand and nodded. "Good deal, Lucille."

"Alrighty, then. I'm going to get out of here. I'm exhausted. I feel like it just keeps piling up. I'll see you in the morning. Don't worry about your soda, I'll get it. You've got bigger fish to fry tomorrow. I think for my prize, I'll need a shopping trip."

He winked at her, stood up and paused at the end of the table. The smile he gave her was mischievous, but she knew he meant absolutely nothing by it. The respect the two had for one another was immense. Nothing

231

would ever be done to break that. "You, ma'am, need to go home and rest. You've got a lot of paying up to do tomorrow. G'night!"

Walking out with a strut, one that he never used, but today he felt it appropriate. He had never had such a strong feeling about something in his life. Deep down he knew that he was on to something. Although he thought he knew what it was, a tiny portion of his brain lacked certainty.

Alison's phone was vibrating as she watched Aaron prance out of the restaurant as if he'd won a major award. Shrugging off her irritation, she glanced at her phone to see who it was. *Seth*. Flicking her phone to the unlock position, she read his text:

Hey, it's Seth. Wasn't sure if you received my messages, so I thought I'd send a text and confirm tomorrow? Hope all is well.

She had thought Seth odd when she first met him, but this just confirmed her assessment.

As his text was of little importance to her, she pocketed the phone, and stared straight ahead. Looking at all the sights in the restaurant reminded her of a 1960s sitcom, set in a southern town. She half expected to see Aunt Bee or Sheriff Taylor walk through the door, whistling the iconic theme song.

But her mind wouldn't relax. What Aaron had just said made her think, but at the same time, she was beginning to question her ability as an experienced investigator. "Robert? Robert? Was he really a master manipulator?"

"Darlin, can I get you somethin' else? You about ready for that chocolate pie?"

Gertrude was the most attentive waitress she'd had in years. However, she was getting on her nerves.

232

"No, I'm great. I'm just leaving. Thanks… I don't need change."

Gertrude took the folded twenty-dollar bill along with the ticket. "Oh, thank you, honey. God bless you."

Draining the remaining tea from her glass, now watered down by the melted ice, she thought about asking for a to-go cup but changed her mind.

Picking up her laptop bag and binder, she made a mental note to transfer some of the notes from her conversation with Aaron, from her computer to paper. Tomorrow, she'd use them when she spoke to Robert.

Walking to the front door, she glanced back towards the tables. Every eye was on her. Unsure why, she smiled in the general direction of the kitchen— feeling awkward and insecure, she shouldered the door open and walked out into the warm, summer air.

Tonight, the humidity was higher than usual. Typical for a Texas summer, the faint sound of thunder could be heard in the distance. The air felt freeing to her. The atmosphere of the café had been relaxing, but the freedom of the night air helped calm her to the core.

The town was dead as she drove down Main Street, heading back to her hotel. Though only a short drive, she valued her time alone more than anything else, as it gave her time to think, and that's what she needed.

Driving down the lonely stretch of road, she pulled into the hotel, and sat in her car. Alone, she closed her eyes, picturing Robert. Seeing him in her mind, standing in the motel room, covered in blood, the thought gave her a twinge of terror.

Alison knew her suspicions were correct. She knew it was Sammy. The evidence pointed back to him, but she couldn't ignore the point Aaron had made. Digging in her bag, she pulled out her laptop. In the stillness of the night, she reviewed the notes she'd taken when listening to him talk.

"He could have staged the entire thing… he could have, oh, yeah, well… I guess that makes sense. He raped her several years ago. The previous murder, okay, wait… that murder."

Murmuring to herself as she scanned the transcription from their conversation, she couldn't believe what she was reading.

Her computer was about to die, so she slid it back in its protective pouch in her bag and flung the door open to find that the humidity had intensified. Smelling rain, she decided to leave her window open. The fresh air would benefit her, and hopefully, help her to relax and easily fall asleep.

In her hotel room, the maid had tidied up earlier in the day. It was always her custom to leave a little something on the bed for the cleaning staff. As a frequent user of hotels, she knew she wasn't the most organized guest. This morning, she left a small bag of chocolates, purchased at the local store. Something as a gesture of niceness, which she knew she'd also appreciate. Throwing her bag on the other bed, its contents spilled out unintentionally. "Shit."

Flinging her clothes off, now soaked with the stench of the greasy café atmosphere, she headed towards the bathroom. Stepping into the shower, she let the hot water run down her back. With her eyes closed, the tension of the day washed away—or so she hoped. It had been so long since she'd had any time away from the field. Making a mental note, she promised herself, after this case was finished, a mandatory two weeks away was in order.

234

She could have stayed in the shower all night, just standing under the hot water. Eventually stepping out of the shower, she caught something out of the corner of her eye.

Since the lights weren't turned on in the bathroom, she could clearly see out the window of her room. Despite the sheer curtains being drawn, the image of a person was very clear to her.

Grabbing her robe that hung in the bathroom, she quickly walked to the door. As she peered out the peephole, she was shocked to see absolutely nothing.

Her brain was playing tricks on her. "Silly girl, all of this Robert talk has you spooked. Go to bed."

She was right, there was nothing there. She was just tired. Pushing the thought out of her mind, she returned to the bathroom to finish her nightly ritual. Knowing she needed to be at the police station early in the morning, she found the bottle of antihistamines tucked away in her bag. Taking a tablet with a gulp of water, she knew the effects would kick in shortly. A solid night's sleep was what was needed. Tonight, she'd achieve that, with the assistance of Prince Histamine.

Alison decided to leave the window slightly cracked, allowing the summer breeze to drift in. The brief terror of seeing a man standing outside her window had left her a few moments ago. Now, she knew she had nothing to worry about.

As she climbed into bed, feeling the coolness of the sheets against her legs, she felt a sudden sense of relaxation. The alarm was set to 5:00 A.M. She'd be at the police station no later than six, ready to begin her day. The breeze blew in through the open window, relaxing her but adding humidity to the room. The air felt soothing to her.

235

With her last thought of the night being about Robert and tomorrow's questioning session, she turned over and drifted into the most peaceful sleep she'd had in years.

Chapter Thirty-Eight

At the sound of a large diesel truck revving its engine in the parking lot, her eyes snapped open. Realizing she'd overslept, she leapt out of bed, threw on the first set of matching clothes she could find and headed out the door. Stepping into her car, she remembered her work bag was still in the room.

"I hate mornings," she muttered under her breath, the irritation evident.

Rushing back into the room, she slipped her bag over her shoulder and grabbed her phone, which she'd also been left behind.

The flood of early morning sun blinded her as she sped down the road, hoping she wouldn't run into any highway patrolmen or police cruisers. In the distance, Fleetham could be seen, as the sun cast its colors across the countryside.

Squinting into the sunlight as she drove, she thought, *This is a new day. A day of hope. But damn the questioning.*

Lying on the passenger seat, her phone began to ring.

Answering it, she heard Robert's voice on the other end.

"Where are you? Ross is here and wants to question me. What the hell is going on? Is there something I don't know? This is absolute bullshit, Alison."

237

She didn't have time to react before he began ranting. "Uh, well, Aaron came to me last night and had some information that he needed to share. I'll be at the station in a few minutes, and we can talk in private. Go in your office and close the door. Don't talk to Ross yet."

Robert slammed the phone down without saying goodbye. Expecting his reaction, she rolled her eyes and continued her drive. Glancing down at the phone, she found Aaron's number. Pressing 'call', she listened as it rang.

On the fourth ring, he answered. "Has he called you yet?"

"Yes, just a second ago. I wanted to speak to him before Ross arrived. He's so diligent, but at the same time… ya know?"

In the background, the noise of an electric shaver echoed through the speaker. "I know. I'm just finishing getting ready. I'll be there in about ten minutes. Where are you?"

Looking at her GPS, which was only showing a highway, she couldn't give him an exact location. "Ten minutes away or so, I think. You know there aren't any suburbs here. I see cows and three tractors. I did pass a herd of deer on the side of the road a few miles back."

She could hear him laughing in the background. "You're a mess. I'll see you later."

After she spoke to him, she did feel better about the day. Anytime she had a mountain of stress on her shoulders, he had always been able to say something to make her calm down.

Straight ahead, the water tower welcomed her, signaling her location. Now she knew she was about five minutes away from the police station. She passed a pickup truck traveling slower than any human could walk. She'd assumed the man in the truck was either checking on his field or out for a morning drive. "Humph, small towns."

With her directional on to signal a left turn, Alison whipped into her usual parking space in front of the police station. Robert's cruiser was already there, which she already knew, as well as Ross' car.

She'd prepared herself during her drive to deal with the stress of listening to Robert, however, she knew that it would be far worse than expected.

Confidently walking into the main entrance, the tension was so thick, you could cut it with a knife. Without needing to say a word to anyone, the expression on their faces was unmistakable. Robert sat on a stool in the back of the office, sipping a cup of coffee—more than likely, knowing him, it had an extra something added to it. Ross sat at the table in the center of the room, typing on his computer. She knew what he was doing and what he was typing. And so did Robert.

Placing her bag down on the table next to Ross, she walked over to Robert.

"Let's go into your office. We need to talk."

Alison didn't wait for him to respond. Turning on her heels, she marched directly into his office and sat in the chair facing his desk. After taking his time to walk the ten feet to his office Robert appeared in the doorway.

Stomping into the room, it was clear to Alison that he was not only furious with her, but quite possibly, had lost all trust in her.

"I want to know what the hell this is all about? Why does Ross want to do a poly on me? Why is this even being discussed? I have a mind to have him escorted out of this office immediately!"

239

Alison sprang from her chair and hurried over to the table where Ross sat. Grabbing her bag, she returned to Robert's office, plunking the obviously worn bag on top of his papers. The laptop was the first thing she took out. Waiting for it to boot up, she read from her notebook.

"Look, I'm sorry, but Aaron brought this to my attention last night during dinner. I think it's something wor..."

"Oh, so now you and pretty boy are doing your thing?"

Ignoring his comment, she turned to the page that had been marked by dog-earing it. "Anyway, this information he told me, it made sense, but I didn't want to think about it—because it was about you. Okay, so remember when we interviewed Sammy? All evidence pointed to him, right? I'm not discounting that at all."

Digging through his top drawer, he pulled out his stainless-steel flask and swallowed half the bottle, or so it seemed to Alison. "But what does it have to do with me?"

"What Aaron surmised was... What if everything had been planted on 'Little Sammy'? What if all the fingerprints were his, but not through him doing anything dishonest? Do you get what I'm saying? If you remember, when we went to his house to search it, we noticed that his front door doesn't close completely. Anyone could walk in. Anyone could plant anything in there. It wouldn't be hard at all."

He leaned back in his chair and folded his arms behind his head, grinning at her. "So, you're talking about me, I guess? I slipped into Sammy's house?"

With the laptop fully booted, and the entire conversation in front of her, she scanned through it, "Let

240

me see. Front door, yeah, this… the body. Here it is. He thinks you had a motive. You raped her several years ago and it was determined that she was minor. There's motive there. A very solid motive, Robert."

Robert stood up and walked behind Alison. Taking his arm and flinging the door as hard as he could, it slammed with a thump, knocking the photograph of him and Seth off the wall. "Now you listen here, 'Miss Thing'. I might be a lot of things, I might've done bad things to women, but I sure as shit didn't kill any of them. This conversation is over…"

Alison's face showed exactly how she felt. She was terrified. The aggression in his voice, as well as the obvious hatred he felt for her, made her extremely uneasy. "Okay, I understand you're upset, but Ross will still perform the test. Please don't drink any more. I want it to be an honest test and I don't want any hiccups. Just off the record, I believe you—it's Aaron who doesn't."

Robert opened the door and walked into the main section of the station. "Okay, let's get this over and done with. I was born ready."

Startled by Robert's sudden approach, Ross quickly turned his head, seeing a man with a bright red face. He'd heard Robert's outburst through the closed door, so he assumed he was still on edge. "I just need to finish this report, then I'll be ready. If you'll sit down, I'll begin momentarily. Alison, would you care to join us?"

Robert flipped a chair around backward and sat down. Drumming his nails on the table, he impatiently waited for Ross to finish typing. Robert hoped the noise would irritate him enough that he'd begin sooner rather than later. "This is complete… I don't know what!" Robert muttered under his breath.

241

Closing his laptop, Ross took the polygraph machine and plugged it into the power source. Alison took a seat behind Robert, in order to clearly see Ross' face. "Robert, will you please turn the chair around and sit properly. Any interference with your posture could possibly affect the results."

Robert did as he was asked, removed his hat, and sat straight up. Applying all the electrodes on his fingers, Ross attached them to the machine. Beginning to sweat, Robert didn't know why as he knew he had nothing to worry about. Nevertheless, it terrified him. He'd seen so many people wrongly accused and thought about himself.

"Okay, Robert. I'm ready. I'll start with a few questions to set the parameters, then we will begin. Do you understand?"

Robert said nothing, simply nodding.

"This is Ross Anderson, polygraph examiner. The time is 7:04 A.M. Polygraph examination with Sheriff Robert Binder of Fleetham Police Department."

"Is your name Robert Binder?"

"Yes."

"Do you live in Fleetham?"

"Yes."

"Are you fourteen years of age?"

"No."

"Did you have underage sex with Tessie Johanan?"

"Yes."

"Did you ever purchase drugs for Tessie or give her drugs of any kind?"

"No."

"Did you strangle Tessie?"

"No."

"Did you kill Tessie Johanan?"

"No."

"Is your son's name Seth?"

"Yes."

Eyeing Alison, Ross shook his head, signifying that Robert had passed his polygraph test without lying. However, she'd seen suspects pass before, even though they were lying throughout the entire test. Sadly, she knew it was subjective, but if correct, could provide a wealth of knowledge.

Robert leaned back in his chair and took a deep breath. "I told you people I didn't do nothing. Yet, we had to do this thing." Throwing the electrodes on the table, he stood up and returned to his office, slamming the door, turning his radio on full blast, music blaring throughout the station.

Ross began to read the printout of the examination. "The exam was fine. Nothing registered on the reading. Let's leave him alone. I know this bothered him."

Alison nodded, and stood up. Looking out the window, she saw the ambulance race down the street. The lights were on, but the siren remained silent. She didn't think twice about seeing the emergency medical team in town. It was an everyday occurrence in any large city. Turning around, she walked straight into Robert's office. "I just want to apologize. I know you're pissed off at me, and more than likely have zero trust in me at the moment. But I wanted to say I'm sorry. I was just doing my job"

Robert's eyes had teared up before Alison entered his office. He sniffed and blew his nose on his handkerchief. "Kid, I know you done what you had to

243

do, but if you truly knew me, you'd know I didn't do this. Are you done with me now?"

Alison knew he cared about her—she had a grudging respect for him as well, despite him being as common as a hillbilly. "Yes, sir. Now, let's get to work. I need Aaron to come by later, so don't kill him. Just let it go, okay?"

He laughed and began to dig through his drawer for his working file on Tessie. "We need to figure something out. I was reading it this morning before 'Martyr Ross' arrived, and something confused me. In the autopsy report... Hell, I saw her body... the heart cut-out on her chest. In this case from years ago, there wasn't no cut-out on the chest. Why?"

"I thought about that, too. Both victims had been tied up, strangled and disemboweled, however, only one had the shape of a heart cut from their chest. I don't have an answer for that. Neither does Aaron. He thinks that most serial killers leave one clue behind—he thinks this person's trait is their mutilation of the body."

Robert's head was down, looking at another photograph he'd not seen before. It was of the motel room after the body had been removed. He remembered seeing the bed without the sheets and the pill bottle on the nightstand, but he'd missed this—on the headboard the shape of a cross had been scratched into the wood.

"Look, did you see this? I wonder if it's important?"

Alison craned her neck in his direction to see what he was referring to. The cross was clearly evident. However, she wasn't sure if it was pertinent to the case. "I'll have Aaron go over the scene and look at this. It's funny, I didn't notice this be..."

244

The front door sprang open, and a man raced into the police station. "Mama's been killed or something! Can anyone help? I don't know what happened. She's gone."

Alison rushed into the front of the station, to find him crying hysterically. "What did you say? What happened? Who's your mother?"

Robert was right behind her and recognized the man as Lester Cresson. His mother, Gertrude, was a waitress at the local café.

"I'm Lester. My mama's name is Gertrude Cresson. I found her this morning when I went to bring her the morning paper. She had fallen on the floor, bleeding from the belly. By the time the ambulance arrived, they told me she was dead."

Alison and Robert looked at each other simultaneously.

Coming over, Ross walked up to Lester. "Don't worry, we'll look into this immediately. In the meantime, you need to stay here and talk to our detective. Sheriff Binder and I will go over to your mother's house. Robert, do you know the way?"

Robert nodded, grabbed his hat off the hat rack by the front door and headed to his cruiser. Ross was right behind him, hurrying to catch up to him. "Look, man, I'm sorry about all of this, but I was only doing what was asked of me."

Robert had completely forgotten about the polygraph and was now focused on this new fiasco. "It's over and done with. I would have done the same thing in your place. We have work to do. Let's drop this."

The two men drove in silence to Gertrude's house, both focusing on the scene that awaited them.

245

Chapter Thirty-Nine

As they parked next to the ambulance outside Gertrude's house, the driver got out and began to brief the sheriff while Ross stayed in the car and called Alison.

"Aaron needs to be here. Now."

Without waiting for her to reply, he hung up the phone and stepped out of the car. This wasn't his comfort zone. He didn't belong in the field, and the procedures that were about to unfold were completely alien to him.

The driver of the ambulance, a new EMT, briefed Robert on the scene that awaited them inside.

"She was on the floor and had bled out. There was a bruise to her neck and her stomach had been cut open. The entire digestive tract had been removed. The autopsy will reveal more. I'll head to the station to give a statement. Nice to meet you, Sheriff Binder."

"Before you go, was there any sign of rape or sexual assault?"

"No. There was nothing I saw to indicate that."

With no further questions, Robert turned to Ross, who looked terrified and completely unsure of what to do next.

"I need Alison and Aaron. Now! This is their department."

Dialing Alison again, Ross listened as it went to voicemail. "We need you now. Hurry, please! Robert wants you and Aaron here immediately!"

246

As he hung up the phone, Alison's car drew to a halt alongside the house. Stepping out of the car, she grabbed her bag and walked over to Robert. "What's going on? Oh, Aaron is right behind me. He should be here in a sec."

Looking as if he had just seen a ghost, Robert couldn't answer her. Taking her hand, he led her to the front door. Opening it, the smell of stale cigarette smoke and greasy food washed over Alison like a tsunami, reminding her of the café.

The two walked into the living room, leaving Ross alone to wait for Aaron. Directly in front of them was the shadowy silhouette of a body. Setting the stage for the events that followed, the first physical evidence of the body they encountered was Gertrude's orthotic shoe, half on, half off.

The puddle of blood was enormous, spreading across the entire kitchen. She was lying on her back but given the distribution of blood on her face and stomach, she appeared to have succumbed face down. The blood had begun to coagulate, leaving patches of blackish-maroon clots adhering to her clothes. The front of her shirt had been cut away, leaving her abdomen exposed.

"Jesus, Mary and Joseph. The same thing. I don't understand. She was our waitress last night at dinner. She was so sweet."

Robert was becoming nauseated, not from the odor in the house, but from the metallic smell of blood that filled the room.

"I hear a car in the driveway, maybe it's Aaron. After this case is closed, I'm going to retire, Alison. I can't do this anymore. Our town doesn't have things like this happen."

247

The front door slammed shut, and footsteps were hard on the hollow flooring. "I came as fast as I could. What happened?"

They stepped aside so Aaron could see the body in front of them. Shocked, he covered his mouth with his hand, "Now, we have a serious problem. Out there somewhere is an active serial killer."

Aaron grabbed his phone and called the medical examiner who picked-up immediately. After filling him in on the situation and giving him the address, Jim said his ETA was half an hour. During the wait, Aaron began to pace about, careful not to step in the blood or contaminate the scene.

"We can't do this now. I don't have any equipment, and there aren't any gowns or shoe covers here," Alison grumbled to the two men.

Aaron stepped back to where the others stood, trying to retrace his footsteps. "I need to make a judgment call here. This isn't my case anymore. It's not yours either, Robert. Alison, you're out too. I need to call head office. With this being a serial killer, we need a trained team to handle this. Alison, I'm sorry to override your authority, but even you must realize that you're not the person for the job."

Although she agreed with him, her pride had been bruised. But she knew she was obliged to comply. "Yes, I know. As much as I hate to say it, I know that. And I agree... sort of. You know me."

Having secured their consent, Aaron stepped outside in order to get a stronger signal. Once his call was connected to the FBI forensics office, he quickly gave them the details and hung up. A full forensics team would arrive at the scene no later than two hours from now.

"Okay, y'all. This is different than Tessie's. Ali, you'll be briefed, only you won't have full rights to the scene or the case. Same goes for all of us."

After hearing his statement, an immense feeling of happiness, exhaustion and relief overcame them all.

"We don't all need to be here... Robert, you and Alison go back to the station and I'll wait here."

Robert tilted his hat towards Aaron. "Thank you. Just so you know, I forgive you. Let's move on, okay?"

Utterly confused by what he was referring to, Aaron frowned. The new case, lying in front of him on the floor making him realize what was important and what wasn't.

***

After working on her laptop for the last couple of hours, Alison stared blankly at the screen. Now, her notes from the last few days were beginning to look as if they'd been written in a foreign language.

Arriving at the police station, Ross announced to Robert and Alison, who were engrossed in what they were doing, "I'm going to head back to the office and finish my report. I need to get out of here... the air is thick with... I don't know what. I'll have my statement ready tomorrow, should the investigation team need it."

The two looked up, waved and returned to their tasks.

Having thought about what she was about to say, Alison began, "This is what I don't get. Sammy's still behind bars. You passed your polygraph test with flying colors. Then, another murder happens a few days after Tessie's. We're clearly missing something here, but I just don't know what it is."

249

Although Robert listened, he was having his own self-doubts. "I know. Well... I don't know. I just don't know anymore."

Alison stood up, walking over to the door that led into the booking room. With her arms folded, she leant against the doorframe, thinking. "I'm going to chat with Sammy. I guess one of us needs to tell him that he's free to go."

Nodding his agreement, Robert turned back to what he was doing. Shrugging, Alison sighed and unlocked the door. Turning the handle, the door creaked open, announcing her arrival into the darkened room. Her hand grazed the cold, damp wall as she searched for the light switch. The fluorescent tubes flickered on with a distinctive clatter. Sammy's cell door waited for her at the other end of the corridor. Her mind went back to the hospital morgue briefly. "Just like the ten-mile-long hallway in the pit of hell."

Locking the door behind her, the echo of metal rubbing against metal vibrated off the concrete walls. "Sheriff, is that's you, sir?"

When Alison arrived in front of his cell, Sammy was sitting on the floor, legs crossed, staring straight ahead. Standing quickly, he almost fell from the sudden shift in position. "Hi, Sammy. I wanted to talk to you about something if that's okay?"

Shaking his head resignedly, he lowered himself on to the bed, where he sat, preparing himself to be questioned. Intense nervousness was apparent as beads of sweat formed on his forehead and his face flushed. "You can relax. I just wanted to talk to you about the town. I don't know much about the history here and was hoping you could fill me in."

250

"Well, ma'am, whatcha wanna know? There's been a lot of stuff that's happened here over the years."

Alison pulled up a metal folding chair, and placed it in front of his cell, the pocket notebook she always carried already in her hand, ready to go. "I know you've lived here all your life, so tell me this, before Tessie, have you ever heard of anyone seriously hurting anyone? Anything like that?"

Sammy looked up at the ceiling, not particularly looking at anything, thinking. "No, ma'am, not since that killin' awhile back."

Alison took notes as he spoke. "Okay, mmhmm, When was that?"

"Maybe… twenty years ago."

"But nothing since then?"

"No, ma'am. Not that I know of."

"What about anyone raping anyone, anything like that?"

"Nothin' I ever heard of."

Alison sat in her chair for a moment, not speaking. Tucking her hair behind her ear, she cringed as the metal scraped across the floor. "Thank you, Sammy, for your help. By the way, I'll get the sheriff to sort the paperwork, then you're free to go."

Sammy closed his mouth and smiled at her.

As she crossed the threshold through to the booking room, she locked the door behind her. The flickering lights continued their fluorescent dance, reminding her of a 1980s disco. Leaving the door through to the police station open, Robert was in front of her, sitting alone at the table, staring at the floor. Stopping for a moment, she watched him. The intense feeling of remorse suddenly became overwhelming. "Robert?"

251

Startled, he whipped his head around, and saw her standing in the doorway. "Yeah, what's good?"

"I forgot to tell you something. Listen, I didn't mention this earlier, but Seth asked me to dinner. I think it would be nice to just get out of here for a bit and relax, ya know?"

He looked shocked. "My Seth?" Remembering what he'd told Seth, he managed to keep his anger in check as he spoke.

Suddenly becoming embarrassed, her manicured finger brushed a strand of hair from her face. "Yeah, nothing big deal. Just dinner, then I'll go back to the hotel. I need a break. This morning was entirely too much, ya know? Let's finish this tomorrow. I'm almost ready to submit my report, anyway. But I will need additional information from the coroner. I have more officers coming to wrap things up tomorrow."

Snatching his hat off the table, he walked to his office. "I'm surprised at you, Alison. Didn't take you for someone who would leave early from nothing. But I guess once you've had your fill, you're ready to quit. I'll tell ya one thing, it's been a hell of a week."

Grabbing her laptop and files, she shoved them in her bag. "Okay, so tonight we need to relax and re-group. Tomorrow, first thing, we'll get back to work. Deal?"

He nodded, saluted her, and walked her to the front door, "Before I go, I best sort those papers out so Sammy can go home too."

Chapter Forty

The bathroom was full of steam as Seth finished his shower. Stepping out of the scalding hot water, he stood naked in front of the mirror, staring at himself. His towel hung on the rack a mere foot away, but he hesitated to grab it. With his obsessive vanity came intense workouts at the gym. His work had paid off and could be seen in his physique, which he admired as his mind drifted, "Oh, you pretty thing. I can't wait until tonight. Once you've spent time with me, you'll never want to go back home."

Grabbing his towel, he wrapped it around his waist, his wet hair framed his face as water dripped down his back. The look of exhaustion hid the usually bright-eyed façade. Spraying himself with his favorite cologne, he suddenly got chills. His cologne always turned him on. Shipped from Europe, it had become one of his trademarks. Passersby would often comment, calling it, 'woodsy, citrusy, or musky'.

As he finished drying, he stepped into the closet and chose the most appropriate outfit for tonight. A simple, black shirt and jeans. "Nothing too fancy. With any luck, they'll be off before I can say hello," he chortled to himself.

Feeling a sudden sting in his arm, he looked down and saw that his shirt had snagged on a fresh scratch dug deep into his left arm. Though the shirt was dark, the fresh blood was soaking into the fibers and staining it. Ripping the shirt off and blotting the bleeding wound with a tissue, he screamed, "That bitch!"

Chapter Forty-One

Alison took her time traveling back to the hotel, partly because of total exhaustion, and partly because she felt nervous about going out with Seth. *He's odd, but he's also very handsome. I guess you just have to learn to deal with certain things and take the rough with the smooth.* Ever since he asked her out, she had been having an internal conflict about tonight, but overwhelmingly her heart had won.

Looking in her rearview mirror, Fleetham was disappearing into the distance. She relished the time away from work, yet in an odd way, loved spending time in the town. She'd told Robert it would be the perfect place to retire, "If it weren't for the murders."

Rounding the corner, her hotel greeted her. The driving time had been barely enough for her to empty her mind of the day's stresses.

Several new vehicles were parked in the hotel parking lot and her usual spot had been taken by a large, moving van. After finding a spot around the corner, she dug in her bag and found her room key card. Using the side entrance, she slipped inside, making her way to her room.

This morning, she'd left an envelope with a gift card to a local restaurant as a token of appreciation for the cleaning staff. Purchased via the concierge, she had him add it to her hotel bill.

255

Entering her room, she found a thank you note placed on her pillow, along with a small, chocolate candy.

She loved to treat people. In a way, she always thought that, by doing a good deed for others, she was doing a good deed for herself. Her thoughts turned to her co-workers as she placed the note inside her suitcase. "I wish everyone truly knew me."

Checking how long she had to get ready, she stepped into the shower. Not waiting for the water to heat fully, she. shivered, loving the chill of the water as she washed her body. She knew she had to wash her hair, as it smelt of cigarette smoke and fried food from Gertrude's house, mingled with the dank and musty odor of the jail.

Rinsing off, she stepped out of the shower and slipped on the glassy floor. Catching herself on the granite countertop, she giggled as she realized how giddy she'd become about tonight. Quickly drying her hair, she ran a brush through it, sprayed on some deodorant and headed to her wardrobe. Choosing the most non-law-enforcement looking outfit she had—a black pantsuit—she threw on her outfit. Her pants, which truly could have been a size larger, detailed her figure. Not usually seen at work, as she had no desire to flaunt her assets, Alison was glad that she had the freedom to do so tonight. "Eat your heart out, weird doctor boy." A grin crept across her face. For the first time since she'd entered Fleetham, she finally felt relaxed.

Her watch told her that she needed to leave. Spritzing her perfume on her neck and down her blouse, she headed out the door, back to her car. The tension began to rise, as well as the anxiety. She hadn't been out with a man in quite some time, so was almost feeling like a high schooler.

The restaurant was twenty minutes away, so she had more time than she had thought. Pulling out of the parking lot, she cruised down the road.

Arriving at the address twenty-nine minutes early, she parked and pulled out her phone. Scrolling through her messages, she found Seth's number and sent him a thoughtful text.

Hi, Seth. I just arrived. I'm really excited about tonight. See you shortly! No rush, I just got here a bit early.

Alison felt like a schoolgirl again. The excitement. The nervous yet sickening feeling. The butterflies. She loved it and missed it terribly. The texting bubbles began to appear.

Alright. See you soon! I can't wait. ☺

Chapter Forty-Two

The forensic team was due in Fleetham to begin its investigation of the second murder. Meanwhile, Aaron remained in Gertrude's house to secure the property, in case curious onlookers decided to have a look-see.

Standing in the doorway, he looked into the kitchen. He hadn't had the chance to fully examine the body—his job was to figure out the nuances of the killer, but frustrated by the wait, his curiosity got the better of him. From his vantage point, he studied Gertrude's body where it lay on the floor.

The front of her shirt had been cut or torn away, he wasn't sure which, because it was caked in dry blood. Instantly, images of Tessie began to play over and over in his mind. "God."

He hadn't noticed it earlier, purely because he was so stunned to see another murder in such a small town. On her chest, a piece of skin had been cut away. Unlike Tessie's, it wasn't that of a heart but in the shape of the letter 'A'.

He scanned the kitchen, not wishing to contaminate the crime scene by stepping inside. Nothing appeared to be out of place, and nothing had been thrown about or knocked over. Apart from the carnage on the floor, the kitchen looked like any normal kitchen should.

On the edge of the sink lay a knife, which he assumed was the one used on the body as blood covered the surface of the blade.

The wound to her chest had bled extensively, unlike Tessie's, which was performed postmortem. The shape was most curious to him.

Gertrude's outstretched arm pointed towards him, her bloodied hand lying outside the crimson pool from her abdomen. Squatting in order to see her hand more clearly, he noticed blood underneath her fingernails. Hanging between her forefinger and middle finger was a sliver of what looked like skin.

Aaron turned away from the kitchen and made a circle through the living room. A typical home, full of Depression glass and family photos, it was the home of a regular, small-town woman.

A brown suede recliner sat in the far corner, beneath a grandmother clock. An overturned ashtray, its ashes and filters strewn all over the floor. Underneath the recliner, something caught his eye. The light from the ceiling lamp cast just enough to illuminate an orange cylinder.

Taking his pen form his pocket, he crouched and ran it underneath the chair, hoping to push the item out.

The cylinder rattled, as his pen knocked it from under the chair with ease. It was a pill bottle. Aaron turned the bottle over, so the label was visible. Expecting to find that it was a medicine that Gertrude took regularly and had accidently dropped, he glanced at the label.

The sudden fear, anxiety and disgust that came over him, made him fall back. Sitting on the floor, he looked up at the ceiling. In this position, he pictured Gertrude fighting for her life as someone came into her home with one objective. To kill.

He leaned forward, thinking he'd misread the name on the bottle, but looked again anyway. The name hadn't changed.

259

Date of fill: April 12, 2019
Medicine: Xanax 0.5 mg
Prescribing physician: Dr. Dominque Bingham
Refills: 3
Instructions: Take one tablet by mouth every 4-6 hours as needed for anxiety/agitation/restlessness.
Patient: Seth Binder

Aaron immediately realized he had wasted so much time waiting for the forensics team, who were already two hours late. Having found the bottle, he started mulling over the evidence. "Surely, it's just a coincidence? No, not the sheriff's son? Get a grip on yourself, man."

The sound of a car crunching on the gravel as it pulled into the driveway interrupted his thoughts. Three cars had arrived, all black. All federally issued.

As the occupants exited, walking silently up the path, he stepped outside to greet them.

"...So, that's all we know. The body is in the kitchen. If you need anything else, let me know. The coroner will be here as soon as you give the go ahead to release the body. Here's his number." Aaron finished, having spent the last fifteen minutes filling them in on what little they knew.

Hurrying to his car, he needed to call Alison to tell her what he'd found. Taking his phone from his pocket, he dialed Alison who didn't pick up, so he left a voicemail.

"Hey, Ali, it's Aaron. Forensics just got here. I just wanted to let you know something. This is different than Tessie's murder. An 'A' was cut into Gertrude's chest, and there is a piece of skin hanging from her fingers. She must have fought back. Good for her. Call me later."

With nothing more that he could do, he decided to go back to his hotel to take a shower and get some rest.

***

Refreshed and having had a bite to eat in his room, Aaron checked his phone once more. Seeing that Alison still hadn't called him back, he tried her number again.

"Hey, where are you? I need to talk to you *now*!"

"Aaron, what in the world is wrong? Are you still working? It's late. I'm about to go to dinner with someone, can I call you back?"

Aaron began to speak, but Alison interrupted him. "I have a text coming in, hang on."

Hey, my car won't start. Could you come and pick me up? I live about five minutes from the restaurant. My address is 489 South Percer Blvd.

"Aaron, I have to go. I was meeting someone for dinner, but his car won't start."

Aaron knew that she didn't know anyone other than her co-workers, since she lived so far away. "Who are you meeting for dinner? I'm a bit jealous it wasn't me." He tried to make light of the situation, not wanting to appear intrusive.

"Oh, just someone I met while I was here. He's free tonight, and I needed a break. I'll text you later, if that's okay? I told Robert I'd be at the station early, so hopefully you can make it too. We've got to knock this out ASAP."

She hung up without giving Aaron a chance to reply. Scrolling through his phone, Aaron looked for anyone whom he knew Alison had become acquainted with while working the case.

261

Jim was first on his list. "Hey, man, what's up?"

"Hi, I just wanted to know if Alison was with you? I need her to work on something for me."

Jim cleared his throat before answering. "No, if you like, I can have her call you if I hear from her."

Aaron's anxiety was rising, unsure of who she was meeting, but had a feeling he already knew the answer to his question. "No, I'll send her a text in a minute. Have a good one."

Aaron hung up without allowing Jim to reply.

Next on his quest to find an answer was Ross. He was fairly certain that Ross wouldn't be with her, but he dialed his number anyway.

"Hello. This is Ross."

His voice sounded tired and drawn. "Hey, it's Aaron. I was just calling to see if Alison is with you? I need her input on something to do with the case."

Yawning deeply on the other end of the phone, Ross replied. "No, she was at the station when I left a while ago. Try there. I want to get an early night. Goodnight."

Ross hung up. Aaron had only one more person on his list to dial.

Thumbing through his contacts until he found Robert's name, he pressed the call button, listening as it rang several times. Answering, with music blaring in the background, Robert snapped, "I'm not working tonight. I went home early. What's wrong?"

Aaron was relieved he'd answered so quickly—he thought he'd be hammered already, as per his normal after work history. "Have you talked to Alison tonight? I need her to help me with something to do with the case."

Robert coughed. A lighter clicked in the background as he took a long drag of his cigarette. "She's out with my boy. He's done got him a woman to take to dinner apparently."

Aaron's heart began to race, his anxiety and fear intensifying. "Where are you?"

"Oh, hi there, darlin'. Sorry, talking to the waitress. I'm at the Rusty Anchor having myself a drink. You comin' over to partake? I came straight from the office and took it easy."

Aaron thought that if he came straight from the police station, all his essentials would be with him... including his gun.

"Stay right there. I'll be with you in a few minutes."

Since his arrival into town, Aaron had seen the bar many times. It was a few blocks away from the motel, but not a spot he would ever choose to hang out at. His car purred to life and stones flung from under the tires as he gunned the engine.

Racing at full speed down the narrow, bumpy road, he arrived at the main junction between the residential and business division. He turned left, towards the edge of town where the neon blue sign of the bar flashed over the early evening sky. A dozen cars were parked in front, mainly older model trucks. The irony of the sheriff's cruiser parked front and center made Aaron snigger. Walking in, he was greeted by a waitress who appeared to be older than his mother. "Hey, hun, find an empty seat and I'll be with ya in a sec."

Spotting Robert sitting alone at a corner table, Aaron rushed over to him and sat down. "I need you to come with me now. We're going over to Seth's house. Alison's in trouble."

263

Robert looked shocked by Aaron's words. "What do you mean? Did Alison have an accident or something? I know she's not used to these country roads and all the animals that stray onto the road every day. What's going on? Let me call Seth."

Aaron grabbed the phone from Robert's hand and pocketed it. "No. Don't call Seth. Listen, when I was at Gertrude's house, waiting for the forensic team to arrive, I saw something under her chair that caught the light. It was a full bottle of medication prescribed for anxiety and Seth's name was on the label. I can't figure out why it would have there, unless Seth was in the house before we got there. Robert, I think he's the one who killed her."

Swiftly standing up, Robert began shouting at Aaron. "You pompous bastard! How dare you accuse my son of something like that! How do you know it was Seth? You don't have an ounce of proof, now, do ya?"

Aaron sat motionless, hoping he'd calm down. "Robert, listen to me. I've thought about this for quite a while. After seeing Tessie's body, and now Gertrude's, I've got a gut feeling about this and I think I'm right. The cuts on both bodies. Remember how perfectly straight they were? And the heart-shaped cut-out? Remember how precise that was? There was one on Gertrude's chest, this time it was in the shape of an 'A'."

Robert stood open-mouthed at this revelation, as Aaron continued, "I sure as hell couldn't do it, and nor could you. But a physician could. In school, they're trained to perform surgical procedures, which involves cutting of a person's tissues."

Robert's face turned bright red and his eyes teared up. "I yelled because I wanted to believe it was a lie. My boy is a doctor, he has spent his entire life living

264

his dream. There's no way he could have done something like this. I know my boy."

Aaron put his hand on Robert's. For the first time since he'd arrived in town, Aaron met a man who he assumed very few people knew. "Come with me. If I'm wrong, I'm wrong, but I have to know. Maybe he came to check on her and the bottle fell out of his pocket. I just have to know what the story is, and make sure Alison is okay. All right?"

Grabbing his hat and gun holster that he'd taken off earlier, Robert remarked, "I don't think I'll need this, but just in case…"

The two walked to Robert's cruiser. "Aaron, you'll have to drive. I done drunk too much. I'll tell you how to get to his house."

Before Robert had fully closed the door, Aaron began driving away. Already being on the edge of town, he pulled away at full throttle. Speeding at ninety miles an hour, determined to get there before what his gut instinct told him would inevitably happen, he prayed that he was wrong.

Chapter Forty-Three

Alison keyed the address into her GPS. Driving out of the restaurant parking lot, she was feeling more nervous than she had been when she arrived. She wasn't fearful about meeting him at his house but felt apprehensive about being physically intimate with him.

The GPS gave her an estimated journey time of three minutes. With the road to his house lined with residential homes, she drove slowly and texted Seth to let him know her ETA.

Be there in 5 min.

She turned on to his street, amazed by the caliber of homes it contained. All newer model houses, each larger than the previous one. Seth's house sat at the end of a cul-de-sac.

Three large oak trees stood sentinel alongside the front sidewalk. The circular drive housed his Porsche. As she pulled into the driveway, right behind his car, the streetlamps added an eerie hue to the lawn.

Alison walked up the entrance steps to the front porch and searched for the doorbell. To the left of the scroll door, an ornate brass 'S' was attached to the brick. In the middle of the letter sat the illuminated doorbell button. Pressing it twice by accident, the Westminster bells played overhead. She'd only heard the deep bell sound once in her life when she was standing under the roof of Westminster Abbey in London.

Suddenly remembering her trip to Europe, she envisioned his house sitting on a large plot of land. *The perfect manor house*, she mused, laughing at the thought.

Answering the door quickly, Seth stood there, his chest exposed through his unbuttoned shirt. She averted her eyes from his bare skin back to his face, realizing she was blushing. "I'm sorry about my car, I don't know what's going on with it. Come in and sit down. I just need to change shirts. I spilled a cup of tea on it and wanted to shift the stain before it set."

Alison watched as Seth disappeared down the hallway and into an open room, its light shining into the hallway. She assumed it was either a bathroom or utility room. Not thinking much about what he was doing, she decided to casually look around the front room in which she stood.

Hanging overhead, a very large crystal light lit the entire front portion of the house. The ceiling, Alison imagined was at least twenty feet high. Rising all the way up to the second floor, it was a true sight to see.

To her immediate left, a library full of books awaited anyone who had a love of literature. Alison poked her head through the massive, carved doors. A large desk sat in the center of the room. The perimeter of the library was encased with books. Built-in bookshelves with a ladder leaning against the wall, dominated the room. A large globe sat to the side of the desk.

In the far corner of the room, situated between a wall of bookcases, a small table housed in an alcove on the side wall held a tiny lamp. Alison walked over to see what was through the small curved entry. Expecting to see a painting hung on the depression in the wall, she was surprised to find a room on the other end.

The room, which was bathed in an odd, reddish light was full of medical equipment, ranging from an operating table to an oxygen machine.

She ran her hand against the carved, oak wall on the inside of the alcove in the library. She saw the crevice that the door slid into and realized a pocket door closed this room off.

Stepping through the passageway, she looked around at the contents of the room.

Curious, she walked over to a porcelain adorned bureau, covered with glass jars full of liquid.

A different shape floated in the liquid inside each small, glass jar. The first jar contained the letter 'B', the next a circle, then a star, then an 'A', then a perfectly carved Christmas tree.

"What the hell? Is this skin?" She surprised herself as she uttered the thought aloud.

"Yes, it is. I couldn't wait to show you."

Standing in the doorway, Seth buttoned his shirt. "What do you think of my collection? If you look on the operating table, you'll see there are pictures, as well."

Alison turned around, startled, and terrified all at the same time. As she walked closer to the operating table, she saw twenty or thirty black and white photos. Of her. It was clear from the various poses that they had been taken by someone who was spying on her. "Seth, what's going on here?"

"Well, you see, I've been watching you for a long time. I did my research. As one of the best forensic detectives in the state, I knew you'd jump at the opportunity to solve a homicide case in a town where nothing ever happens. So, I fixed it for you and gave you a life. Sadly, someone had to lose theirs in order to do that."

Alison slowly reached under her jacket for her gun. Unaccustomed to being out without her gun, an immediate feeling of terror overwhelmed her when she realized she didn't have it with her.

"Oh, don't worry, Alison. You're not going to go through what that piece of trash Tessie went though. I have spent my life perfecting my abilities. Didn't' Dad tell you?"

Alison was confused as Robert hadn't told her anything about Seth, other than discussing his profession. "What do you mean, Seth?"

"Maybe he doesn't know, after all. Don't they say that confession is good for the soul?"

Alison backed away, keeping the operating table between her and Seth as she saw the manic glint in his eyes.

"I guess it all started when I was in high school. I was always the loner who didn't fit in, so I had to amuse myself. I remember creeping into the girl's locker room and finding a used tampon wrapped in a paper towel. Unwrapping it, I inhaled the metallic smell of blood, making me aroused and yearning for more. Ironically, it was probably the main reason for choosing my profession."

As he paused, Alison felt for her phone in her pocket, but must have left it in her car. Looking around, she frantically searched for anything on the table to defend herself with, stopping when he began speaking again.

"My lust for blood led me to begin experimenting. Oh, well it started with the animals. I used to find stray animals and then moved on to domestic stock. The authorities were baffled. Eventually, when I was in my first year of med school, I killed a man.

269

Imagine the thrill it gave me when I saw you reading about it in the library yesterday. It was then that I knew this would all work between us."

Alison couldn't believe what she was hearing. "What about the woman in Dallas a couple of years back, and… Gertrude? Did you kill them too, Seth?"

"Yes, but I killed them for you, ya know. Before that, there was my psychiatrist. Everyone thought he had committed suicide, but that's what they were meant to think."

It was clear to Alison that he found pleasure in death and the macabre. Reaching behind her, she grasped one of the glass jars and turned around, looking for a window to jump out of. "So, where do I fit into all this?"

Ignoring her question, Seth laughed and began to dig his nail into the cut on his arm. Making it bleed, he raised his fingers and licked the blood off, closing his eyes as he was doing so. "I wanted to be a doctor so badly. Actually, I wanted to be a surgeon, but my dumbass shrink stopped that. Said I was 'too destructive but had a brilliant mind'. So, that's why I had to kill him."

Her palms were sweating as she sidled towards the door, getting as close as she could to Seth. "I'm getting a headache. The light is bothering me. Let's go back in the library."

Seth leaned against the wall and stared at her. "I watch you at night. I have hidden a camera in your room and can see everything. I couldn't wait to take you out on a date and get to know you better. I want to keep you here. I think you'd make me very happy, and I could give you everything you ever wished for. Aren't you excited, baby?"

"Seth, you need help." Alison hefted the glass jar and threw it at the window. The jar smashed into a thousand pieces, leaving broken glass and liquid all over the floor. The window remained untouched, other than a wet impression on the glass.

"You can throw everything in this house at my windows. They won't break. Go ahead, I want to see you move anyway. I think it's sexy."

Alison rushed from wall to wall, looking for anything that remotely resembled a weapon. The window on the far wall was covered by a drape. Pulling it back, she peered outside in the hope that someone would see her, or that she'd see a neighbor. Greeting her from the yard was a brick wall. The house, apart from the front façade was surrounded by a ten-foot tall brick, retaining wall. "I had to do something. I can't leave my prizes all alone and unprotected. I told you, I did all of this for you, ya know."

"You crazy son-of-a-bitch. You only met me a few days ago. Leave me alone!" Alison began to scream at the top of her lungs.

"Scream all you like. The house is like a cave. You can hear everything inside, but nothing on the outside. Go ahead and try it. But I don't like a raspy voice on a girl, so you might want to stop now."

Seth walked to where Alison stood and put his hand on her cheek. "Shhh, shhh, pretty girl. I won't hurt you, you know. Do you trust me? You're so pretty, and I love you so much. Come here, let me hold you."

As he grabbed her, Alison could sense his heat and sweat against her skin, feeling disgusted and terrified at the same time. Her heart was pounding in her chest from the few seconds encased in his arms.

271

Feeling his hand reach down below her waist, grazing her stomach, a sudden flood of goosepimples covered her entire body. "Oh, baby, I knew I'd get this reaction. No one else responded like this to me. I knew you were the one."

Beginning to cough, Alison started to dry heave, making him release his grip on her.

Free, she ran towards the table and grabbed another jar of liquid. Throwing it at him, she hoped to hit his head, but he had enough time to deftly move out of the way. "You're only making this worse for yourself, Alison. Come to daddy. Come here, my sweet girl."

Reaching into his pocket, he pulled out a syringe full of a clear liquid. Pulling the cap off with his teeth, he walked slowly over to her. She tried to dart away, but his strength and quick reflexes outwitted her. Grabbing her arm in a vise-like grip, he pulled her to him.

Taking the syringe, he slid it into her jugular vein. The pain from the needle being inserted made her feel faint as the waves of nausea and the sudden dizziness from the shock of it all, began to sweep over her.

Seth's hand switched positions, with his thumb hovering over the plunger. Watching, as if in slow motion, the pad of his thumb moved closer to its goal.

Out of the corner of her eye, she saw a shadow cross the library wall—the shadow of someone walking.

"Help, in here. Hurry, he's trying to kill me. Hurry!"

Seth laughed, but held the needle as still as if he were a marble statue. "I told you, girl, no one will hear you. Shut up and try to relax. This will be painless as long as you cooperate."

Since his back faced the doorway, Seth was unable to see what was happening behind him. He assumed Alison was scared and attempting to summon help that he knew wouldn't come.

A tiny flash of light followed by a deafening crack came from the doorway. Seth's hand immediately relaxed and fell to his side. Taking advantage of the momentary respite, Alison yanked the syringe out of her neck and flung it to the floor. Wrapping his arms around her, Seth attempted to keep his balance. Outweighing her by nearly a hundred pounds, his weight forced them both to the ground.

Seth lay on top of her, blinking rapidly, blood pouring from the left side of his chest, saturating Alison's jacket and shirt.

The shadow appeared in full form now, Aaron trailing Robert as they entered the secret room. Robert hovered above both of them, his gun outstretched. His face was covered in tears. Tears of pain. Tears of emotional anguish. He'd just shot his son, but more importantly, realized that his son was a person who he didn't truly know. He'd lived a lie his entire life.

Seth moved his hand to his chest, attempting to cover the bleeding wound. As he did, the drowsiness began to set in. Attempting to push him off her, the pain in Alison's right shoulder prevented her from exerting much force.

Reaching over with her left hand, she felt the site of the pain. The bullet had pierced her left shoulder and lodged in the bone. The agony was excruciating, but she managed to push it out of her mind and shoved him onto his back.

Twisting his head toward his father, he smiled. "I love you, Daddy."

273

Robert lowered his gun, knowing that he had little time to spend with his dying son. "You're no son of mine. A lifetime of lies. That's all you were."

Seth smiled at him. Taking the deepest breath he could manage, he opened his mouth to speak his final words, "blood is blood, Daddy."

The End

Acknowledgments

The reference to Robert D Hare is a direct quote from him, which can be found at www.healthyplace.com

Thank you for reading my book Deceit: A Life of Lies. I hope you enjoyed reading it as much as I enjoyed writing it. Can I ask a favor of you? Would you please take a couple of minutes and leave a review on Amazon or Goodreads. As a self-published author, we rely on your feedback.

Thanks.

Mark R Hopkins

Young Enough to Sell

Sitting on his bed, savoring a crystal snifter of brandy, Christof opened his laptop, logging on to the Tor server. Once his encrypted email had been entered, he scrolled through the hundreds of ads, until he found the post that intrigued him the most.

Thin, petite, blonde, STD free, very submissive and verbal. Twelve years old.

Christof clicked on the post, waiting for the full advert to load. The photos that were included in the listing, not only intrigued him but also gave him immense levels of excitement. The girl was standing in line at the school cafeteria, ordering lunch. Her school uniform, while modest by academia standards, sent chills down his arm. The mystery as to what was hidden beneath her red-plaid skirt made him all the more fascinated. Licking his lips, he stared at the photo.

"You've no idea. You've no idea." As he clicked the button to move to the next picture, he began to lose interest. The second photo was of the girl walking along the aisle of a grocery store. Nothing to excite, but merely to show the item for sale in its entirety. The third photo showed the girl for sale sitting next to what Christof assumed was her friend, who he wished was included in the purchase. An African American female, who appeared to be the same age as the blonde girl, but with the look of an imported porcelain doll.

Realizing that he'd have to settle for the petite, blonde girl, he entered his opening bid. The auction had gone live four hours ago. Already, the bidding had reached $276,102. Unsure why she had received that much attention, he knew he had to get in on the action. Determined to win, he added an alert to notify him of future bids and entered $300,000.

Although he had the funds, he knew that he'd be required to use Bitcoin. With a confirmation message sent to his account, the notification was set. Sipping his brandy, he thought about what he'd do if he ended up winning the auction. "What I'll do to you. You'll be shared with my friends and kept under lock and key. You'll be mine, girl. JoJo will watch over you."

When his laptop pinged, the anticipation surged through him as he opened the message. A man from Austria had outbid him. "Eurotrash. You can't afford this. You have no idea of my capabilities."

This time, far exceeding the European bidder, he entered $425,000, way below his maximum of $1,000,000, but he was prepared to pay even more. Christof wanted her. He'd bought girls in the past, but there was something about this one that made him want to have her immediately. "The innocence," he whispered to himself.

Moments later, he received a confirmation message that his bid had been accepted. Minimizing the screen, his previous browser page popped up revealing his latest newsletter that he'd been editing, aimed at the masses who subscribed.

Educated in the northeastern United States, he moved to the deep south in his early thirties. Settling in Houston, he began his work as an apprentice at a large counseling firm. Working his way up the ranks, he became the leading clinical psychologist, specializing in addiction issues. A former addict himself, he had the "street cred" to fully immerse himself into the minds of his patients. Although he was a religious man, he didn't attend church regularly.

His addiction wasn't drugs or alcohol, but sex. In college, his fraternity brothers introduced him to the world of sadistic rape. Typically, at a drunken party, the goal, at least for his brotherhood, was to claim as many girls as they could—he learned early on, the term "claim" meant sex.

With his desire for control, as well as pleasure, this wasn't a difficult task for him to complete. Outranking his fellow brothers by nearly fifty percent, his numbers earned him the right to be president of their organization. With the premise of helping those who were less fortunate, his fraternity provided everyone well, particularly Christof.

Finding a lonely girl on campus, befriending her, and ultimately taking advantage of her was never a problem for him. The task became harder when he attempted to take control of older, more mentally mature

279

women. With the power of street drugs, he quickly resolved that issue. His first true sadistic encounter was a week before his college graduation. Meeting her at a bar, he knew she was the one. A graduate student, majoring in accounting, she had the brains of Einstein. Sadly, her knowledge didn't include common sense. Easily purchasing a popular sedative in the right part of town, he'd slipped it into Milly's drink. She was tall, attractive, and according to what she told him, a virgin. Once the sedative had taken effect, he took her back to his apartment and began his attack.

Halfway through, she began to awaken, leaving Christof only one choice, so he restrained her using a method that was similar to the photos he'd seen earlier on the *Dark Web*. The thought of tying women up, excited him so much that he only sought mates who were interested in this form of play. Unfortunately, they were few and far between, leaving him to purchase his fantasies. Quickly, he became a frequent shopper on the online trafficking auction.

A notification that the auction was soon to end interrupted his musings. Maximizing the screen, he could see the live updates as the clock ticked down. "This is it. You little minx, you're about to be mine."

11, 10, 9, 8, 7, 6, 5, 4, 3, 2, 1…

It was over. A pop-up message alerted him that he'd been the highest bidder, and payment was remitted. Accessing his online bank, an account he kept specifically for the purchasing of his "play time", he sent an electronic transfer of $425,000.

His heart raced faster and faster. He knew he'd need to make travel arrangements for his purchase. His warehouse was on the other side of town, where his assistant in these matters was ready and willing to handle anything he asked of her. Formerly a sex trade worker, she understood what the girls went through, what they felt, and what their owners needed. Playing devil's advocate, she was constantly torn between the pain of the victim and the desire of the owner.